WATCHING

(THE MAKING OF RILEY PAIGE—BOOK 1)

BLAKE PIERCE

BOOKS BY BLAKE PIERCE

THE MAKING OF RILEY PAIGE SERIES
WATCHING (Book #1)
WAITING (Book #2)

RILEY PAIGE MYSTERY SERIES
ONCE GONE (Book #1)
ONCE TAKEN (Book #2)
ONCE CRAVED (Book #3)
ONCE LURED (Book #4)
ONCE HUNTED (Book #5)
ONCE PINED (Book #6)
ONCE FORSAKEN (Book #7)
ONCE COLD (Book #8)
ONCE STALKED (Book #9)
ONCE LOST (Book #10)
ONCE BURIED (Book #11)
ONCE BOUND (Book #12)
ONCE TRAPPED (Book #13)

MACKENZIE WHITE MYSTERY SERIES
BEFORE HE KILLS (Book #1)
BEFORE HE SEES (Book #2)
BEFORE HE COVETS (Book #3)
BEFORE HE TAKES (Book #4)
BEFORE HE NEEDS (Book #5)
BEFORE HE FEELS (Book #6)
BEFORE HE SINS (Book #7)
BEFORE HE HUNTS (Book #8)
BEFORE HE PREYS (Book #9)

AVERY BLACK MYSTERY SERIES
CAUSE TO KILL (Book #1)
CAUSE TO RUN (Book #2)
CAUSE TO HIDE (Book #3)
CAUSE TO FEAR (Book #4)
CAUSE TO SAVE (Book #5)
CAUSE TO DREAD (Book #6)

CHAPTER ONE

Riley sat hunched on her bed staring at her psychology book. She couldn't concentrate, not with all the noise in the room. That song was blaring again—Gloria Estefan's "Don't Let This Moment End."

How many times had she heard that stupid song just this evening? It seemed to be blasting out of every dorm room these days.

Riley yelled over the music at her roommate …

"Trudy, *please* let this moment end! Or this song, anyway. Or just shoot me maybe."

Trudy laughed. She and their friend Rhea were sitting on Trudy's bed on the other side of the room. They'd just finished doing each other's nails and were now waving their hands around in the air to dry them.

Trudy yelled back over the music, "Sure, I will, *not*."

"We're torturing you," Rhea added. "No peace until you go out with us."

Riley said, "It's Thursday night."

"So?" Trudy said.

"So, I've got an early morning class tomorrow."

Rhea said, "Since when do you need sleep?"

"Rhea's right," Trudy added. "I've never known such a night owl in my life."

Trudy was Riley's best friend, a blonde with a huge, goofy grin that charmed pretty much everybody she met, especially guys. Rhea was a brunette—prettier than Trudy and somewhat more reserved by nature, although she tried her best to keep pace with Trudy's gregariousness.

Riley let out a groan of despair. She got up from her bed and walked over to Trudy's CD player, turned the music down, then climbed back onto her bed and picked up the psych book again.

And of course, right on cue, Trudy got up and turned the music back up again—not as loud as before, but still too loud for Riley to be able to concentrate on reading.

Riley slammed her book shut.

"You're going to make me resort to violence," she said.

Rhea laughed and said, "Well, at least it would be a change. If you keep sitting there all scrunched up like that, you'll get stuck in that position."

Trudy added, "And don't go telling us you've got to study. I'm in that psych class too, remember? I know you're reading way ahead in that stupid book—weeks ahead maybe."

Rhea let out a gasp of mock horror. "Reading ahead? Isn't that, like, illegal? Because it sure ought to be."

Trudy nudged Rhea and said, "Riley likes to impress Professor Hayman. She's got a thing for him."

Riley snapped, "I do *not* have a thing for him!"

Trudy said, "Sorry, my mistake. Why *would* you have a thing for him?"

Riley couldn't help thinking …

Just because he's young and cute and smart?

Just because every other girl in the class has a crush on him?

… but she kept her thoughts to herself.

Rhea held her hand out and studied her nails.

She said to Riley, "How long has it been since you got any action? Sex-wise, I mean."

Trudy shook her head at Rhea.

"Don't ask," she said. "Riley has taken a vow of chastity."

Riley rolled her eyes and told herself …

Don't even dignify that with a snotty reply.

Then Trudy said to Rhea, "Riley's not even on the pill."

Riley's widened with shock at Trudy's indiscretion.

"Trudy!" she said.

Trudy shrugged and said, "It's not like you swore me to secrecy about it or something."

Rhea mouth had dropped open. Her horror seemed genuine this time.

"Riley. Say it ain't so. Please, please tell me she's lying."

Riley growled under her breath and said nothing.

If only they knew, she thought.

She didn't like to think about her rebellious teen years, much less talk about them. She'd been lucky not to get pregnant or catch some horrible disease. In college, she'd cooled off a lot of things—including sex, although she always carried a box of condoms in her purse just in case.

Trudy pointedly turned the music back up.

Riley heaved a sigh and said, "OK, I give up. Where do you want to go?"

"The Centaur's Den," Rhea said. "We need some serious drinkage."

"Where else is there?" Trudy added.

Riley swung her legs off her bed and got on her feet.

"Am I dressed OK?" she asked.

"Are you kidding?" Trudy said.

Rhea said, "The Den's grungy, but not *that* grungy."

Trudy walked over to the closet and rummaged through Riley's clothes.

She said, "Do I have to be like your mom or something? Here's what you need to wear."

Trudy took out a spaghetti-strapped crop top and a nice pair of jeans and handed them to Riley. Then she and Rhea went out into the hall to round up some of the girls on their floor to join them.

Riley changed clothes, then stood looking at herself in the long mirror on the closet door. She had to admit, Trudy had picked out a good look for her. The crop top flattered her slender, athletic body. With her long dark hair and hazel eyes she could pass for a college party girl.

Even so, it felt oddly like a costume, not like Riley at all.

But her friends were right, she did spend a lot of time studying.

And surely there was such a thing as overdoing it.

All work and no play ...

She pulled on a denim jacket and whispered to herself in the mirror ...

"Come on, Riley. Get out there and live a little."

*

When she and her friends opened the door to the Centaur's Den, Riley was almost overcome by the familiar but suffocating smell of cigarette smoke and the equally suffocating noise of heavy metal music.

She hesitated. Maybe this outing was a mistake after all. Were the grinding chords of Metallica a musical improvement over even the numbing monotony of Gloria Estefan?

But Rhea and Trudy were behind her, and they pushed her on inside. Three other girls from the dorm followed them in, then headed straight for the bar.

3

Peering through the smoky air, Riley saw some familiar faces. She was surprised to find so many here on a weeknight.

Most of the space was a dance floor where moving beams and sparkles flashed across kids who were happily writhing to a chorus of "Whiskey in the Jar."

Trudy grabbed both Riley and Rhea by the hands.

"Come on, let's dance, the three of us!"

It was a familiar tactic—girls would dance together until they caught the eyes of some guys. It wouldn't be long before they'd all be dancing with guys instead of each other—and drinking like crazy.

But Riley was in no mood for that—or for the noise, for that matter.

Smiling, she shook her head and pulled her hand away from Trudy.

Trudy looked hurt for a moment, but it was too loud in here to have an argument about it. Then Trudy stuck her tongue out at Riley and pulled Rhea out onto the dance floor.

Yeah, real mature, Riley thought.

She pushed through the crowd to the bar and bought herself a glass of red wine. Then she headed downstairs, where tables and booths filled a basement room. She found an empty booth where she could sit down.

Riley liked it a lot better down here than upstairs. True, the cigarette smoke was even thicker, enough to sting her eyes. But it was less frenzied, and quieter too, although muffled music from upstairs still thudded down through the floorboards.

She sipped her wine slowly, remembering her reckless teenage drinking all too well. She'd always managed to get whatever she wanted to drink from seedy adult connections in the little town of Larned. Whiskey had been her booze of choice in those days.

Poor Uncle Deke and Aunt Ruth, she thought. Out of her anger and boredom, she'd put them through more than their share of trouble.

She kept telling herself …

Maybe I'll make it up to them someday.

Her thoughts were interrupted by a male voice.

"Hey."

Riley looked up and saw a big, muscular, reasonably good-looking guy holding a mug of beer and gazing down at her with a rakish, confident smile.

4

Riley squinted—an expression that silently asked …

"Do I know you?"

Of course, Riley knew exactly who it was.

It was Harry Rampling, the quarterback for the university football team.

Riley had seen him take this same approach with lots of girls—presenting himself without introduction, because he took it for granted that he was already known far and wide as God's gift to all the women on campus.

Riley knew that this tactic usually worked. Lanton had a lousy football team, and Harry Rampling wasn't likely to wind up with a career in professional football, but he was a hero here in Lanton all the same, and girls were usually all over him.

She simply stared at him with a quizzical expression, as if she had no idea who he might by.

His smile faded a little. It was hard to tell in the dim light, but Riley suspected that he was blushing.

Then he walked away, apparently embarrassed but unwilling to stoop to the indignity of actually introducing himself.

Riley took a sip of her wine, enjoying her small victory and a bit of solitude.

But then she heard another male voice.

"How did you do that?"

Another guy was standing beside her booth holding a beer. He was well dressed, well built, somewhat older than she was, and he immediately struck Riley as markedly more attractive than Harry Rampling.

"How did I do what?" Riley asked.

The guy shrugged.

"Repulse Harry Rampling like that. You got rid of him without saying a word, not even so much as a 'fuck off, buster.' I didn't know that was even possible."

Riley felt strangely disarmed by this guy.

She said, "I sprayed myself with jock repellant before I came here."

As soon as the words were out, she thought …

Good God, I'm being witty with him.

What the hell did she think she was doing?

He smiled, enjoying the little joke.

He slipped uninvited into the seat across from Riley and said, "My name is Ryan Paige, and you don't know me from Adam, and

5

I won't blame you if you forget my name in five minutes or even sooner. I can assure you that I'm eminently forgettable."

Riley was startled by his audacity.

Don't introduce yourself, she told herself.

But she said aloud …

"I'm Riley Sweeney. I'm a senior. Psychology major."

She felt herself blushing now.

This guy was smooth, all right. And his pickup technique was so casual that it didn't seem like a technique at all.

Forgettable, hah, Riley thought.

She was already sure she wasn't going to forget Ryan Paige anytime soon.

Be careful with him, she told herself.

Then she said, "Um—are you a student here at Lanton?"

He nodded and said, "Law school. I'm finishing up this year too."

He said it as though there was no reason for her to be impressed.

And of course, Riley was impressed.

They sat talking for a while—she didn't know how long exactly.

When he asked her what she planned to do after graduation, Riley had to admit that she wasn't sure.

"I'll look for a job of some kind," she told him. "I guess I'll have to figure out a way to go to graduate school if I'm going to work in my field."

He nodded approvingly and said, "I've been making inquiries with several law firms. A couple of them look promising, but I need to consider my next step really carefully."

As they talked, Riley realized that whenever their eyes met and their gazes held steady for a moment, a slight tingle ran through her body.

Was that happening to him, too? She noticed that he did look away suddenly a few times.

Then, during a lull in the conversation, Ryan finished his beer and said, "Look, I'm sorry to rush off, but I've got a class in the morning and some studying to do."

Riley was almost dumbstruck.

Wasn't he going to make a pass at her?

No, she thought. *He's got too much class for that.*

Not that he didn't have his sights on her—she was sure he did.

But he knew better than to move on her too fast.

Impressive, she thought.

She managed to reply, "Yeah, me too."

He smiled a sincere-looking smile.

"It was nice to meet you, Riley Sweeney."

Riley smiled back.

"It was nice to meet you too, Ryan Paige."

Ryan chuckled and said, "Aw, you remembered."

Without another word, he got up and left.

Riley's mind boggled at all that hadn't happened. They hadn't exchanged phone numbers, she hadn't mentioned which dorm she was in, and she still had no idea where he lived. And he hadn't even asked her out on a real future date.

It wasn't because he didn't expect there to be a real date, she was sure of that.

No, he was simply confident. He was sure their paths would cross again soon, and he expected chemistry to kick in.

And Riley more than half-believed he was right.

Just then she heard Trudy's voice call out.

"Hey, Riley! Who was the cute guy?"

Riley turned and saw Trudy coming down the stairs, carrying a full pitcher of beer in one hand and a mug in the other. Three other girls from their dorm were tagging along behind her. They all looked pretty drunk.

Riley didn't reply to Trudy's question. She only hoped Ryan was out of earshot by now.

As the girls approached the table, Riley asked …

"Where's Rhea?"

Trudy looked all around.

"I dunno," she said in a slurred voice. "Where *is* Rhea?"

One of the other girls said, "Rhea went back to the dorm."

"What!" Trudy said. "She left and didn't tell me?"

"She did tell you," another girl said.

The girls were all about to climb into the booth with Riley. Rather than get trapped in there with them, Riley got up from her seat.

"We should all go home," she said.

With a flurry of protests, the girls seated themselves, giggling and obviously settling in for a long night.

Riley gave up on them. She walked upstairs and out the front door. Outside, she took a deep breath of cool, fresh air. It was

March and sometimes cold at night here in the Shenandoah Valley of Virginia, but the chill was welcome after the stuffy, smoke-filled bar.

It was a short, well-lit walk back to the campus and her dorm. She felt that the evening had turned out pretty well. She'd only had a glass of wine, just enough to be relaxing, and there had also been that guy …

Ryan Paige.

She smiled.

No, she hadn't forgotten his name.

*

Riley was sleeping deeply and dreamlessly when something jarred her awake.

What? she wondered.

At first, she thought maybe someone had shaken her by the shoulder.

But no, that wasn't it.

As she stared into the darkness of her dorm room, she heard the sound again.

A shriek.

A voice filled with terror.

Riley knew that something terrible had happened.

CHAPTER TWO

Riley was out of her bed and on her feet before she was fully awake.

That sound had been horrible.

What was it?

When she switched on the light beside her bed, a familiar voice grumbled from across the room, "Riley—what's going on?"

Trudy was lying in her own bed fully clothed, shielding her eyes against the light. She obviously had collapsed there in a fairly inebriated state.

Riley had slept right through her roommate's arrival.

But she was awake now.

So were others in the dorm. She could hear alarmed voices calling out from the rooms nearby.

Riley went into motion, shoving her feet into slippers, pulling on her robe, and opening their room door. She stepped out into the hallway.

Other room doors were swinging open. Girls were poking their heads out, asking what was wrong.

And Riley could see at least one thing that was wrong. About halfway down the hall, a girl was collapsed on her knees, sobbing.

Riley raced toward her.

Heather Glover, she realized.

Heather had been with them at the Centaur's Den. She'd still been there with Trudy and the others when Riley left.

Now Riley knew—it was Heather she'd heard screaming.

She also remembered …

Heather is Rhea's roommate!

Riley reached the sobbing girl and crouched beside her.

"What's wrong?" she asked. "Heather—what happened?"

Sobbing and choking, Heather pointed to the open door next to her.

She managed to gasp …

"It's Rhea. She's—"

Heather suddenly threw up.

Dodging the spray of vomit, Riley stood up and peered into the

9

room door. In the light shining in from the hallway, she could make out something spread out on the floor—a dark liquid. At first she thought it was spilled soft drink.

Then she shuddered …

Blood.

She'd seen blood pooled like this before. There was no mistaking it for anything else.

She stepped into the doorway and quickly saw that Rhea lay sprawled across her single bed, fully clothed and with her eyes wide open.

"Rhea?" Riley said.

She peered closer. Then she gagged.

Rhea's throat was slashed almost from ear to ear.

Rhea was dead—Riley knew that for certain.

It wasn't the first murdered woman she'd seen in her life.

Then Riley heard another scream. For a moment she wondered if the scream might be her own.

But no—it was coming from right behind her.

Riley turned, and there in the doorway stood Gina Formaro. She'd also been partying at the Centaur's Den that night. Now her eyes were bulging and she was trembling all over, pale with shock.

Riley realized that she herself felt remarkably calm, not scared at all. She also knew that she was probably the only student on the whole floor who wasn't already in a state of panic.

It was up to her to make sure things didn't get even worse.

Riley gently took Gina by the arm and led her out of the doorway. Heather was still there on the floor where she had vomited, still sobbing. And other wandering students were beginning to make their way toward the room.

Riley pulled the room door closed and stood in front of it.

"Stay back!" she yelled at the approaching girls. "Stay away!"

Riley was surprised at the force and authority in her own voice.

The girls obeyed, forming a crowded semicircle around the dorm room.

Riley yelled again, "Somebody call nine-one-one!"

"Why?" one of the girls asked.

Still crouched on the floor with a pool of vomit in front of her, Heather Glover managed to croak out …

"It's Rhea. She's been murdered."

Suddenly a wild mix of girls' voices exploded in the hallway—some screaming, some gasping, some sobbing. A few of the girls pushed toward the room again.

"Stay back!" Riley said again, still blocking the doorway. "Call nine-one-one!"

One of the girls who owned a little cell phone was carrying it in her hand. She made the call.

Riley stood there wondering …

What do I do now?

She only knew one thing for certain—she couldn't let any of the girls into the room with the body. There was enough panic on the floor already. It would only get worse if more people saw what was in that room.

She also felt sure that no one was supposed to walk around in …

In what?

A crime scene, she realized. That room was a crime scene.

She remembered—she was sure it must be from movies or TV shows—that the police would want the crime scene to be as untouched as possible.

All she could do was wait—and keep everybody out.

And so far she was being successful. The semicircle of students began to break up, and girls wandered off into smaller groups, disappearing into rooms or forming little clusters in the hallway to share their horror. There was a lot of crying now, and some low, animal-like wailing. A few more cell phones were appearing, those who owned them calling parents or friends to report their versions of the disaster.

Riley thought that probably wasn't a good idea, but she had no way to stop them. At least they were staying away from the door that she guarded.

And now she was starting to feel her own share of horror.

Images from her early childhood flooded Riley's brain …

Riley and Mommy were in a candy store—and how Mommy was spoiling Riley!

She was buying her lots and lots of candy.

They were both laughing and happy until …

A man stepped toward them. He had a weird face, flat and featureless, like something out of one of Riley's nightmares. It took Riley a second to realize that he was wearing a nylon stocking over his head—the kind that Mommy wore on her legs.

And he was holding a gun.

He started yelling at Mommy ...

"Your purse! Give me your purse!"

His voice sounded as frightened as Riley felt.

Riley looked up at Mommy, expecting her to do as the man said.

But Mommy had turned pale and was shaking all over. She didn't seem to understand what was going on.

"Give me your purse!" the man yelled again.

Mommy just stood there, clutching her purse.

Riley wanted to tell Mommy ...

"Do as the man says, Mommy. Give him your purse."

But for some reason, no words came out of her mouth.

Mommy staggered a little, as if she wanted to run but couldn't make her legs move.

Then there was a flash and a loud, terrible noise ...

... and Mommy fell to the floor, landing on her side.

Her chest was spurting deep red, and the color soaked her blouse and was spreading out in a puddle on the floor ...

Riley was yanked back to the present by the sound of approaching sirens. The local cops were arriving.

She felt relief that the authorities were here and could take over ... whatever it was that had to be done.

She saw that boys who lived on the second floor were coming down and asking the girls what was going on. They were also in various stages of dress—shirts and jeans, pajamas and robes.

Harry Rampling, the football player who had approached Riley back at the bar, made his way toward where she was standing against the closed door. He pushed past the girls still hovering there and stared at her for a moment.

"What do you think *you're* doing?" he snapped.

Riley said nothing. She saw no point in trying to explain—not with the police about to appear at any second.

Harry smirked a little and took a menacing step toward Riley. He'd obviously been told about the dead girl inside.

"Get out of the way," he said. "I want to see."

Riley stood even more firmly than before.

"You can't go in there," she said.

Harry said, "Why not, little girl?"

Riley stared daggers at him, but she was wondering ...

What the hell do I think I'm doing?

Did she really think she could keep a male athlete from going in there if he decided to?

Oddly enough, she had the feeling that she probably could.

She'd certainly put up a fight, if it came to that.

Fortunately, she heard the clatter of footsteps entering the hall, then a man's voice calling out …

"Break it up. Let us through."

The clump of students broke up."

Someone said, "Over there," and three uniformed cops made their way toward Riley.

She recognized all of them. They were familiar faces around Lanton. Two of them were men, Officers Steele and White. The other was a woman, Officer Frisbie. A couple of campus cops were also tagging along.

Steele was overweight, and his reddish face made Riley suspect that he drank too much. White was a tall guy who walked with a constant slouch and whose mouth always seemed to be hanging open. Riley didn't think he seemed especially bright. Officer Frisbie was a tall, sturdy woman who had always struck Riley as friendly and good-natured.

"We got a call," Officer Steele said. He huffed at Riley. "What the hell's going on here?"

Riley stepped away from the door and pointed to it.

"It's Rhea Thorson," Riley said. "She's—"

Riley found that she couldn't finish the sentence. She was still trying to get it through her head that Rhea was dead.

She just stepped aside.

Officer Steele opened the door and slouched past her into the room.

Then came a loud gasp as he exclaimed …

"Oh my God!"

Officers Frisbie and White both hurried inside.

Then Steele reappeared and called out to the onlookers, "I need to know what happened. Right now."

There was a general murmur of alarmed confusion.

Then Steele fired a series of questions. "What do you know about this? Was this girl in her room all evening? Who else was here?"

More confusion followed, with some girls saying that Rhea hadn't left the dorm, others saying that she went to the library, others that she'd gone out on a date, and of course a few who said that she'd gone out drinking. Nobody had seen anybody else here. Not until they heard Heather screaming.

Riley took a breath, getting ready to shout the others down and tell what she knew. But before she could speak, Harry Rampling pointed at Riley and said …

"This girl's been acting all weird. She was standing right there when I got here. Like maybe she'd just come out the door."

Steele stepped toward Riley and growled …

"Is that right? You've got some explaining to do. Start talking."

He seemed to be reaching for his handcuffs. For the first time, Riley started to feel a trace of panic.

Is this guy going to arrest me? she wondered.

She had no idea what might happen if he did.

But the woman cop said sharply to Officer Steele, "Leave her alone, Nat. Can't you see what she was doing? She was guarding the room, making sure nobody else got in. We've got her to thank that the crime scene isn't hopelessly contaminated."

Officer Steele backed away, looking resentful.

The woman shouted to the onlookers, "I want everybody to stay exactly where you are. Nobody moves, d'you hear? And keep talking to a minimum."

There were nods and murmurs of assent from the group.

Then the woman grabbed Riley by the arm and started to escort her away from the others.

"Come with me," she whispered sharply to Riley. "You and I are going to have a little talk."

Riley gulped anxiously as Officer Frisbie led her away.

Am I really in trouble? she wondered.

CHAPTER THREE

Officer Frisbie kept a firm grip on Riley's arm the whole way down the hall. They went through a pair of double doors and wound up standing at the base of the stairs. At last the woman released her.

Riley rubbed her arm where it hurt a little.

Officer Frisbie said, "Sorry to get rough there. We're in kind of a hurry. First of all, what's your name?"

"Riley Sweeney."

"I've seen you around town. What year are you in college?"

"A senior."

The woman's stern expression softened a little.

"Well, first of all, I want to apologize for how Officer Steele talked to you just now. Poor guy, he really can't help it. It's just that he's … what's the word my daughter would use? Oh, yeah. A dick."

Riley was too startled too laugh. Anyway, Officer Frisbie wasn't smiling.

She said, "I pride myself on having pretty reliable gut instincts—better than the 'good old boys' I'm stuck working with, anyway. And right now my gut is saying that you're the one person around here who might be able to tell me exactly what I need to know."

Riley felt another wave of panic as the unsmiling woman took out a notepad and got ready to write.

She said, "Officer Frisbie, I really have no idea—"

The woman interrupted her.

"You might be surprised. Just go ahead—tell me about what your night's been like."

Riley was puzzled.

What my night's been like?

What did that have to do with anything?

"From the beginning," Frisbie said.

Riley replied slowly, "Well, I was sitting in my room trying to study, because I've got a class tomorrow morning, but my roommate, Trudy, and my friend Rhea …"

Riley suddenly fell silent.

My friend Rhea.

She remembered sitting on her bed while Trudy and Rhea had been across the room doing their nails and playing Gloria Estefan too loud and generally making nuisances of themselves, trying to get Riley to go out with them. Rhea had been so lively—laughing and mischievous.

No more.

She'd never hear Rhea's laugh or see her smile again.

For the first time since this horrible thing had happened, Riley felt close to tears. She sagged against the wall.

Not now, she told herself sternly.

She straightened up and took a deep breath and continued.

"Trudy and Rhea talked me into going to the Centaur's Den."

Officer Frisbie gave Riley an encouraging nod and said, "About what time was this?"

"Around nine-thirty, I think."

"And was it just the three of you who went out?"

"No," Riley said. "Trudy and Rhea got some other girls to come. There were six of us all together."

Officer Frisbie was jotting down notes quickly now.

"Tell me their names," she said.

Riley didn't have to stop to think.

"There was me—and Trudy Lanier and Rhea, of course. And Cassie DeBord, and Gina Formaro, and Rhea's roommate, Heather Glover."

She stood there silently for a moment.

There must be more, she thought. Surely she could remember something more to tell the police. But her brain seemed stuck on her immediate group—and on the image of her friend dead in that room.

Riley was about to explain that she hadn't spent much time with the others at the Centaur's Den. But before she could say anything else, Officer Frisbie abruptly put her pencil and notebook back in her pocket.

"Well done," she said, sounding very businesslike. "That's exactly what I needed to know. Come on."

As Officer Frisbie led her back into the hallway, Riley wondered …

"Well done"?

What did I even do?

The situation in the hall was the same as before, with a small

16

mob of stunned and horrified students standing around while Officer White looked on. But there were two new arrivals.

One was Dean Angus Trusler, a finicky and easily agitated man who was mingling among the students, getting some of them to tell him what was going on despite their orders not to talk.

The other newcomer was a tall, vigorous-looking older man wearing a uniform. Riley recognized him at once. He was Lanton's police chief, Allan Hintz. Riley noticed that Officer Frisbie didn't look surprised to see him—but she didn't look at all pleased, either.

Standing arms akimbo, he said to Frisbie, "Mind telling us why you're keeping us waiting, Frisbie?"

Officer Frisbie tossed him a look of barely disguised disdain. It was obvious to Riley that their working relationship was strained at best.

"I'm glad to see someone got you out of bed, sir," Officer Frisbie said.

Chief Hintz frowned.

Trying his best to look as authoritative as the police chief, Dean Trusler stepped forward and spoke to Hintz sharply.

"Allan, I don't like the way you and your people are handling this. These poor kids are terrorized enough without being bossed around. What's this all about—telling them to stay put and stay quiet, with no explanations? Some of them just want to go back to their rooms and try to get some sleep. Some want to get out of Lanton altogether and go home to their families for a while—and who can blame them? Some even wonder if they need to hire lawyers. It's time you told them what you want from them. Surely none of our students are suspects."

As the dean kept ranting, Riley wondered how he could be so sure that the murderer wasn't right here in the hallway. She found it hard to imagine any of the girls committing such a horrible crime. But what about the guys? What about a big tough jock like Harry Rampling? Neither he nor any of the other guys looked like they'd just slashed a girl's throat. But maybe after a shower and a quick change of clothes …?

Steady, Riley told herself. *Don't let your imagination run away with you.*

But if it wasn't a student, then who could have been in Rhea's room?

She struggled again to remember if she had seen anyone else with Rhea at the Centaur's Den. Had Rhea danced with any guy?

Had a drink with someone? But Riley still came up with nothing.

Anyway, questions like that didn't seem to matter. Chief Hintz wasn't listening to a word Dean Trusler was saying. Officer Frisbie was whispering to him and showing him the notes she'd taken while talking to Riley.

When she finished, Hintz said to the group, "OK, listen up. I want five of you to come to the common room."

He rattled off the names Riley had given to Officer Frisbie, including her own.

Then he said, "The rest of you, go to your rooms. Guys, that means go back to your floor. Everybody stay put for the night. Don't go outside this building until you're notified otherwise. And don't plan on leaving the campus anytime soon. We're likely to have questions for many of you."

He turned to the dean and said, "Make sure all the students in the building get the same message."

The dean's mouth was hanging open with dismay now, but he managed to nod his assent. The hall was filled with murmurs of confused dissatisfaction as the girls obediently dispersed to their rooms and the guys headed back upstairs.

Chief Hintz and Officers Frisbie and White led Riley and her four friends down the hall. Along the way, Riley couldn't help but glance into Rhea's room. She glimpsed Officer Steele probing around inside. She couldn't see the bed where she had found Rhea, but she was sure that the body was still there.

It didn't seem right somehow.

How long till they take her away? she wondered. She hoped they had at least covered her up, hidden the horrible slashed throat and open eyes from view. But she supposed the investigators had more important things to attend to. And maybe they were all used to such sights anyhow.

She was sure that she would never forget the sight of Rhea dead and that pool of blood on the floor.

Riley and the others went obediently into the well-furnished common room and sat down on various chairs and sofas.

Chief Hintz said, "Officer Frisbie and I are going to talk with each of you individually. While we do, I don't want any of the rest of you to talk to each other. Not one word. Do you hear me?"

Without even glancing at each other, the girls nodded nervously.

"And for now, don't even use your phones," Hintz added.

They all nodded again, then just sat there staring at their hands, at the floor, or off into space.

Hintz and Frisbie led Heather into the adjoining dorm kitchen while Officer White stood slouching vigilantly over Riley, Trudy, Cassie, and Gina.

After a few moments, Trudy broke the silence. "Riley, what the hell—?"

White interrupted, "Be quiet. Chief's orders."

Silence fell again, but Riley saw that Trudy, Cassie, and Gina were all staring at her. She looked away.

They think it's my fault they're here, she realized.

Then she thought—maybe it was true, maybe she shouldn't have spilled their names. But what was she supposed to do, lie to a police officer? Still, Riley hated the distrustful vibes she was getting from her friends. And she couldn't really blame them for feeling that way toward her.

What kind of trouble are we in, anyway? she wondered. *Just for going out together?*

She was especially worried about Heather, who was still in the kitchen answering questions. The poor girl had been especially close to her roommate, Rhea. Of course, this was a nightmare for everybody, but Riley couldn't begin to imagine how hard it must be for Heather.

Soon they heard the dean's voice stammering uneasily over the dorm's PA system.

"This is Dean Trusler. I—I'm sure all of you know by now that something terrible just happened on the girls' floor. You have orders from Police Chief Hintz to stay in your rooms tonight and not leave the dorm. A police officer or a campus official might come by your room to talk with you. Be sure to answer any and all questions. For now, don't plan on leaving campus tomorrow, either. You'll all be getting additional notification soon."

Riley remembered something else the chief had said …

"We're likely to have questions for many of you."

He was starting with Riley and the other four girls right now.

It was starting to make sense to her. After all, they'd been together with Rhea shortly before she was killed. But what did Hintz think the girls might know?

What does he think I might know? she wondered.

Riley couldn't imagine.

At last, Heather came out of the kitchen, accompanied by

Officer Frisbie. Heather looked pale and sick, as if she might start vomiting again. Riley wondered—where was Heather going to spend the night? She couldn't very well go back to the room she had shared with Rhea.

As if overhearing Riley's thoughts, Officer Frisbie said, "Heather is going to spend the rest of the night in the RA's room."

Heather walked shakily out of the common room. Riley was glad to see that the resident assistant met her at the doorway.

Officer Frisbie called for Gina to come into the kitchen, where Hintz was still waiting. Gina got up stiffly and followed the woman through the swinging door, leaving Riley, Trudy, and Cassie sitting in uncomfortable silence. It seemed to Riley that time had slowed down as they waited.

Finally, Gina reemerged. Without a word to the others, she walked through the common room and out the other door. Then Officer Frisbie asked for Cassie, who went next into the kitchen.

Now there were only Riley and Trudy sitting there in chairs across from each other. As they waited, Trudy kept giving Riley angry and reproachful glances. Riley wished she could explain what she had said during her short conversation with Officer Frisbie. All she'd done was answer a simple question. She hadn't accused anyone of doing anything bad.

But Officer White was still looming over them, and Riley couldn't say a single word.

Finally, Cassie came out of the kitchen and went back to her room, and Trudy was next to be called into the kitchen.

Riley was now alone with Officer White, feeling isolated and afraid.

With nothing to distract her, she kept flashing back to poor Rhea's body, her wide open eyes, and the pool of blood. Now those images were mixed with memories of her own mother lying dead—so long ago, but still so horribly vivid in her mind.

How could something like that be happening here and now, in a college dormitory?

This can't be real, she thought.

Surely she wasn't really sitting here bracing herself to answer questions that she couldn't possibly know the answers to.

Surely one of her best friends hadn't just been savagely murdered.

She had almost convinced herself of the unreality of the moment when Officer Frisbie led Trudy out of the kitchen. With a sullen expression, Trudy left the common room without so much as a glance at Riley.

Officer Frisbie nodded at Riley, who got up and obediently followed her into the kitchen.

This can't be happening, she kept telling herself.

CHAPTER FOUR

Riley sat down at the table in the kitchen, across from Chief Hintz. For a moment the chief just stared across at her, holding his pencil over a notepad. Riley wondered if she was supposed to say something.

She glanced up and saw that Officer Frisbie had positioned herself off to one side, leaning against a counter. The woman had a rather sour expression on her face, as if she wasn't very happy with the interviews. Riley wondered if Frisbie was annoyed by the girls' responses or by the way her boss had been asking questions.

Finally the chief said, "First of all, did the victim ever give you any reason to think she feared for her safety?"

Riley was jolted by that word …

Victim.

Why couldn't he just refer to her as Rhea?

But she needed to answer his question.

Her mind raced back over recent conversations, but she only remembered innocuous exchanges like the one she and Trudy and Rhea had had earlier tonight about whether Riley was on the pill.

"No," Riley said.

"Did anyone wish her ill? Was anyone angry with her recently?"

The very idea seemed odd to Riley. Rhea was—had been—so pleasant and amiable that Riley couldn't imagine anyone being mad at her for more than a few minutes.

But she wondered …

Did I miss any signs?

And had the other girls told Hintz anything Riley herself didn't know?

"No," Riley said. "She got along with pretty much everybody—as far as I knew."

Hintz paused for a moment.

Then he said, "Tell us what happened when you and your friends arrived at the Centaur's Den."

A rush of sensations came back to Riley—Rhea and Trudy physically pushing her through the door into the thick fog of cigarette smoke and the deafening music …

Did she need to get into all that?

No, surely Hintz only wanted to hear bare-boned facts.

She said, "Cassie and Heather and Gina headed straight to the bar. Trudy wanted me to dance with her and Rhea."

Hintz was reviewing notes he'd taken from the other girls, who of course had told him what they'd known about Riley's actions, including the fact that Riley had left them to go downstairs.

"But you didn't dance with them," he said.

"No," Riley said.

"Why not?"

Riley was startled. Why could her reluctance to dance possibly matter, anyway?

Then she noticed Officer Frisbie giving her a sympathetic look and shaking her head. It seemed obvious now that the woman thought Hintz was being a bit of an asshole, but there really wasn't anything she could do about it.

Riley said slowly and carefully, "I just … well, I wasn't in much of a party mood. I'd been trying to study, and Rhea and Trudy had pretty much dragged me there. So I bought a glass of wine and headed on downstairs."

"Alone?" Hintz asked.

"Yeah, alone. I sat down in a booth by myself."

Hintz thumbed through his notes.

"So you didn't talk to anyone else while you were at the Centaur's Den?"

Riley thought for a moment, then said, "Well, Harry Rampling came over to my table …"

Hintz smiled a little at the mention of Harry's name. Riley realized that, like most of the community, the chief probably thought pretty highly of the school's quarterback.

He asked, "Did he sit down with you?"

"No," Riley said. "I brushed him off."

Hintz frowned with disapproval, apparently annoyed that any girl would have the poor judgment to reject a true hero like Harry Rampling. Riley was starting to feel a little exasperated. Why was her taste in guys any business of Hintz's, anyway? What did it have to do with what had happened to Rhea?

Hintz asked, "Did you talk to anyone else?"

Riley gulped.

Yes, she *had* talked to someone else.

But was she going to get the guy in trouble by talking about him?

She said, "Um … a law student came over to my booth. He sat down with me and we talked for a while."

"And then?" Hintz asked.

Riley shrugged.

"He said he had studying to do, and he left."

Hintz was jotting down some notes.

"What was his name?" he asked.

Riley said, "Look, I don't see why he's important. He was just another guy at the Centaur's Den. There's no reason for you to think—"

"Just answer my question."

Riley swallowed hard and said, "Ryan Paige."

"Had you met him before?"

"No."

"Do you know where he lives?"

"No."

Riley was momentarily glad that Ryan had managed to keep himself so mysterious, without giving her so much as his address or phone number. She saw no reason why she should be answering any questions about him at all, and she sure didn't want to get him into any trouble. It seemed almost kind of stupid that Hintz was pushing her about it. And Riley could tell by how Officer Frisbie rolled her eyes that she felt the same way.

Hintz tapped his pencil eraser against the table and asked, "Did you see Rhea Thorson with anybody in particular at the Centaur's Den? Aside from the friends you went with, I mean?"

Riley was starting to feel more frustrated than nervous.

Didn't Hintz understand anything she'd been saying?

"No," she said. "Like I said, I went off by myself. I didn't see Rhea at all after that."

Hintz kept tapping his eraser, looking at his notes.

He asked, "Does the name Rory Burdon mean anything to you?"

Riley thought quickly.

Rory …

Yes, the first name was familiar, anyway.

She said, "Rhea seemed to be kind of interested in him, I guess. I saw her dancing with him a few other times at the Centaur's Den."

"But not tonight?"

Riley fought down a sigh. She wanted to say …

How many times do I have to tell you, I didn't see Rhea at all after I got there?

Instead, she simply said, "No."

She figured Rory must have been there tonight as well, and that the other girls had told Hintz they'd seen Rhea hanging on him.

"What do you know about him?" Hintz asked.

Riley paused. What little she did know seemed too trivial to mention. Rory was a tall, skinny, awkward guy with thick glasses, and all the girls except Riley had teased Rhea for being interested in him.

She said, "Not much, except he lives off campus somewhere."

She realized that Hintz was just staring at her again, as if he expected her to say something more.

Does Hintz consider him a suspect? she wondered.

Riley was sure that the chief was way off base if he did suspect Rory. The guy had struck her as shy and gentle, not the least bit aggressive.

She was about to say so to Hintz, but the police chief glanced down at the papers in front of him and moved on with his questions.

"When did you leave the Centaur's Den?" he asked.

Riley made the best guess she could about the time—it had been pretty late.

Then Hintz said, "Did you see any of your friends before you left?"

Riley remembered the girls staggering down the stairs, and how Trudy had been carrying the pitcher of beer when she'd asked …

"Hey, Riley! Who was the cute guy?"

Riley said, "Trudy and Heather and Gina and Cassie all came downstairs. They said Rhea had already gone. That was when I left."

As Hintz jotted down notes, Riley's head started to fill with questions of her own. She remembered asking where Rhea was, and Trudy had said …

"I dunno. Where is Rhea?"

… and then Heather had said …

"Rhea went back to the dorm."

Riley wondered—what did Heather or any of the other girls know about Rhea's departure?

Did they know whether she had left the Centaur's Den alone or not?

And what had they told Hintz about it?

Riley wished she could ask, but knew that she mustn't.

"Did you leave the bar alone?" Hintz asked.

"Yeah," Riley said.

"And you walked all the way back to the dorm alone?"

"Yeah."

Hintz's frown deepened as he glared at her.

"Are you sure that was wise? The school offers an escort service for crossing the campus at night. Why didn't you call for it?"

Riley gulped. This seemed to her like the first really good question Hintz had asked so far.

She said, "I guess I always felt safe walking on campus at night. But now …"

Her voice faded.

Now things are really different, she thought.

Hintz frowned again.

"Well, I hope you use better judgment in the future. Especially when you've been drinking too much."

Riley's eyes widened.

"I only had one glass of wine," she said.

Hintz squinted at her. She could tell by his expression that he thought she was lying. The other girls must have admitted to drinking a lot, and he assumed that Riley had as well.

She resented his attitude, but she quickly told herself that whatever Hintz thought of her didn't matter right now. It would be stupid and petty of her to get pissed off about it.

Hintz kept jotting things down and said, "That will be all—for now. You must obey the same rules as everybody else in the dorm. Stay in your room tonight. Don't plan on leaving the campus until you're notified otherwise. We might want to ask you more questions soon."

Riley was oddly startled.

Is that it? she wondered.

Was the interview really over?

Because she sure still had questions, even if Hintz didn't.

One question in particular had been welling up in her mind ever since she had discovered Rhea's body. She remembered stepping into Rhea's dimly lit room and seeing her severed throat and her wide open eyes—but she hadn't stopped to really look closely at her body.

In a halting voice, she said to Hintz …

"Could you tell me … do you know …"

She suddenly realized how hard it was going to be to even ask the question.

She continued, "Before she died … before she was killed … was Rhea …?"

She couldn't bring herself to say the word …

Raped.

And from Hintz's blank expression, Riley could tell that he really couldn't figure out what she was trying to ask.

Fortunately, Officer Frisbie did understand.

She said, "I can't say for sure—the medical examiner is still on his way here. But I don't think she was sexually assaulted. It looked to me like her clothes weren't disturbed during the attack."

Breathing a little easier, Riley gave Frisbie a look of silent gratitude.

The woman nodded slightly, and Riley left the kitchen.

As Riley headed out of the common room, she found herself wondering yet again what the other girls had told Hintz—for example, whether Rhea had left the bar alone or not. Did they know anything about what had happened to Rhea that Riley didn't know? After all, they'd been with her until she'd decided to leave.

As Riley walked down the hall, she saw that a couple of campus cops were standing outside Rhea's room door, which was now taped off with crime scene tape. She shuddered at the thought that Rhea's body was still in there, awaiting the arrival of the medical examiner. Riley found it hard to imagine anyone sleeping in that room ever again—but of course, it wouldn't be vacant forever.

Riley opened the door to her room, which was dark inside except for some light spilling in from the hall. She saw Trudy turn over in her bed to face the wall.

She's still awake, Riley thought.

Maybe now they could talk, and Riley could get some answers to her questions.

Riley closed the door and sat down on her own bed and said, "Trudy, I was wondering if maybe we could talk about our interviews."

Still facing the wall, Trudy replied …

"We're not supposed to talk about it."

Riley was startled by the sharp, icy tone of Trudy's voice.

"Trudy, I don't think that's true, at least not anymore. Hintz didn't say anything like that to me."

"Just go to sleep," Trudy said.

Trudy's words cut through Riley painfully. And suddenly, for the first time, Riley felt tears welling up in her eyes, and a sob rose up in her throat.

It was bad enough that Rhea had been brutally murdered.

Now her best friend was angry with her.

Riley got under the covers. Tears streaked down her face as something began to dawn on her …

Her life had been changed forever.

She couldn't yet begin to imagine how.

CHAPTER FIVE

The next morning Riley sat in the university auditorium along with other glum-looking students. Although the general campus mood was depressed, she had to wonder if everybody else there felt as miserable as she did. She thought that some of them looked more annoyed than saddened. A few seemed nervous, as though they were frightened by every movement around them.

How do we ever get over something like this? she wondered.

But of course, not everyone had been close to Rhea. Not everyone had even known her. They would surely be horrified at the thought of a murder on campus, but for many of them it wouldn't be personal.

It was personal for Riley. She couldn't shake off the horror that had hit her at the sight of Rhea's …

She couldn't bring herself to think the words she needed. She couldn't yet think of her friend as a dead body, in spite of what she had seen last night.

The all-campus assembly today seemed completely disconnected from what had happened. It also seemed to be dragging on forever, making her feel even worse.

Chief Hintz had just finished giving a stern lecture about campus safety and promising the killer would soon be apprehended, and now Dean Trusler was going on and on about how to get things back to normal here at Lanton University.

Good luck with that, Riley thought.

Classes were canceled for today, Trusler said, but they would resume on Monday. He said he understood if some students might not feel ready to go back to classes so soon, and also if some of them might want to go home to be with their families for a few days, and the school's counselors were ready to help everybody deal with this horrible trauma, and … and … and …

Riley tuned out and stifled a yawn as the dean rattled earnestly on, not saying anything useful as far as she was concerned. She'd barely slept at all last night. She had just drifted off to sleep when the medical examiner's team had noisily arrived. Then she'd stood in her doorway watching in silent horror as the team carted away a sheet-covered form on a gurney.

Surely, she'd thought, *that can't be someone who was laughing and dancing hours ago. That can't really be Rhea.*

Riley hadn't gone to sleep at all after that. She couldn't help but envy Trudy, who seemed to have been out cold the whole night—probably, Riley guessed, from all the alcohol she had consumed earlier.

Early this morning the dorm resident assistant had announced this meeting over the intercom. Trudy had still been in bed when Riley left. When Riley had come to the assembly, she hadn't seen Trudy anywhere in the auditorium.

Riley looked around now, but still didn't spot her. Maybe she was still in bed.

She's not missing much, Riley thought.

She also didn't see Rhea's roommate, Heather, anywhere. But Gina and Cassie were sitting a couple of rows ahead of her. They'd brushed past Riley on the way in to the meeting—apparently still mad at her for giving their names to the cops.

Last night Riley had understood why they might feel that way, but now it was starting to seem childish. It was also extremely hurtful. She wondered if her friendships were ever going to mend.

Right now, that "normal" the dean was talking about seemed gone forever.

At long last the meeting came to an end. As the students poured out of the building, reporters were waiting outside. Right away they descended on Gina and Cassie, asking them all kinds of questions. Riley guessed that they'd managed to find out who Rhea's companions had been that night before her murder.

If so, they probably knew about Riley too. But so far they hadn't spotted her. Maybe it was a lucky thing that Gina and Cassie had brushed Riley off this morning. Otherwise, she'd be right there with them, stuck answering impossible questions.

Riley quickened her step to avoid the reporters, wending her way among the other students. As she went, she could hear the reporters prodding Gina and Cassie over and over with the same question …

"How do you feel?"

Riley felt a tingle of anger.

What kind of question is that? she wondered.

What did they expect Gina and Cassie to say in reply?

Riley had no idea what she herself would say—except maybe

to tell the reporters to leave her the hell alone.

She was still awash in confused and terrible feelings—numbing shock, lingering disbelief, gnawing horror, and so much else. The worst feeling of all was a kind of guilty relief that she hadn't met Rhea's fate.

How could she or her friends put any of that into words?

What business did anyone have asking them that, anyway?

Riley made her way to the cafeteria in the student union. She hadn't had any breakfast yet, and was just starting to realize she was hungry. At the buffet she scooped up some bacon and eggs and poured herself some orange juice and coffee. Then she looked around for a place to sit.

Her eyes quickly fell on Trudy, who was sitting alone at a table, facing away from the others in the room and eating her own breakfast.

Riley gulped anxiously.

Did she dare try to join Trudy at the table?

Would Trudy even talk to her?

They hadn't exchanged a single word since last night when Trudy had bitterly told Riley to go to sleep.

Riley summoned up her courage and maneuvered her way across the room to Trudy's table. Without saying anything, she put her tray on the table and sat down beside her roommate.

For a few moments Trudy kept her head low, as if she didn't notice Riley's presence.

Finally, without looking at Riley, Trudy said, "I decided to skip the meeting. How was it?"

"It sucked," Riley said. "I should have skipped it too."

She thought for a moment, then added, "Heather wasn't there either."

"No," Trudy said. "I hear her parents came this morning and took her straight home. I guess nobody knows when she'll be coming back to school—or even *if* she'll be coming back."

Trudy finally looked at Riley and said, "Did you hear about what happened to Rory Burdon?"

Riley remembered how Hintz had asked her about Rory last night.

"No," she said.

"The cops showed up at his apartment late last night pounding on his door. Rory had no idea what was going on. He didn't even know what had happened to Rhea. He was scared to death he was going to get arrested, and he didn't even know why. The cops questioned him until they eventually figured out that he wasn't their guy, and then they left."

Trudy shrugged slightly and added, "The poor guy. I shouldn't have mentioned his name to that stupid police chief. But he just kept asking all these questions, I didn't know what else to say."

A silence fell between them. Riley found herself thinking about Ryan Paige, and how she'd mentioned his name to Hintz. Had the cops also paid Ryan a visit last night? It didn't seem unlikely, but Riley hoped not.

Anyway, she felt relieved that Trudy was at least willing to talk to her. Maybe now Riley could explain.

She said slowly, "Trudy, when the cops first got there, that woman cop asked me what I knew, and I couldn't lie about it. I had to say you'd been out last night with Rhea. I also had to tell her about Cassie and Gina and Heather."

Trudy nodded. "I get it, Riley. You don't need to explain. I understand. And I'm sorry … I'm sorry I treated you like …"

Suddenly Trudy was quietly sobbing, her tears falling freely into her breakfast tray.

She said, "Riley, was it my fault? What happened to Rhea, I mean?"

Riley could hardly believe her ears.

"What are you talking about, Trudy? Of course not. How could it be your fault?"

"Well, I was so stupid and drunk last night, and I wasn't paying any attention to what was going on, and I don't even remember when Rhea left the Centaur's Den. The other girls said she left alone. Maybe if I …"

Trudy's voice faded away, but Riley knew what she was leaving unsaid …

"… maybe if I'd just walked Rhea home."

And Riley, too, felt a terrible pang of guilt.

After all, she might well ask herself the same question.

If she hadn't gone off by herself at the Centaur's Den, and *if* she'd been around when Rhea got ready to leave, and *if* she'd offered to walk Rhea home …

That word, *if* …

Riley had never imagined how awful a word could be.

Trudy kept crying quietly, and Riley didn't know what to do to make her feel better.

She half-wondered why she wasn't crying herself.

Of course, she had cried in her own bed last night. But surely she hadn't cried enough—not over something this terrible. Surely there was still more crying in store for her.

She sat picking at her breakfast as Trudy wiped her eyes and blew her nose and settled herself down a bit.

Trudy said, "Riley, the thing I keep wondering is *why*? Why Rhea, I mean? Was it something personal? Did somebody hate her enough to kill her? I don't see how that's even possible. Nobody hated Rhea. Why would anybody hate Rhea?"

Riley didn't reply, but she'd been wondering the same thing. She also wondered whether the cops had found any answers yet.

Trudy continued, "And was it somebody we know who killed her? Is maybe one of us next? Riley, I'm scared."

Again, Riley didn't reply.

She felt sure, though, that Rhea had known her murderer. She didn't know why she was sure—it wasn't like she was a cop or knew anything really about criminals. But something in her gut told her that Rhea had known and trusted her killer—right up until it had been too late to save herself.

Trudy looked at Riley steadily, then said, "You don't seem to be scared."

Riley felt taken aback.

For the first time, it dawned on her …

No, I'm not scared.

She'd been feeling every other sort of awful emotion in the world—guilt, grief, shock—and yes, horror. But her horror was somehow different from fear for her own life. The horror she felt was for Rhea herself, horror at the awfulness of what had happened to her.

But Riley wasn't afraid.

She wondered—was it because of what had happened to her mother all those years ago, the sound of that gunshot, the sight of all that blood, the incomprehensible loss she still struggled with even today?

Had the most terrible trauma she had ever suffered made her stronger than other people?

For some reason, she almost hoped not. It didn't seem quite right to be strong like that, strong in ways that other people weren't.

It just didn't seem quite …

It took Riley a few seconds to think of the word.

Human.

She shivered just a little, then said to Trudy, "I'm heading back to the dorm. I really need to get some sleep. Want to come with me?"

Trudy shook her head.

"I just want to sit here for a while," she said.

Riley got up from her chair and gave Trudy a quick hug. Then she emptied her breakfast tray and left the student union. It wasn't a long walk back to the dorm, and she was relieved not to see any reporters along the way. When she got to the front door of the dorm, she paused for a moment. Now it occurred to her why Trudy hadn't wanted to come back with her right now. She just wasn't ready to face the dorm again.

As Riley stood at the door, she too felt weird about it. Of course, she'd spent the night there. She lived there.

But having spent some time outside, where a return to normality had been declared, was *she* ready to go back inside the building where Rhea had been killed?

She took a deep breath and walked on in through the front door.

At first she thought she felt OK. But as she continued into the hallway, the feeling of strangeness deepened. Riley felt as if she were walking and moving underwater. She headed straight to her own room and was about to open the door when her eyes were drawn toward the room farther down the hallway, the room that Rhea and Heather had shared.

She walked to it and saw that the door was shut and sealed off with police tape.

Riley stood there, suddenly feeling horribly curious.

What did it look like in there right now?

Had the room been cleaned up since she'd last seen it?

Or was Rhea's blood still there?

Riley was seized by an awful temptation—to ignore that tape and open that door and walk right inside.

She knew better than to give in to that temptation. And of course the door would be locked.

But even so …

Why do I feel this way?

She stood there, trying to understand this mysterious urge. She began to realize—it had something to do with the killer himself.

She couldn't help thinking …

If I open that door, I'll be able to look into his mind.

It made no sense, of course.

And it was a truly terrifying idea—to look into an evil mind.

Why? she kept asking herself.

Why did she want to understand the killer?

Why on earth did she feel such unnatural curiosity?

For the first time since this whole terrible thing had happened, Riley suddenly felt really afraid …

… not *for* herself, but *of* herself.

CHAPTER SIX

The following Monday morning, Riley felt deeply uneasy as she slipped into her seat for her advanced psychology class.

It was, after all, the first class she'd attended since Rhea's murder four days earlier.

It was also the class she'd been trying to study for before she and her friends had gone to the Centaur's Den.

It was sparsely attended today—many students here at Lanton didn't feel ready to get back to their studies just yet. Trudy was here too, but Riley knew that her roommate was also uncomfortable with this rush to get back to "normal." The other students were all unusually quiet as they took their places.

The sight of Professor Brant Hayman coming into the room put Riley a bit more at ease. He was young and quite good-looking in a corduroy-clad academic sort of way. She remembered Trudy telling Rhea …

"Riley likes to impress Professor Hayman. She's got a thing for him."

Riley cringed at the memory.

She certainly didn't want to think she had a "thing" for him.

It was just that she'd first studied with him back when she'd been a freshman. He hadn't been a professor yet, just a graduate assistant. She'd thought even then he was a wonderful teacher—informative, enthusiastic, and sometimes entertaining.

Today, Dr. Hayman's expression was serious as he put his briefcase on his desk and looked at the students. Riley realized that he was going to get right to the point.

He said, "Look, there's an elephant in this room. We all know what it is. We need to clear the air. We need to discuss it openly."

Riley held her breath. She felt sure she wasn't going to like what was going to happen next.

Then Hayman said …

"Did anybody here know Rhea Thorson? Not just as an acquaintance, not just someone you'd sometimes run into on campus. Really well, I mean. As a friend."

Riley cautiously put up her hand, and so did Trudy. Nobody

else in the classroom did.

Hayman then asked, "What kinds of feelings have the two of you been going through since she was killed?"

Riley cringed a little.

It was, after all, the same question she had overheard those reporters asking Cassie and Gina on Friday. Riley had managed to avoid those reporters, but was she going to have to answer that question now?

She reminded herself that this was a psychology class. They were here to deal with these kinds of questions.

And yet Riley wondered …

Where do I even begin?

She was relieved when Trudy spoke up.

"Guilty. I could have stopped it from happening. I was with her at the Centaur's Den before it happened. I didn't even notice when she left. If only I'd just walked her home …"

Trudy's voice trailed off. Riley gathered up the nerve to speak.

"I feel the same way," she said. "I went off to sit by myself when we all got to the Den, and I didn't pay any attention to Rhea. Maybe if I had …"

Riley paused, then added, "So I feel guilty too. And something else. Selfish, I think. Because I wanted to be alone."

Dr. Hayman nodded. With a sympathetic smile he said, "So neither of you walked Rhea home."

After a pause, he added, "A sin of omission."

The phrase startled Riley a little.

It seemed oddly ill-suited to what Riley and Trudy had failed to do. It sounded too benign, not nearly dire enough, hardly a matter of life and death.

But of course, it was true—as far as it went.

Hayman looked around at the rest of the class.

"What about the rest of you? Have you ever done—or failed to do—the same sort of thing in a similar situation? Have you ever, shall we say, let a female friend walk somewhere alone at night when you really ought to have walked her home? Or maybe just neglected to do something that might have been important to someone else's safety? Not taken away somebody's car keys when they'd had a drink too many? Ignored a situation that might have resulted in injury or even death?"

A confused murmur passed among the students.

Riley realized—it was really a tough question.

After all, if Rhea hadn't been killed, neither Riley nor Trudy would have given their "sin of omission" a moment's thought.

They'd have forgotten all about it.

It was hardly any surprise that at least some of the students found it hard to remember one way or the other. And the truth was, Riley herself couldn't remember for sure about herself. Had there been other times when she'd neglected to look out for someone's safety?

Might she have been responsible for the deaths of others—if it weren't for sheer dumb luck?

After a few moments, several reluctant hands went up.

Then Hayman said, "What about the rest of you? How many of you just can't remember for sure?"

Almost all the rest of the students raised their hands.

Hayman nodded and said, "OK, then. Most of you may well have made the same mistake at one time or another. So how many people here feel guilty for the way you acted or the thing you probably should have done but didn't do?"

There was more confused muttering and even a few gasps.

"What?" Hayman asked. "None of you? Why not?"

One girl raised her hand and stammered, "Well ... it was different because ... I suppose because ... nobody got killed, I guess."

There was a general murmur of agreement.

Riley noticed that another man had stepped into the classroom. It was Dr. Dexter Zimmerman, the chairman of the Psychology Department. Zimmerman seemed to have been standing just outside the door listening to the discussion.

She'd had one class with him the semester before last—Social Psychology. He was an older, rumpled, kindly-looking man. Riley knew that Dr. Hayman looked up to him as a mentor—almost idolized him, actually. A lot of students did too.

Riley's own feelings about Professor Zimmerman were more mixed. He'd been an inspiring teacher, but somehow she didn't relate to him the way most others did. She wasn't sure exactly why.

Hayman explained to the class, "I asked Dr. Zimmerman to stop by and take part in today's discussion. He should really be able to help us out. He's just about the most insightful guy I've ever known in my life."

Zimmerman blushed and chuckled a little.

Hayman asked him, "So what do you make of what you just

heard from my students?"

Zimmerman tilted his head and thought for a moment.

Then he said, "Well, at least some of your students seem to think there's some kind of moral difference at work here. If you neglect to help someone and they get hurt or killed, it's wrong—but it's all right if there don't happen to be any bad consequences. But I don't see the distinction. The behaviors are identical. Different consequences don't really change whether they're right or wrong."

A hush fell over the classroom as Zimmerman's point started to sink in.

Hayman asked Zimmerman, "Does that mean that *everybody* here should be wracked with guilt right along with Riley and Trudy?"

Zimmerman shrugged.

"Maybe just the opposite. Does feeling guilty do anybody any good? Is it going to bring the young woman back? Maybe there are more appropriate things for all of us to be feeling right now."

Zimmerman stepped in front of the desk and made eye contact with the students.

"Tell me, those of you who weren't very close to Rhea. How are you feeling toward these two friends of hers right now—Riley and Trudy?"

The classroom was silent for a moment.

Then Riley was astonished to hear a few sobs break out in the classroom.

One girl said in a choked voice, "Oh, I just feel so awful for them."

Another said, "Riley and Trudy, I wish you didn't feel guilty. You shouldn't. What happened to Rhea was terrible enough. I just can't imagine the pain you're feeling right now."

Other students echoed their agreement.

Zimmerman gave the class an understanding smile.

He said, "I guess most of you know that my specialty is criminal pathology. My life's work is about trying to understand a criminal's mind. And for the last three days, I've been struggling to make sense of this crime. So far, I'm only really sure of one thing. This was personal. The killer knew Rhea and wanted her dead."

Again, Riley struggled to comprehend the incomprehensible …

Someone hated Rhea enough to kill her?

Then Zimmerman added, "As awful as that sounds, I can assure you of one thing. He won't kill again. Rhea was his target, no one else. And I'm confident the police will find him soon."

He leaned against the edge of the desk and said, "I can tell you one other thing—wherever the killer is right now, whatever he's doing, he's not feeling what all of you seem to be feeling. He is incapable of sympathy for another person's suffering—much less the actual *empathy* I sense in this room."

He wrote down the words "sympathy" and "empathy" on the big whiteboard.

He asked, "Would anybody care to remind me of the difference between these two words?"

Riley was a bit surprised that Trudy raised her hand.

Trudy said, "Sympathy is when you care about what somebody else is feeling. Empathy is when you actually *share* somebody else's feelings."

Zimmerman nodded and jotted down Trudy's definitions.

"Exactly," he said. "So I suggest that all of us put aside our feelings of guilt. Focus instead on our capacity for empathy. It separates us from the world's most terrible monsters. It's precious—most of all at a time like now."

Hayman seemed to be pleased with Zimmerman's observations.

He said, "If it's OK with everybody, I think we should cut today's class short. It's been pretty intense—but I hope it has been helpful. Just remember, you're all processing some pretty powerful feelings right now—even those of you who weren't very close to Rhea. Don't expect the grief, shock, and horror to go away anytime soon. Let them run their course. They're part of the healing process. And don't be afraid to reach out to the school's counselors for help. Or to each other. Or to me and Dr. Zimmerman."

As the students got up from their desks to leave, Zimmerman called out …

"On your way out, give Riley and Trudy a hug. They could use it."

For the first time during the class, Riley felt annoyed.

What makes him think I need a hug?

The truth was, hugs were the last things she wanted right now.

Suddenly she remembered—this was the thing that had turned her off about Dr. Zimmerman when she had taken a class with him. He was way too cuddly for her taste, and he was all touchy-feely about lots of things, and he liked to tell students to hug each other.

That seemed kind of weird for a psychologist who specialized in criminal pathology.

It also seemed odd for a man so big on empathy.

After all, how did he know whether she and Trudy wanted to be hugged or not? He hadn't even bothered to ask.

How empathetic is that?

Riley couldn't help think that the guy was a phony deep down.

Nevertheless, she stood there stoically while one student after another gave her a sympathetic hug. Some of them were crying. And she could see that Trudy didn't mind this attention at all. Trudy kept smiling through her own tears with every hug.

Maybe it's just me, Riley thought.

Was something wrong with her?

Maybe she didn't have the same feelings as other people.

Soon all the hugging was over, and most of the students had left the room, including Trudy. So had Dr. Zimmerman.

Riley was glad to have a moment alone with Dr. Hayman. She walked up to him and said, "Thanks for the talk about guilt and responsibility. I really needed to hear that."

He smiled at her and said, "Glad to be of help. I know this must be very hard for you."

Riley lowered her head for a moment, gathering up her nerve to say something she really wanted to say.

Finally she said, "Dr. Hayman, you probably don't remember, but I was in your Intro to Psych course back in my freshman year."

"I remember," he said.

Riley swallowed down her nervousness and said, "Well, I've always meant to tell you … you really inspired me to major in psychology."

Hayman looked a bit startled now.

"Wow," he said. "That's really nice to hear. Thank you."

They stood looking at each other for an awkward moment. Riley hoped she wasn't making a fool of herself.

Finally Hayman said, "Look, I've been paying attention to you in class—the papers you write, the questions you ask, the ideas you share with everybody. You've got a good mind. And I've got a feeling … you've got questions about what happened to your friend that most of the other kids don't think about—maybe don't even *want* to think about."

Riley gulped again. He was right, of course—almost uncannily right.

Now this *is empathy,* she thought.

She flashed back to the night of the murder, when she'd stood outside Rhea's room wishing she could go inside, feeling as if she'd learn something important if she could only walk through that door at that very moment.

But that moment was gone. When Riley had finally been able to go inside, the room was all cleaned up, looking as if nothing had ever happened there.

She said slowly …

"I really want to understand … *why*. I really want to know …"

Her voice faded. Did she dare say tell Hayman—or anybody else—the truth?

That she wanted to understand the mind of the man who had murdered her friend?

That she almost wanted to *empathize* with him?

She was relieved when Hayman nodded, seeming to understand.

"I know just how you feel," he said. "I used to feel the same way."

He opened a desk drawer and took out a book and handed it to her.

"You can borrow this," he said. "It's a great place to start."

The title of the book was *Dark Minds: The Homicidal Personality Revealed.*

Riley was startled to see that the author was Dr. Dexter Zimmerman himself.

Hayman said, "The man is a genius. You can't begin to imagine the insights he reveals in this book. You've simply got to read it. It might change your life. It sure changed mine."

Riley felt overwhelmed by Hayman's gesture.

"Thank you," she said meekly.

"Don't mention it," Hayman said with a smile.

Riley left the classroom and broke into a trot as she headed out of the building toward the library, eager to sit down with the book.

At the same time, she felt a twinge of apprehension.

"It might change your life," Hayman had told her.

Would that be for the better, or for the worse?

CHAPTER SEVEN

In the university library, Riley sat down at a desk that was in a little enclosure. She put the book on the desk and sat staring at the title—*Dark Minds: The Homicidal Personality Revealed,* by Dr. Dexter Zimmerman.

She wasn't sure why, but she was glad she had chosen to start reading the book here rather than in her dorm room. Perhaps she simply didn't want to be interrupted or be asked what she was reading and why.

Or maybe it was something else.

She touched the cover and felt a strange tingling …

Fear?

No, that couldn't be it.

Why would she be frightened of a book?

Nevertheless, she felt apprehensive, as if she was about to do something forbidden.

She opened the book and her eyes fell on the first sentence …

Long before committing a murder, the killer has the potential to commit that murder.

As she read the author's explanations for that statement, she felt herself slipping into a dark and terrible world—an unfamiliar world, but one that she felt mysteriously fated to explore and try to understand.

Turning the pages, she was introduced to one murderous monster after another.

She met Ted Kaczynski, nicknamed the "Unabomber," who used explosives to kill three people and injure twenty-three others.

And then there was John Wayne Gacy, who loved to dress as a clown and entertain children at parties and charitable events. He was liked and respected in his community, even while he secretly went about sexually assaulting and murdering thirty-three boys and young men, many of whose bodies he hid in the crawl space of his house.

Riley was especially fascinated with Ted Bundy, who

eventually confessed to thirty murders—although there might have been many more. Handsome and charismatic, he had approached his female victims in public places and easily won their trust. He described himself as "the most cold-hearted son of a bitch you'll ever meet." But the women he killed had never recognized his cruelty until it was too late.

The book was full of information about such killers. Bundy and Gacy had been remarkably intelligent, and Kaczynski had been a child prodigy. Both Bundy and Gacy had been raised by cruel, violent men, and they had suffered brutal sexual abuse when they'd been young.

But Riley wondered—what had turned them into killers? Plenty of people were traumatized in childhood without turning to murder.

She pored over Dr. Zimmerman's text looking for answers.

According to his assessment, homicidal criminals knew right from wrong, and they were also aware of the possible consequences for their actions. But they were uniquely able to shut off that awareness in order to commit their crimes.

Zimmerman also wrote what he had said in class—that killers lacked any capacity for empathy. But they were excellent imposters who could feign empathy and other ordinary feelings, making them hard to spot—and often likeable and charming.

Nevertheless, there were sometimes visible warning signs. For example, a psychopath was often someone who loved power and control. He expected to be able to attain grandiose, unrealistic goals without much effort, as though success was simply his due. He'd use any means to achieve those goals—nothing was out of bounds, however criminal and cruel. He typically blamed other people for his failures, and he lied easily and frequently …

Riley's mind boggled at Zimmerman's wealth of information and insights.

But as she read, she kept thinking about the first sentence in the book …

Long before committing a murder, the killer has the potential to commit that murder.

Although murderers were different in many ways, Zimmerman seemed to be saying that there was a certain kind of person who was destined to kill.

Riley wondered—why weren't such people spotted and

stopped before they could even get started?

Riley was anxious to keep reading and find out whether Zimmerman had any answers to that question. But she glanced at her watch and realized that a lot of time had passed since she'd fallen under the book's spell. She had to go right now, or she'd be late for her next class.

She left the library and headed across campus, clutching Dr. Zimmerman's book as she walked along. About halfway to her class, she couldn't resist the pull of the book, and she flipped it open and skimmed parts of the text as she walked.

Then she heard a male voice say …

"Hey, watch out!"

Riley stopped in her tracks and looked up from her book.

Ryan Paige was standing on the sidewalk right in front of her, grinning at her.

He seemed highly amused by Riley's distracted state of mind.

He said, "Wow, that must be some book you're reading. You almost plowed right into me there. Could I have a look?"

Thoroughly embarrassed now, Riley handed him the book.

"I'm impressed," Ryan said, thumbing through a few pages. "Dexter Zimmerman is a flat-out genius. Criminal law isn't my focus, but I took a couple of classes with him as an undergrad, he really blew me away. I've read some of his books, but not this one. Is it as good as I figure it must be?"

Riley simply nodded.

Ryan's smile faded.

He said, "Terrible thing, what happened to that girl Thursday night. Did you happen to know her?"

Riley nodded again and said, "Rhea and I were in the same dorm—Gettier Hall."

Ryan looked shocked.

"Wow, I'm so sorry. It must have been awful for you."

For a moment Riley flashed back to the scream that woke her up on that horrible night, the sight of Heather collapsed and sick in the hall, the blood on the dorm room floor, Rhea's wide open eyes and slashed throat …

She shuddered and thought …

He's got no idea.

Ryan shook his head and said, "The whole campus is on edge—has been ever since it happened. The cops even came by my place that night, woke me up, asked me all kinds of questions. Can you believe it?"

Riley cringed a little.

Of course she could believe it. After all, she was the one who gave Ryan's name to the police.

Should she admit it? Should she apologize?

While she was trying to decide, Ryan shrugged and said, "Well, I guess they must have talked to lots of guys. I hear she was at the Centaur's Den that night, and of course I was too. They were doing their job. I understand. And I sure hope they catch the bastard who did this. Anyway, what happened to me is no big deal—not compared to how this must be for you. Like I said, I'm really, really sorry."

"Thanks," Riley said, looking at her watch.

She hated to be rude. In fact, she'd been hoping to run into this handsome guy again. But right now she was going to be late for class—and besides, she somehow wasn't in the state of mind to enjoy even Ryan's company.

Ryan handed the book back to her, as if he understood. Then he tore a small piece of paper out of a notebook and jotted something down.

A bit shyly, he said, "Look, I hope this doesn't seem to be out of line, but … I just thought I'd give you my phone number. Maybe you'd just like to talk sometime. Or not. It's up to you."

He handed her the bit of paper and added, "I wrote my name down too—in case you'd forgotten."

"Ryan Paige," Riley said. "I hadn't forgotten."

She recited her own phone number for him. She worried that it must seem brusque of her to tell him her number instead of writing it down for him. The truth was, she was glad to think she might see him again. She was just having trouble acting all friendly to anybody new right now.

"Thanks," she said, putting the paper in her pocket. "I'll see you later."

Riley brushed right past Ryan and headed toward her class.

She heard Ryan call out behind her, "I hope so."

*

As the rest of the school day passed, Riley read snatches of Zimmerman's book whenever she got a chance. All day long she couldn't help wondering—might Rhea's killer be like Ted Bundy, a charming man who had managed to engage Rhea's trust?

She remembered what Dr. Zimmerman had said in class that morning …

"The killer knew Rhea and wanted her dead."

And unlike Bundy, Rhea's killer was finished. He would seek no other victims.

At least according to Dr. Zimmerman.

He seemed so positive, Riley thought.

She wondered how he could be so certain.

Later that evening, Riley and Trudy were in their dorm room studying quietly together. Little by little, Riley started feeling restless and impatient. She wasn't sure why.

Finally she got up from her desk, put on her jacket, and headed for the door.

Trudy looked up from her homework and asked, "Where are you going?"

"I don't know," Riley said. "Just out for a little while."

"Alone?" Trudy asked.

"Yeah."

Trudy shut her book and looked at Riley anxiously.

"Are you sure that's a good idea?" she asked. "Maybe I should come along. Or maybe you should call the campus escort service."

Riley felt a surprising burst of impatience.

"Trudy, that's ridiculous," she said. "All I want to do is take a little walk. We can't live like this—always afraid something awful might happen. Life has to go on."

Riley was startled by the sharpness of her own words. And she could see by Trudy's expression that her feelings were hurt.

Trying to speak more gently, Riley said, "Anyway, it's not very late. And I won't stay out long. I'll be safe. I promise."

Trudy didn't reply. She silently opened her book and started reading again.

Riley sighed and walked out into the hallway. She stood there for a few moments wondering …

Where do I want to go?

What do I want to do?

Slowly came a vague realization …

I want to go back.

She wanted to know how Rhea's death had happened.

CHAPTER EIGHT

With relentless questions about Rhea's death dogging her mind, Riley stood still and looked up and down the dorm hallway.

This was where it started, she thought.

She found herself picturing the place on Thursday night, the moment after she reluctantly agreed to go to the Centaur's Den with her friends.

She had just put on her denim jacket over a flattering crop top and stepped out into the hallway. Trudy and Rhea had been rounding up the other girls for their outing—Cassie, Gina, and Heather.

Riley remembered the bustle of immature excitement in the air—the promise of drinking, dancing, and maybe some guys.

She also remembered how disconnected she'd felt from all that.

She retraced the group's steps down the hall and continued on outside.

It was already dark out—not as dark as it had been that night, but the lamps along the pathways were on, so it was easy for Riley to visualize how things had looked at the time.

As she walked the way they had all taken, Riley remembered lagging behind the others, tempted to head back to her room to resume her studies. Cassie, Gina, and Heather had clustered together, chattering and giggling. Rhea and Trudy had walked side by side, playfully punching each other in the arm over some joke that Riley hadn't been able to hear.

Riley kept visualizing all that had happened as she followed their route off campus and into the surrounding streets. Soon she arrived at the entrance to the Centaur's Den, as they had that night. She remembered being pushed ahead into the smoky, noisy bar.

As she walked on inside now, the place was markedly less crowded than it had been that night. It was also quieter. Alanis Morissette's "Uninvited" was playing on the jukebox, softly enough for Riley to be able to hear the nearby cracking of billiard balls. And there were no moving light beams or sparkles flashing over the empty dance floor.

But Riley could vividly remember the din and chaos of that

night—how "Whiskey in the Jar" had blared so loudly that the whole place vibrated, and how Heather, Cassie, and Gina had headed straight toward the bar, and how Trudy had grabbed both Riley and Rhea by the hands and yelled over the music …

"Come on, let's dance, the three of us!"

As she stood looking at the now-empty dance floor, Riley remembered shaking her head and pulling her hand away, and how Trudy had looked hurt and then stuck out her tongue at her and then went right on dancing with Rhea.

Had that been the last time Riley had seen Rhea—at least alive?

She remembered heading downstairs to be by herself. The next time she'd seen her friends was when they'd come stumbling drunkenly down the stairs and Trudy had been wielding a full pitcher of beer.

Riley had asked Trudy …

"Where's Rhea?"

Trudy hadn't known, but one of the other girls—Heather, Riley thought—had said that Rhea had already gone back to the dorm.

Riley swallowed hard at the realization—yes, the last time she had ever seen Rhea alive was right here on this dance floor.

She felt a renewed rush of guilt, and the awfulness of that word *if* …

If maybe I'd just stayed and danced with them …

But she reminded herself of what Dr. Zimmerman had said about guilt—that it wasn't going to bring Rhea back …

"Focus instead on our capacity for empathy."

Riley wondered—was that what she was trying to do right now, by reliving what she and her friends had gone through that night?

Was she trying to empathize?

If so, with whom?

She had no idea.

All she knew was that her curiosity was growing by the moment.

She simply wanted to *know*—without really having any idea what she expected to find out.

Riley turned away from the dance floor and noticed a couple of guys playing pool. One of them was Harry Rampling, the football player who had approached her downstairs that night.

Riley watched as Harry took a pool shot that didn't put any balls in any pockets. Riley thought it was a dumb shot. She was a pretty good pool player herself.

Then Harry made eye contact with her and sneered a little.

He stepped over to his opponent, who was getting ready to take a shot of his own, and whispered something in his ear while looking at Riley. Then the two guys chuckled snidely, so Riley was sure that whatever Harry had said about her was gross and insulting.

She felt a flash of anger. She more than half-wanted to walk right over and demand to know what Harry had said about her, and then insist that he apologize.

But she didn't want to get distracted from the task at hand.

Instead, she stood looking at him for a moment, wondering whether the police had paid him a visit that night. After all, she'd mentioned his name to Chief Hintz, the same as she'd mentioned Ryan's.

But she remembered Hintz's approval at the mention of Harry's name and his disapproval when Riley said she'd brushed him off. Of course the chief thought far too highly of the football hero to ever suspect him of murder. Riley wondered if maybe he'd been wrong.

Should she maybe go over and ask Harry some questions?

What good would that do? she thought.

After all, she wasn't a cop. She'd have no idea how to go about it.

Besides, the fact that he thoroughly disgusted her was hardly any reason to suspect him. Really, as far as the murder was concerned, he was no different from Ryan Paige—just another guy who had happened to be at the Centaur's Den that night.

She gazed around the room for a moment. Someone else had been there that night, either in the club or waiting outside. She kept thinking that she should be able to remember more faces from that night. But of course the police had questioned everyone who had been here and come up with no suspects.

Riley turned toward the bar. Sitting on a stool alone drinking a beer was a tall, lanky guy with thick glasses. Riley recognized him right away. He was Rory Burdon, who'd been surprised by a police visit that night. Right now he appeared to be lost in thought.

She walked over to the stool next to him and asked, "Is it OK if I sit down?"

Rory snapped out of his reverie and looked at Riley with surprise.

Then he shrugged and said, "Sure."

Riley sat down and ordered a beer for herself.

Rory asked her, "You were one of Rhea's friends, weren't you? I saw you with her sometimes."

Riley nodded.

Rory sat staring at his beer for a moment.

Then he said, "I've been a wreck ever since. I didn't go to any classes today, and I don't guess I will tomorrow. I can't get it through my head what happened. I'd been dancing with her just a little while before she left."

Then he shook his head and said, "Who would do that to a nice girl like Rhea?"

Riley didn't know what to say. It certainly wasn't a question she knew the answer to. Surely the only person who did know the answer was the killer himself.

Rory took a sip of his beer and said, "The cops came to my apartment that night. That was how I found out about it. It was awful. I don't mean it was awful getting questioned like that. The cops were just doing their job. It was just such an awful way to find out."

He looked at Riley with a curious expression.

"How did you find out about it?" he asked.

Riley shuddered deeply.

"I found her body," she said.

Rory's eyes widened.

"Oh, I'm so sorry," he said. "It was so stupid to ask."

"It's OK," Riley said. "You couldn't have known."

Riley sipped on her own beer. They were both quiet for a moment.

Then Rory said slowly and cautiously …

"I don't know if I should tell you this. The truth is, I haven't told this to anybody else …"

Then he fell quiet again.

Riley felt a twinge of expectation. Was he going to tell her something about what had happened to Rhea?

Then he said, "I had a real crush on Rhea. What happened to her hit me really hard."

Riley was startled. She remembered how Rhea's friends had teased her over her "thing" about Rory.

Should she tell Rory that Rhea had felt the same way about him?

Rory continued, "She was really nice to me. She even danced

with me from time to time—like she did that night. I'm sure it was just to be friendly, and I knew better than to ask her out on a real date or anything like that. The thing is …"

He paused again.

Then he said, "I remember when she left that night. I was standing nearby when she told her friends she was going back to her room. I was kind of worried. I thought maybe she shouldn't walk there alone. But …"

His face twisted with emotion.

"I thought about going over to her and asking if she wanted me to walk her to the dorm. But I was … too scared, can you believe it? I thought if I offered to walk her home—well, maybe she'd take it the wrong way. Maybe she'd get weirded out and think I was trying to stalk her or something."

He seemed to be fighting back tears now.

"If I'd gone with her, maybe it wouldn't have happened," he said. "But I was too much of a coward."

Riley shivered a little. She felt a sudden aching all over at that awful word, "coward."

This is empathy, she thought.

And it wasn't a pleasant feeling, experiencing someone else's emotional pain.

She was glad of one thing, though. She'd been right not to tell him that his crush on Rhea had been requited. Then he'd know for sure that Rhea would have let him walk him home if he'd simply asked.

That would make him feel much, much worse.

But she had to say something. She couldn't just let him go on feeling like this.

She said, "You weren't a coward. A lot of people feel this way—people who knew her, I mean. I do too. I was here that night, and I didn't even …"

Her voice faded a moment.

Then she said, "I think we've all got to realize—it wasn't our fault. We weren't responsible for what happened. Someone else did it, and that person needs to be found and made to pay for it. It's wrong—really, really wrong to blame ourselves."

Rory's face seemed to relax a little.

Riley figured she must be saying the right thing. She almost added …

"Life goes on."

… but she managed to stop herself.

After all, that old cliché simply wasn't true.

The events of last week proved it.

Rory said, "I wish I'd gotten to know her better."

Riley thought sadly …

Yeah, me too.

She patted Rory on the shoulder and said, "You just take care of yourself, OK?"

Rory nodded and took another sip of his beer. Without finishing her own, Riley got up from the bar and walked away. As she passed the pool table, she was glad that Harry Rampling and his pal were too immersed in their game to notice her.

When Riley stepped outside, the sudden burst of cool night air reminded her of when she'd left the Centaur's Den Thursday night. She stopped and stood there, not far from the door, not sure what she wanted to do next.

Little by little, an unsettling feeling came over her …

He was here, she thought.

The murderer stood where I am right now, waiting.

She didn't know why, but she felt absolutely sure of it.

In fact, she could feel exactly what he had felt as he'd waited— his heightened awareness, his quickening breath and pulse, his eager anticipation.

She shuddered as she realized …

I'm empathizing with him.

It was a truly terrifying idea—as terrifying in its way as the sight of Rhea's body.

She wondered—did she dare surrender to this feeling?

Did she dare descend into the darkness of his mind?

I've got to do this if I can, she told herself firmly. *I've got to find out what happened to Rhea.*

CHAPTER NINE

Riley stopped herself in mid-thought.

What do you mean? she asked herself. *What do you think you're doing?*

And yet she couldn't drive the idea out of her mind—that she could somehow be getting a glimpse of the killer's actual sensations.

She stepped back from the doorway and leaned against the building's outside wall, taking deep breaths and trying to force herself to think rationally.

Surely, she told herself, *you don't believe that you can find out what happened to Rhea by paying attention to ...*

... to what?

But even as she stood there arguing with herself, she knew that she was sensing something real. She was getting some insight into what had happened here.

And she had to learn whatever she could.

Just as she felt sure he must have done, she stepped backward until she was hidden in the shadows near the door to the Centaur's Den.

She imagined the door opening and Rhea stepping outside alone.

He sees her, she thought. *But she doesn't see him.*

She wondered for a moment—had he been waiting especially for Rhea?

She remembered again what Dr. Zimmerman had said ...

"The killer knew Rhea and wanted her dead."

But now Riley realized that her rational mind was also engaged alongside this new rush of sensation, and she felt some doubts about the professor's explanation. For example, how would the killer have known for sure that Rhea would choose to walk home alone that night, and not surrounded by friends? Could he have been lying in wait here for any girl who might unwisely decide to leave the Centaur's Den by herself?

Might Zimmerman be wrong?

Riley didn't know. She just knew that she needed to use her

own instincts along with her own logic.

Now she was finding it easier to imagine Rhea blithely continuing on her way down the street. She remembered the boots Rhea had been wearing that night, and now she could almost hear them clacking against the pavement, and she could visualize the sharp outline of her figure under the streetlights.

For a few moments she stood where the killer must have stood, waiting for Rhea to get some distance away. Then she started to walk in the same direction. Riley was wearing sneakers, so her own footsteps were quiet. She guessed that the killer must have been wearing soft-soled shoes of some kind as well. He would have wanted to remain as silent as he possibly could.

Riley continued walking some thirty or forty feet back from where she imagined Rhea to be until she got to the campus, with its winding paths lighted by lamps. As she felt the killer must have done, she started to close the distance between them.

As she got closer, she realized that even her sneaker-clad feet would have become audible to Rhea—and so would the killer's footsteps.

Did Rhea look back to see who was following her?

Maybe.

Or maybe she just quickened her pace.

Riley began walking faster to keep up with her.

She must have gotten scared, she thought.

And eventually, Rhea must have dared to look back.

Riley could visualize her face under the lamplight, could see her expression clearly.

She could see a half-smile of relief on her face.

She knew him, Riley realized.

But how well did she know him?

Perhaps just well enough to be relieved, Riley guessed.

Reassured, Rhea probably slowed her footsteps down to an ordinary pace.

Riley could feel the killer's mounting satisfaction, and his eager expectancy.

Everything was going exactly as he had hoped.

And she could hear him calling out to her in a soft, friendly voice ...

"Hey, it's late. Would you like someone to walk with you?"

Riley imagined Rhea slowing to a near stop and replying in with a shy laugh ...

"Yeah, maybe that would be a good idea."

Riley could feel the killer's exultation now as he walked toward Rhea.

She could also sense him thinking …

This one will do.

She'll do just fine.

Riley suddenly froze in her tracks, jolted out of her uncanny feeling of connection with the killer.

She was stunned by the impressions that had flooded her mind, giving her imagination and her logic a power she hadn't felt before.

But the sensations were gone now.

Try as she might, she couldn't imagine what had happened after he'd joined his all-too-trusting victim here on the path.

But maybe that was just as well, after all.

Did she really want to visualize the murder itself as vividly as she had the events leading up to it?

She tried to shake off the feeling of palpable evil she had just allowed herself to experience, but the horror wouldn't leave.

She wondered …

What did I think I was doing?

She remembered what Dr. Zimmerman had said about empathy.

"It separates us from the world's most terrible monsters."

But what happened to people who started empathizing with monsters? Might they become monsters themselves?

Her skin crawled at the very idea.

She remembered something else Dr. Zimmerman had said.

"This was personal. The killer knew Rhea and wanted her dead."

Surely he'd known what he was talking about—much better than Riley possibly could.

And yet, deep down in her gut, she felt sure he'd been wrong.

The killer had known Rhea, but only a little—maybe not much more than her name.

And she had known him just well enough to not be frightened by him, to trust him to walk her to her dorm.

He'd had nothing personal against her. She just happened to be the girl who walked out of the Centaur's Den alone while he'd been waiting.

Riley also felt sure that the killer wasn't finished yet. If he wasn't stopped, he would claim another victim.

It was only a matter of time.

She wondered—if Zimmerman had been wrong about that, what about the police?

Did they understand the kind of monster they were dealing with?

She tried to tell herself it wasn't her business …

What do I think I am, a cop?

Anyway, what could she possibly do about it?

Without stopping to think, she broke into a run. She ran all the way off campus and then the remaining four blocks to the Lanton police station. She paused outside the building to catch her breath, then went on inside.

A uniformed woman was sitting at the front desk.

She asked Riley, "Can I help you?"

Riley's heart was still pounding, both from excitement and from running.

She said, "I need to talk to somebody about—about the girl who was murdered on Thursday night."

The woman squinted at her.

"Do you have new information?" she asked.

Riley opened her mouth to speak, but didn't know what to say.

Did she have new information?

No, all she had was a vague but overpowering hunch.

She felt a hand on her shoulder and heard a male voice behind her.

"I know you. What are you doing here?"

Riley turned around and saw the big, reddish face of Officer Steele, the cop who had shown up when she'd been blocking the doorway to Rhea's room. Riley remembered that he hadn't been pleased to see her then.

"You've got some explaining to do," he'd said. *"Start talking."*

She didn't guess he was any happier to see her right now.

She stammered, "I just—I want to know how the investigation is going."

Steele's face wrinkled with irritation.

"I sure don't know what business that is of yours," he said.

Riley felt a flash of anger.

"Rhea was my friend," she said. "That makes it my business. And nobody has heard any news at all."

Steele shook his head as if he were about to say no.

But before he did, the woman behind the desk said, "Go ahead,

Nat. Tell the poor kid what you can. It can't hurt."

Steele let out a low growl of irritation.

Then he said, "We've been scouring Lanton for clues, questioning people left and right. We're now pretty sure of one thing. Whoever did it was just passing through town. He's not in Lanton anymore."

Riley almost gasped with surprise.

"You mean—Rhea didn't even know him?"

"No, he was probably a total stranger."

Riley could hardly believe her ears. This completely contradicted what her own instincts had told her just now.

It even contradicted what Dr. Zimmerman had said in class.

She really didn't know what to say now.

Officer Steele said, "We're checking into similar murders around the country. Maybe the killer has done the same thing elsewhere. If so, maybe we can get the FBI involved, but ..."

He shrugged without finishing his sentence. Riley knew what he was leaving unsaid.

"We don't have much hope of that."

She also felt sure that the local cops weren't trying very hard.

It was all she could do not to blurt out what she knew—or thought she knew. But Steele already didn't like her. It wouldn't help to make him think she was out of her mind.

But she couldn't leave without trying to make herself heard. She remembered the woman cop who had been at the crime scene—Officer Frisbie.

When she'd gotten Riley alone, she'd said ...

"Right now my gut is saying that you're the one person around here who might be able to tell me exactly what I need to know."

For some reason, Frisbie had believed in Riley even when Steele hadn't.

She also believed in gut feelings.

Maybe she'd listen to Riley.

She said, "Is Officer Frisbie here? I want to talk to her."

Steele scowled sharply at Riley.

"Do you have any information?" he asked.

Riley wanted to say ...

Yes, and you're going about this completely wrong.

But she just couldn't. She had nothing to say that this close-minded man would pay any attention to.

Steele said, "If you've got information, you can tell me about it right now. Otherwise, you're wasting the department's time."

He turned and walked away.

Riley looked at the uniformed woman at the desk.

"Please," she said, "could you just tell me where I could find Officer Frisbie?"

The woman looked a little reluctant to say no.

"Sorry," the woman said. "If you've got a tip, just say so. If not, you'd better be on your way."

Riley left the building, feeling weighed down by discouragement.

What was going on, anyway?

Dr. Zimmerman had been so sure that Rhea's killing had been personal—and also an isolated event.

The cops seemed to think something completely different—that the killer was some kind of drifter who'd just come through and killed a girl at random, and might well be committing such killings elsewhere.

How could they have such conflicting theories?

And why did Riley feel so sure that both theories were wrong?

She trudged her way slowly back to the campus.

As she wended her way along the lighted paths, she found herself wondering …

Is he out tonight?

She stopped in her tracks and turned slowly around, watching and listening. Even by the lamplight, she couldn't see very far into the winding, wooded paths.

Even so, she felt a palpable dark presence in the air.

He's here, she thought. *He's watching me.*

She felt sure of it.

She was surprised not to be terrified. She wanted to confront the killer face to face—even if it meant fighting for her life.

It would be better than drowning in the uncertainty she felt right now.

She was tempted to yell out …

"Come out! Show yourself!"

But she stopped herself.

What good would it do? Who could she expect to show up except maybe some campus cops, who'd be pissed off that she'd raised a false alarm?

As surely as she felt the presence of the killer, she knew better than to think he'd come out at her command.

If he really had her in his sights, he intended either to kill her right now or let her go.

She couldn't make him decide one way or the other.

She stood there waiting silently for a few long moments. Then she remembered when she'd retraced the killer's footsteps, how she'd imagined Rhea quickening her pace when she'd heard him approach.

She realized …

I'm doing this wrong.

He didn't want to attack anyone who wasn't afraid. He wanted his prey to be helpless.

By showing bravery, she'd spoiled herself as bait.

In fact, she felt his awful presence waning as he slipped away into the night.

Then she continued on her way back to her dorm, still mulling over the sensations she had experienced.

She'd never felt anything like that before.

Or had she?

Back when she was a child, after her mother's death, hadn't she sometimes relived that awful event from some point of view other than her own?

Hadn't she also relied on flickers of a similar insight to steer clear of her father when his temper made him dangerous?

Then Riley asked herself the most important question.

Could she use a sensitivity developed in her terrible childhood to find out what had happened to Rhea?

She only knew that she had to try.

Riley whispered to the unseen and unknown killer, wherever he might be …

"You won't get away—not forever. I'm going to make sure of it."

CHAPTER TEN

The whole dorm was eerily quiet as Riley walked through the hallway toward her room. It was late, of course. But even at this time of night, somebody on the floor was usually playing music, oftentimes too loud. Nobody seemed to be in the mood for that kind of thing anymore.

Life is different here now, Riley thought.

She wondered if things would ever get back to the way they'd been before Rhea's murder.

She opened her door quietly, hoping not to awaken Trudy. But as soon as Riley stepped into the darkened room, she heard Trudy's voice call out.

"Riley!"

Riley felt a jolt of alarm. Trudy sounded desperate. Riley clicked on the light and saw Trudy sitting upright in her bed.

"Trudy!" Riley said. "What's the matter?"

"What's the matter?" Trudy echoed. "I haven't been able to get a wink of sleep since I went to bed. I've been worried sick about you. Do you have any idea how long you've been gone? I didn't know what to do. I wondered whether I should call the police."

Riley sat down on the bed next to her roommate.

"I'm sorry I upset you," she said. "I'm fine."

Trudy shook her head.

"No, you're not fine. Something's wrong. You're acting all crazy, staying out so late when a murderer is out there somewhere. I know, I know—Zimmerman says what happened to Rhea is personal and nobody else is going to get killed. But I can't help feeling scared. Where were you, anyway? What were you doing?"

Riley fought down a sigh.

If she told her everything she'd been doing, Trudy would think she really *was* crazy. Still, her roommate deserved at least some explanation.

"I stopped by the Centaur's Den," Riley said. "I had a beer. And I ran into Rory Burdon and talked to him a little. He's taking things kind of hard."

Riley paused, then added, "Did you know Rory had a crush on

Rhea?"

Trudy's eyes widened.

"No!" she said. "The poor guy. Did you tell him how Rhea felt about him?"

Riley shook her head.

"No, he was feeling bad enough as it was. He feels awfully guilty. He thinks he should have walked her home that night."

Trudy cringed and lowered her head. Riley suddenly realized she'd said the wrong thing.

After all, she knew that Trudy felt the same way—only worse, maybe. She'd been too drunk to even notice when Rhea had left.

Riley figured she'd better change the subject.

"I also went to the police station," she said.

"Why?" Trudy asked.

Riley hesitated, then said, "I don't know, I … I guess I just wanted to know if they were getting anywhere with … you know."

Trudy sat silently. She seemed anxious to hear what Riley would say next.

Riley said, "They seem to think it was someone Rhea didn't even know—someone just passing through town. They think he's gone by now. They also think maybe he's done the same sort of thing in other places. They said that maybe the FBI could help."

Trudy looked puzzled.

"But Dr. Zimmerman said …"

"Yeah, I know," Riley said. "But the police see it differently. Anyway, nobody seems to think any of the rest of us are in any danger."

Trudy stared into space.

"I wish I could believe that," she said.

I wish I could believe that too, Riley thought, remembering the feeling she'd just had of the killer being nearby—watching her.

Suddenly Trudy startled Riley by hugging her tightly.

She started crying and said, "Oh, Riley, don't scare me like this anymore, please? I know there's not supposed to be any reason to be scared anymore, but I can't help it. You're my best friend. And the idea of losing you after what happened to Rhea …"

Trudy was too overwhelmed to talk anymore. She sobbed in Riley's arms.

Riley didn't know what to do or say. Could she really promise not to go off on her own like this again?

Why not? she thought.

It seemed only reasonable.

But nothing Riley had experienced a little while ago had felt reasonable. She'd felt driven by the moment of terrible connection she'd felt with the killer. Would she be able to resist the pull if she felt that connection again? Was this really the last time she'd go out into the night alone trying to find him, to understand him?

She gently disentangled herself from Rhea's arms.

"I'm sorry I scared you," she said. "I'll try not to do it again. Anyway, it's late, and you should get some sleep. I should too. I'm going to take a shower."

Rhea nodded, seeming calmer now.

Riley gathered up her pajamas and robe, turned off the light, and left the room.

As she headed for the bathroom, a wave of exhaustion swept over her. It had been a long, strange, troubling day. She really needed to get some rest before tomorrow's classes.

But she somehow doubted she was going to sleep very well tonight.

*

A gunshot rang out.

Little Riley was in the candy store again, and she could smell powder smoke.

A bad man had just shot her mommy.

She dropped her handful of candy and called out ...

"Mommy!"

But when she looked at the crumpled figure on the floor, it wasn't Mommy at all.

It was another woman, younger than Mommy, and blood was pouring out of her throat. She was dead and her eyes were staring up at little Riley.

And for some reason, as if she knew her from some other time or place, little Riley knew her name.

"Rhea," she said.

She fought down her terror and turned around and looked up at the man with the stocking over his head.

Smoke was still coming out of his pistol.

"Who are you?" she demanded, trying not to sound like the little girl she was. "Show me your face."

The man stared at her through the stocking for a moment.

Then he slowly pulled it off his head, and ...
It wasn't a man at all.
It was another woman.
And little Riley knew who the woman was.
It was Riley herself—all grown up!

Riley was awakened from her nightmare by the sound of the room phone ringing.

She opened her eyes and saw morning light streaming in through the window. Trudy lay sound asleep in her bed. Riley considered letting the phone ring until the answering machine kicked in. But the ringing and the sound of the outgoing message would surely wake up Trudy for no good reason.

Riley climbed out of bed and answered the phone.

A gruff male voice spoke to her.

"Hey, girl."

Riley recognized the voice right away—and she wasn't very happy to hear it.

It was her father.

But what was he doing calling her? He didn't even have a telephone.

He must be calling from a payphone in town.

But why? she wondered.

"Hi, Daddy," she said.

A silence fell.

For a few seconds Riley wondered ...

Does either one of us have anything else to say?

Things had been strained between them for many years.

From time to time they both tried to reach out and mend fences, and Riley even visited him in his cabin in the Appalachian Mountains every year or so. They seldom really fought, but when they did things could get really bad. Try as both of them might, they were never quite comfortable together.

"How are you doing?" Riley asked.

She heard a long, familiar growl.

"Well, you know how it is. It's not deer season, so I'm fishing. Trout mostly. The fishing hasn't been too bad."

The mention of fishing brought back scenes of fishing with her father, and also shooting smaller game—squirrels, crows, and groundhogs. Riley had no taste for hunting deer, so she never did that with him. The country around his cabin was beautiful, even if

64

she felt uneasy in his company. He had bought the cabin soon after retiring as a Marine captain.

It was lonely up there, especially during winters. But her father liked it that way. He'd always been a hard man who generally didn't get along with people, and real bitterness had set in after Riley's mother had been murdered.

Another silence fell. Riley knew that it was her cue to say something about herself.

But should she tell him what had happened during the last few days?

How would he react?

She said, "Daddy, there's been a murder here. Right here in my dorm, on my floor. A girl I knew really well. Her throat was slashed. Nobody knows who did it."

There was more silence now. Riley wondered if he was going to say anything at all.

"Well," he finally said slowly, "you know how to watch out for yourself."

Riley felt oddly stung. It took a moment for her to realize why. She'd studied about this very thing in psychology—a problem called a "double bind," when someone gave conflicting messages to someone else.

And in this case, her father was definitely giving her conflicting messages.

On one hand, he was letting her know that she wasn't worthy of his worry and concern. On the other hand, he was telling her that she was tough like he was, and maybe he even admired her a little.

Riley simply had no way of harmonizing those two messages. At least her studies helped her understand why that was so troubling.

Then her father asked, "What's your major these days?"

Riley swallowed down her irritation. She knew what was coming. They'd had this talk before.

"Psychology," she said.

"That's no good," he said, "You should think about changing majors."

Riley felt an urge to explain why he was wrong. But an old, familiar instinct kicked in to stop her.

If she told him the truth—that she liked studying psychology, and besides, this was the second semester of her senior year and it was too late to change—he would lose his temper and the call would end badly.

"I'll think about it, Daddy," she lied, hoping that resolved the issue.

But she sensed that the conversation was already taking an unpleasant turn.

He said, "Girl, it's time you figured something out. You're just not cut out for a normal life. There's no point trying to fit in, trying to live and work like other people do. It's not in your blood. It's not in your nature."

Now Riley felt on the verge of losing her temper.

She'd heard this speech lots of times—and it was the double bind all over again.

Was her father telling her that she was somehow exceptional and destined to do great things in life?

Or was he just telling her that she was some kind of freak?

She certainly didn't know. She felt pretty sure he didn't know either.

Anyway, it was time to end the conversation.

"It was nice of you to call, Daddy," she said. "I've got to go get ready for class."

Yet another silence fell.

As she often did, Riley sensed that her father was struggling to find words to say something he desperately wanted to say, but just couldn't.

"OK," he finally said. "Write to me from time to time."

The call ended. Riley sat there feeling sad and empty—and also worried.

Those words echoed through her head …

"You're just not cut out for a normal life."

Her father had told her that many times, and she'd usually managed to ignore it.

But now, after what had happened last night, she couldn't help but wonder …

Is he right?

After such a rocky childhood and teenage years, she had sometimes desperately craved the kind of normalcy she saw everywhere in the world around her—a husband, children, a stable career, a comfortable future.

But now she couldn't help but feel that things had changed, literally overnight.

What did it mean that she found it so easy, so compelling, to empathize with a murderer, to see the world through his eyes, however briefly?

Riley tried to shake off her worry.

It was time to get ready for her day.

CHAPTER ELEVEN

As Riley sat at her desk trying to read her textbook for Professor Hayman's class, her mind kept drifting to a different book, the one sitting in her desk drawer—*Dark Minds: The Homicidal Personality Revealed,* by Dexter Zimmerman.

She knew she really should have returned it to Professor Hayman by now. He'd lent it to her two weeks ago, and she'd read it three times. He hadn't asked for it back—in fact, he hadn't talked to her about it at all. Maybe he'd forgotten that he'd lent it to her.

Even so, it seemed wrong to just hang onto something that wasn't hers.

Surely I don't plan to read it again, she thought.

But the spell of the book kept drawing her back into the strange and forbidden worlds that it described in detail.

Why would I be drawn to homicidal personalities? she wondered.

Why is it interesting to learn about awful human beings? Why do I want to know about what made them that way?

She realized that she was even more interested in how they got caught, and in why it took so long for some of them to be caught.

At least that's got to be a healthy interest, she told herself.

Even so, she was sure than none of her friends shared any part of her fascination.

In fact, her roommate, Trudy, was the reason the book was stuck away in the desk drawer. When that book had been sitting out on Riley's little bookshelf, Trudy had shuddered visibly every time she noticed it.

Obviously, the mere sight of Zimmerman's book had made Trudy uncomfortable, so Riley had hidden it away.

But why was she hanging onto it?

Riley's thoughts were interrupted by the ringing of her phone, and she wondered who it could be. She seldom got calls from anybody here in her dorm room. She hoped it wasn't her father again—talking to him once every few months was more than enough for her.

She kept remembering what he'd said the last time she'd talked to him …

"You're just not cut out for a normal life."

She sure didn't need to hear any more of that kind of thing right now, especially with her questions about that book rattling around in her head.

She decided to let the phone ring. The outgoing message tape played, with Trudy's voice explaining that she and Riley couldn't come to the phone but if the caller left a message they would return the call.

At the sound of the beep, a short silence followed. Riley guessed it was someone tentatively trying to decide whether to leave a message or not.

Then came a male voice.

"Uh … I'm calling for Riley Sweeney. Riley, you probably don't even remember my name, but …"

Riley smiled.

Of course she remembered his name.

It was Ryan Paige.

She picked up the phone and said, "Hey."

"Um, this is Ryan. Ryan Paige. We met a couple of weeks ago."

Riley tried to act a little surprised.

"Oh, yeah. I remember. What's up?"

"Well, I was just kind of thinking about what to do over the weekend, and I kind of wondered if you might want to get together. Maybe for dinner and a movie. I hear *The Matrix* is good. Have you seen it?"

"No," Riley said.

Then she said nothing. She felt a bit guilty to realize that she was enjoying his awkwardness, but she still waited for him to continue.

Finally he said, "What do you think?"

"Sounds nice," she said.

There was another pause. Then before she could think about it, Riley blurted …

"What are you doing tonight? I mean, maybe we could just have a drink or something."

She felt her face redden with embarrassment.

How uncool was that?

But there was no taking it back. She was glad Ryan couldn't see her face.

"I'd like that," he said. "How does Pooh-Bah's Pub sound to you?"

Riley was a little startled. Pooh-Bah's was an upscale bar that she and her friends never really thought about going to. But if that was what Ryan wanted …

"Sure," she said.

"OK," he said. "When do you want me to pick you up?"

He's got a car! Riley thought.

Trying to regain her cool, she said, "How about eight-thirty? I'll be through studying by then."

"That sounds fine with me. I'll call you when I get there."

Call me? Riley wondered.

Then she realized …

He's got a cell phone too.

Finally Ryan said, "I'm looking forward to seeing you."

"Yeah, I—I'm looking forward to seeing you too."

She hung up, still feeling thoroughly embarrassed.

"What are you doing tonight?" she'd asked.

What did she think she was doing? Since when had she been overeager like that?

But she quickly rationalized …

Maybe it was a smart thing to do.

After all, tonight would be no big deal—just a chance to find out if she and Ryan hit it off, minus all the formalities like a movie and dinner. It would be easier to break it off early if she wanted to. And then Riley could decide whether she liked him enough to bother going on a real date with him.

But then she worried …

What if I like him but he doesn't like me?

She groaned aloud.

She really couldn't win either way. It was either go on a semi-date tonight that might end badly for her, or spend the whole rest of the week in suspense about how a real date was going to go.

Anyway, she still had some studying to do before Ryan came to get her. She opened her book to where she'd left off before the call.

But now she had a hard time concentrating—not from apprehension about her almost-date. She was worried about somebody else.

Trudy.

Trudy had gone to the library after dinner, which ought to have been no big deal. But lately, even that *was* a big deal. Riley's

70

roommate really hadn't been her old sprightly self in the two weeks since Rhea's murder.

She'd been sticking to a strict, restrictive routine. She went to her classes, and to lunch and dinner at the student union, but almost nowhere else, ever. She spent the rest of her time holed up in her room, sometimes studying, sometimes just sitting quietly, staring into space or down at her own hands. She seldom even played the pop diva music that usually annoyed Riley so much.

Riley knew that she hadn't been her own self lately, either. But she was working on getting back to normal. She wasn't completely successful, but at least she wasn't letting what had happened to Rhea completely disrupt her life.

Riley had been glad when Trudy announced that she was going out to the library for a while. She'd even cautiously told Trudy so, although she was careful not to make too big a deal out of it— Trudy was awfully touchy these days.

But now she couldn't help but wonder how Trudy's little outing was going.

Was she feeling overwhelmed and discouraged?

Riley tried to remind herself that she wasn't responsible for Trudy's emotional well-being. She knew that Trudy had been spending some time with the campus counselors, and it was up to them to help her get over this. But so far, they didn't seem to be doing a lot of good—at least as far as Riley could tell.

Riley glanced at her watch and saw that time was slipping by. She needed to finish studying quickly and get dressed to go out with Ryan.

A sort-of date, she thought as she turned the pages of her textbook. *Does that mean things actually are getting back to normal?*

Finishing up her senior year and getting through graduation would be stressful enough.

Surely there would be no more terrible things happening.

But as for things getting back to normal, Riley couldn't help but wonder …

Is there any such thing as "normal" anymore?

CHAPTER TWELVE

It was getting dark by the time Trudy started home from the library. She really hadn't gotten any studying done there, but that hadn't even been the point, really.

She was proud of herself for what she had done. For a while she had looked over a selection of newly acquired books on a shelf. Then she had sat down and leafed through some of her class notes.

And now she even had the good sense to be amused at her own pride at accomplishing those minuscule tasks. She knew that amusement was a good sign.

At that moment, Trudy was feeling a little better about herself.

This simple outing had been her counselor's idea. An evening trip to the library was supposed to be a way for Trudy to test herself, to try to conquer her fears.

"Baby steps," Trudy's counselor kept saying.

But right now, this didn't seem much like a baby step.

More like a "giant leap," she thought.

Still, Trudy tried to convince herself that it was necessary. She kept remembering what Riley had said not long after Rhea's murder …

"We can't live like this—always afraid something awful might happen."

It was true, of course. Trudy knew that she needed to snap out of the chronic fearfulness that seemed to rule her life these days.

So she'd taken a few baby steps, or made that first giant leap, however anybody wanted to think of it.

Even so, she realized that she was walking along the lighted campus paths rather briskly, at a much faster pace than usual. Even the sight of other students walking not too far away wasn't as reassuring as she'd thought it would be. Every slight shadow between buildings or dark spot behind shrubbery seemed threatening.

She told herself that surely no murderous monster was lying in wait anywhere nearby, not while the campus was still fairly active.

Trudy realized that she was losing touch with the bit of self-satisfaction she'd just experienced back at the library. But somehow she couldn't make herself feel better.

What if the other students in sight went away? What if everybody else suddenly disappeared and left her alone on the maze of pathways, a perfect target for a murderous monster?

She knew that her thoughts were irrational, but she had lost control over them now.

By the time she was about halfway to the dorm, Trudy's heart was pounding and she was almost hyperventilating. She wondered now—what had been the point of trying to test herself like this?

She had thought her counselor was wise to recommend that she go out. She had been proud of making the effort. But all she was managing to do was scare herself to death.

I might as well give it up, she thought. *I should just stay inside,*

Of course, cowering in a dorm room sure didn't seem like much of a life. But she reminded herself that there were only about two months until graduation. If she could make it through until then, pass her exams and graduate, she could go back home and stay there until she felt it was safe to go out.

When Trudy got to the dorm entrance, she let herself in and stood just inside the door gasping for breath.

At last, she felt like she could breathe again.

As she walked toward the room she shared with Riley, she glanced farther down the hallway toward the one where Rhea's body had been found. She'd been avoiding walking through that part of the hall anymore. She'd dreaded the very idea of simply walking past that room.

But she reminded herself of her counselor's motto …

"Baby steps."

Maybe she could at least take some baby steps here indoors. Maybe this was a fear she could conquer right now. There were no other students in the hall at the moment to see if she failed.

Trudy passed by her own room and continued down the hall. The hallway seemed to get longer as she walked along, and the room that scared her seemed to retreat farther and farther away. Instead of quickening her pace like she had coming home from the library, Trudy found herself moving more slowly.

She almost wondered …

Maybe I'll never get there.

But she finally found herself standing in front of the door that had been closed for two weeks now. It seemed weirdly huge and brooding, like some kind of enormous tombstone. She felt dwarfed and daunted by that door.

She knew that no one was living in the room now. Heather hadn't returned to school. She'd emailed her friends, including Trudy, that she was taking a year off from college and might apply somewhere else in the fall. And of course, no one else wanted to move in there—at least not yet.

Trudy wondered—how long would it be before anyone did live there again?

Next year, maybe?

Longer?

Trudy couldn't imagine that it would be anytime soon. Surely it wouldn't be at least until all the students who currently occupied this floor were gone, taking with them the awful memory of that night.

She found it strange to consider—eventually, Rhea's murder would be nothing more than a part of the dorm's history, a story students might tell each other for fun, to scare each other into nervous giggles and nightmares.

Trudy began to wonder …

Is the door locked?

Surely it was, the room being unoccupied and all.

She could find out if it was locked right now, just by reaching out and trying the doorknob.

Just then, a noise startled her almost out of her skin.

She turned and saw that it was Riley coming out of their own room.

"Hey, Riley," she called out.

Riley turned and looked surprised to see Trudy.

"Hi, Trudy," she said.

Trudy and Riley walked toward one another.

"I see you're back from the library," Riley said. "How did …?"

Riley's voice faded. Trudy could pretty well guess what she wanted to ask. It had been pretty obvious when Trudy had left their room that her little outing was all about facing her fears.

Trudy managed to smile a little.

"It went OK," she said.

I didn't get murdered, anyway, she thought.

An awkward silence fell.

Trudy noticed that Riley was looking quite nice, wearing a long, slim maxi skirt, a simple V-neck blouse, and boots that gave her outfit a nice casual touch. She wanted to ask Riley where she was going. But Riley had been a bit defensive lately whenever Trudy asked questions about her comings and goings.

Finally Riley said hesitantly, "Uh, I'm just going out for a while. I don't think I'll be long. I'll call if you if I'm going to be late. I hope that's … OK."

Trudy winced a little as she remembered the scene she'd made when Riley had come in the Monday after the murder. She knew Riley had been staying in a lot more lately out of consideration for her.

"Of course it's OK," Trudy said. Forcing a laugh she added, "What am I, your mother?"

Riley laughed a bit uneasily.

"OK," she said. "I'll see you later."

Riley turned and continued on her way out of the building. Trudy went on into their room, locked the door behind her, and sat down on her bed.

In a few moments, she started to feel a little safer and breathed more easily.

But she wondered …

What does that say about me?

She certainly didn't feel as though she'd succeeded in conquering any fears.

For a few moments back at the library, she'd thought she had. Now she wondered if maybe she never would.

But was she going to stay cooped up right here in her room?

Maybe—just maybe—she could summon up the nerve to go down to the common room to study and have a snack.

A real adventure, she thought wryly. *Maybe in a little while.*

She wondered again about where Riley might be going. Riley seemed different these days. She seemed distracted a lot, and some of her moods struck Trudy as dark and strange.

But, she told herself, it wasn't as if her own moods were exactly sunny and normal.

It was that book, Trudy thought.

Riley spent way too much time reading that book—the one she knew was in Riley's desk drawer, the one about homicidal killers.

What's been going on in her mind? she thought.

Trudy remembered something she'd said to Riley during her emotional outburst that night when Riley had gone out alone …

"You're my best friend. And the idea of losing you after what happened to Rhea …"

Trudy felt a knot of sorrow in her throat.

Was that what was happening?

In a way, was she losing Riley as surely as she'd lost Rhea?

CHAPTER THIRTEEN

When Riley left the dorm, the only car she saw waiting outside was a nice-looking Ford Mustang. She hesitated for a moment. It seemed to her to be a pretty classy vehicle for a student, even one in law school.

At that moment, Ryan Paige got out of the Mustang and waved to Riley. He walked around and opened the passenger door for her, showing a touch more gallantry than she was used to from guys. She was beginning to feel that this evening might be more unusual than she had expected.

As Riley walked to the Mustang and got in, she was aware that Ryan was looking her over with a pleased expression on his handsome features. Of course she took a good look at him too. The truth was, she thought he was just a wee bit overdressed for such an impromptu almost-date, with a dark vest over an expensive blue shirt unbuttoned at the collar.

She wondered—might he be a little too formal and old-fashioned for her taste?

As Ryan got in and started driving, he asked, "How have you been doing?"

Riley sensed that the question was more than merely polite. After all, Ryan knew that she had been friends with Rhea and that she had found the body.

"OK, I guess," she said. "It's been a weird time."

"It sure has," Ryan said. "The whole school seems like a different place. Everybody's so uptight and nervous, and there are all these rumors going around. And there's so much suspicion. I've heard of guys getting ostracized just because they're kind of odd and eccentric, treated like they were murderers. It's not healthy."

Riley didn't reply, but she certainly didn't disagree. She remembered that the police had questioned poor awkward Rory Burdon. She wondered if maybe he, too, was being treated with suspicion these days on account of his visit from the cops. She hoped not.

Ryan gave her a concerned glance, and she realized that she had been sitting there frowning.

"Oh, I'm sorry," he said. "Maybe I shouldn't be talking about
…"

"It's OK," Riley said.

But she didn't volunteer any thoughts of her own on the subject.

It was only a short drive to Pooh-Bah's Pub. When they got to the front entrance, of course Ryan opened the door for Riley. She'd never been here before, but it was as upscale and posh as she'd expected—a bit of a shock to her system after the familiar grunginess of the Centaur's Den.

The place was nicely lit, revealing burnished woodwork and leather upholstery. Instead of the blare of rock music, jazz was playing quietly. Ryan led Riley over to a comfortable, private booth.

Soon a young woman wearing a white shirt and a thin black necktie came over to take their drink orders.

"Hi, Nyssa," Ryan said to her with a smile.

"Hi, Ryan," the server said, smiling back at him.

Riley wondered—was Ryan a regular at this swank place?

Just how rich was he, anyway?

The woman took their orders for glasses of red wine. After some tentative shyness, they began to talk a little—but not about the murder. As far as Riley was concerned, that was a relief.

Before long, Riley began to feel pretty comfortable with her date. In spite of the setting, he began to seem more and more like just a regular guy. And like almost every guy Riley had ever known, he loved to talk about himself. He managed to mention his grades, which were of course excellent, and that he had his own apartment. Soon he was regaling Riley with his promising future, which he said just might include high political office.

As she encouraged his account with brief responses, Riley automatically sorted the more likely from the improbable. She knew better than to take that last bit about his future seriously. Most of the male law students she'd met were sure they'd be president someday. Still, Ryan struck her as genuinely hard-working and conscientious. She didn't doubt that he really was going to succeed in life.

After a while, his autobiographical spiel slowed to a halt, and he began to look just a little bit embarrassed.

Riley was amused.

She was familiar with this phase of a date, in which a guy

realizes he's been talking all about himself way too long and it's time to show some interest in the girl.

"So," he said. "Psychology."

Riley smiled at how he'd managed to abbreviate the question. In full, she figured it went something like …

"What the hell do you think you're going to do with a psychology degree?"

At least he remembered what her area of study was.

Riley shrugged.

"I guess I'm just interested in human nature," she said.

Ryan tilted his head with interest.

He said, "Maybe the dark side of human nature, judging from your reading habits. That book of Zimmerman's you were reading looked pretty grim."

Riley didn't know what to say. She was actually puzzled herself by the dark turns her thoughts had been taking lately.

Ryan leaned back and looked at Riley as if he were studying her.

He said, "My guess is you've had some pretty unsettling experiences at one time or another—stuff that you don't talk about much. Am I right?"

Riley winced.

Between the murder of her mother and her difficult childhood and teenage years, Ryan was definitely not wrong.

"Maybe," she said.

Ryan's expression changed. Riley sensed that he realized he'd touched on something she preferred to leave alone, and that he was looking for some way to change the subject.

She certainly hoped so.

Then Ryan said, "Well, tell me some of the stuff you've learned about human nature from your studies so far."

He laughed nervously and added, "What about me, for instance? I've been sitting here carrying on about myself like an egocentric jerk—which I hope I'm not, by the way. But surely you've been able to figure out a few things about me that I haven't actually talked about."

Riley felt a curious tingle. She had to admit, it was kind of an interesting question.

What *could* she tell about Ryan Paige that he hadn't already told her?

She sat there observing him carefully.

"You dress nice," she said, checking out his expensive blue shirt and vest again. "But not too nice—not preppy nice. You're not some pampered brat. If you were from a rich family, you'd have been bragging about it by now."

He smiled a little. Riley sensed that she was right so far.

She continued, "My guess is you come from a working-class background. Your dad is maybe—what? A construction worker?"

Ryan's expression now showed a touch of surprise.

He said, "A plumber, actually."

Riley was a bit surprised herself now. Her guess hadn't been very far off.

"And your mom?" Riley asked.

"You tell me," Ryan said.

Riley thought for a moment.

Then she said, "Well, she's not a stay-at-home mom. Your family needs the extra income. Some kind of day job. But not skilled work, like your dad …"

Ryan nodded and said, "She works as a clerk in a greeting card store. She's been working there since I was big enough to go to kindergarten."

Riley was really starting to get into this little exercise.

She was also liking what she was figuring out about Ryan.

"You live pretty well for a college student," she said. "There's your car, for instance—a nice Ford Mustang. But …"

She paused as she remembered the feel of the car.

Then she said, "You bought it used. Or you made a good trade for it—maybe a car that your parents bought you as a high school graduation gift or something like that."

Ryan's eyes had widened.

She continued, "You work hard, and not just in your studies. I'm pretty sure you've worked your way through school, made your own way—night jobs during your undergraduate years, and you still work summers at least …"

Riley paused again, trying to imagine what kind of job Ryan might have had.

Suddenly she remembered the familiar look he had exchanged with the young woman who had served them.

And now she realized …

No, it wasn't because he's a regular customer.

She said. "You've worked right here at Pooh-Bah's—as a bartender, I'll bet."

80

Riley could tell by Ryan's startled expression that she was right.

She was feeling quite energized now as hunches kept coming to her.

"You're an only child," she said. "And that's part of why you drive yourself really hard. You want your parents to be proud of you, because you're all they've got. You're really hungry for success. And you figure that the best way to *become* successful is to *act* successful."

Ryan's mouth had dropped open.

"How am I doing so far?" Riley asked.

Ryan just nodded with a surprised and uneasy smile.

"Do you want to hear more?" she asked.

"Um ... I don't think so," he said.

His words took her aback. He didn't sound exactly pleased with her insights.

Maybe I went a little too far, she thought.

Then Ryan said, "Forget about psychology. You should be a cop."

Riley felt really stung now.

There was an edge to his voice that told her he didn't mean that in a nice way.

He was saying that she was definitely not what he'd expected—and not the kind of girl he was interested in, either.

After all, she thought ...

What kind of future lawyer wants to date a would-be cop?

Not that Riley wanted to be a cop—not by any means.

She thought about saying so, but quickly thought better of it.

I've said too much already, she figured.

Riley and Ryan finished their drinks pretty much in silence. Neither of them mentioned the possibility of an end-of-the-week date with dinner and a movie. The truth was, Riley felt it was just as well. Ryan was obviously an especially insecure young male, and even though she was intensely attracted to him, she didn't think he suited her.

As Ryan drove her home, Riley remembered the flow of insights she'd spouted earlier.

Where did all that come from? she wondered.

She'd always known she was pretty observant, but this kind of behavior was new for her—especially the part where she told someone what she was figuring out about them.

When Ryan pulled up in front of the dorm, he unbuckled his seat belt as if he intended to walk her to the door—purely for her safety, she was sure. A goodnight kiss was definitely not in the works.

"It's OK, I'm good," she said, getting out of the car alone.

She walked inside the dorm and looked out through the glass door as Ryan drove away in his nice Ford Mustang.

She suddenly felt terribly sad.

Life had changed so much since Rhea had died.

Riley knew that *she* had changed—and she was still changing in ways she couldn't seem to predict.

What did all this mean for her future?

She sighed, and as she walked toward her room she only felt sure of one thing …

Whatever that future was going to be like, Ryan Paige wasn't going to be part of it.

CHAPTER FOURTEEN

When Riley opened the door to her dorm room, a small light was blinking in the darkness. The answering machine was signaling a new message.

Who could that be? she wondered.

For a fleeting moment she imagined it might be Ryan calling her from his car …

"Hey, Riley, we forgot to talk about getting together later this week …"

Of course she knew it wouldn't be him—and it was just as well. She certainly didn't want a repeat of the awkward outing they'd just had. No, they hadn't hit it off, and that was that. She didn't even feel sad about it.

She stepped quietly into the room, thinking that Trudy must already be asleep.

But Trudy wasn't in her bed.

Riley felt a twinge of alarm. Going to the library had been a big deal for Trudy. Surely she hadn't gone out anywhere tonight.

Is she OK?

Riley flicked on the light switch and saw a note on the table next to the answering machine. She picked it up and read it.

Just went down to the common room to study awhile.

There was a little heart drawn below the message.

Riley breathed a little easier. Trudy was just in the dorm's big living room at the end of the hall.

But that message machine light was still blinking.

Who had called, anyway? Could it possibly be anyone she would want to talk to?

She sure didn't want to talk to her father again anytime soon.

Finally she reminded herself that she was being silly and played the tape. She heard a female voice …

"Hey, guys … this is Kyra. I just thought I'd …"

As the voice fell silent for what sounded like an indecisive moment, Riley realized…

Kyra. Rhea's older sister.

The voice continued …

"I'm sorry to bother you, I just … Give me a call, OK?"

The caller left her phone number, and the message ended with a beep.

Riley remembered Kyra well. She'd graduated from Lanton three years ago, and had come back to visit her younger sister a few times. When she did, she'd also hang out with Riley and Trudy.

She was a robust and hearty young woman with a contagious sense of humor—more like Trudy than her rather reserved younger sister.

Or at least more like Trudy used to be, Riley thought.

But her voice on the tape sounded troubled and worried—which of course was hardly any surprise.

Since the call had just come in twenty minutes ago, Riley figured it wasn't too late to return it.

She dialed the number and Kyra answered.

"Hey, Kyra," she said. "This is Riley."

"Hi, Riley," Kyra said. "Thanks for getting back to me so fast."

A silence fell. Although Riley had sent Rhea's family a card, she guiltily realized she hadn't gotten in touch with Kyra personally.

Riley stammered, "I'm—I'm so, so sorry about what happened."

"Yeah," Kyra said. "How are you coping?"

Riley was startled at the question, coming as it did from Rhea's own sister.

"Never mind me," Riley said. "How about you and your folks?"

She heard Kyra heave a deep sigh.

"It's been really, really rough. I flew home as soon as I heard about it, and Mom and Dad are having an especially hard time. It just doesn't seem real. I can't even …"

She fell silent again.

Then she said, "We had a really private funeral service and burial. The whole town was in too much shock to do more than that. But we're having a little memorial service here at the house this

84

Sunday. It's going to be really weird for me—the people here will all be family and small-town friends, a lot of folks I haven't really talked with very much in recent years. I don't even feel like I know them anymore, and they sure don't know me. I feel a lot closer to you and Trudy. Actually, I think Rhea did too."

Riley swallowed hard. She knew what was coming.

Kyra said, "Oh, Riley—I wish the two of you would come too. It would help me a lot."

Riley didn't speak for a moment.

Finally she said, "Kyra, Trudy and I don't have a car, but … there's bus service between here and Herborn, isn't there?"

"That's right. There's a morning bus from Lanton that will get you here in time. I could meet you at the bus station."

She knew it wasn't going to be easy spending the afternoon among Rhea's grieving friends and relatives.

But she knew she couldn't refuse.

That would just be wrong.

"Sure, I'll come," she said. "I'll ask Trudy if she'll come too. Thanks for inviting us."

"Thank *you*," Kyra said, sounding relieved.

As soon as Riley hung up, she wished she'd asked Kyra a few questions. For example, were the police keeping Rhea's family informed about any progress they were making toward catching her killer? Because Riley hadn't heard any news to speak of at all, nor had anyone else she knew of.

Maybe she'd have time to talk to Kyra about all that on Sunday.

Anyway Riley had to get Trudy in on this right away. She went to the common room, where Trudy was nestled on a sofa reading a textbook. A few other girls were clustered in front of the TV, watching some kind of late night show. They paid no attention to Riley and Trudy.

Riley sat down next to her roommate.

"Trudy, we just got a call from Kyra."

Trudy closed her textbook and her eyes widened.

"Oh!" she said. "How's she doing?"

"She's … well, you know," Riley said with a shrug. She really had no idea how to answer that question.

Then Riley said, "Her family in Herborn is having a memorial service on Sunday. We're both invited."

Trudy's mouth dropped open and her face turned pale.

"Oh, Riley," she said in a near-whisper. "Are you going?"

"I've got to, Trudy. So do you. Kyra sounds like she really needs us there."

Trudy sat staring into space for a moment.

Then she said, "Riley, I can't. I'm sorry but I just … can't."

Riley was shocked.

"Why not?" she asked.

Trudy stammered, "It's just … I'm still … Riley, you know perfectly well I'm having trouble coping. I'd never be able to get through it. I'd just fall apart and make things worse for everybody."

Riley was starting to feel a little angry now, but she tried not to show it.

"Trudy, I think … well, maybe it would do you some real good. What do you think your counselor would say? Maybe it's even what you need. It might give you some …"

"Closure," Trudy said, finishing Riley's thought. "Yeah, I know. And you might be right but …"

Her voice faded.

Finally she said in a shaking voice, "I can't. I really can't."

Riley just stood there for a moment, trying to think of some way to persuade Trudy to go to the service with her. But she couldn't think of anything else to say. She was sure that Trudy wasn't going to change her mind—not even if she took the next few days to think about it.

Trying to keep a note of bitterness out of her voice, Riley said, "I'll call Kyra back and tell her—"

"No," Trudy said. "I'll get in touch with her. I'm pretty sure I've got her email address."

Riley fought down a sigh. There really wasn't anything left to say. She left Trudy alone in the common room without saying another word.

On the way back to her room, Riley hesitated and then came to a stop. She stood outside one closed door. She'd been stopping here like this quite a lot during the last couple of weeks. She couldn't even explain to herself exactly why.

Maybe she hoped she'd get some kind of information, even just a gut feeling, about what had happened inside that room on that terrible night.

But so far, she hadn't felt much when she stood here, except a sad sense of Rhea's absence.

And of course, she was sure the door must be locked and she

couldn't go inside even if she wanted to.

As if to prove this to herself, she reached out and held the doorknob.

To Riley's astonishment, the knob turned easily and the door opened.

Somebody forgot to lock it, she realized.

So, did she actually want to go inside?

Yes, she did.

Riley cautiously stepped into the room and turned on the light. She pulled the door shut behind her.

The room seemed weirder than she'd even expected—completely stripped of anything that had belonged to either Rhea or Heather. One of the beds had been removed and the mattress on the other looked especially bare and stark. And the blood had been scrubbed off the floor so thoroughly that Riley could still smell the cleaning fluids used.

And yet …

A strange feeling stirred within her, not unlike her earlier experience of following in the killer's footsteps along the campus paths.

Riley shuddered.

Did she really want to invite the killer's presence again?

On the other hand, how could she do otherwise?

Whatever this was, maybe—just maybe—she'd learn something important, perhaps even who the killer really was.

She told herself she was letting her imagination go wild.

But Riley realized that deep inside she was accepting this strange experience as something real.

She closed her eyes and pictured the room as it had been when Rhea and Heather had lived here—cheerfully messy, with unmade beds and belongings scattered everywhere and posters on the walls.

Then the real horror kicked in …

She was standing over Rhea's body, not dead yet, gasping and writhing as blood spurted out of the gaping wound in her throat. Riley felt the killer's fingers wrapped around the knife handle as he looked down at the gleaming blade stained with blood.

She felt a smile of satisfaction form across his face.

The killer was looking forward to doing this same thing again—and yet he was reminding himself …

"I'm not in any hurry."

Riley's eyes snapped open and the spell was broken. She was

trembling.

Although the episode had been brief, it was much more intense than what she had experienced on the campus paths.

Should she try to get into that state of mind again, see if she could learn more about the killer?

She closed her eyes and breathed slowly …

… but nothing happened.

Still, she didn't feel the least bit discouraged.

Instead, she felt something that she hadn't felt since Rhea had been murdered.

In a way she couldn't yet understand, she was in pursuit of the murderer.

As long as she could glimpse the world through his eyes, if only fleetingly and occasionally, she had more power over him than he could ever understand.

She whispered aloud to the unseen presence …

"I'm watching you."

Then she turned off the light, left the room, shut the door, and headed back to her own room.

She realized that something new was happening to her.

And that it just might change everything.

CHAPTER FIFTEEN

Riley felt terribly ill at ease at Sunday's memorial service. More than that—she felt positively alien, as if she were an ill-prepared visitor from another planet.

Rhea Thorson's family lived in an attractive home that was all cream-colored and beige, and so well kept it looked newer than it really must have been. The living room was packed with family and friends, all of whom obviously knew and cared about each other.

Riley shifted uncomfortably in her chair and wondered …

What must it feel like to really *belong* like all these people?

She'd certainly never experienced anything like it in any of the places she'd called home over the years.

Rhea's older sister, Kyra, had met Riley at the Herborn bus station this morning and had driven her here just in time for the service. Riley had been hastily introduced to Rhea's parents and siblings and a handful of relatives, then took her place in one of the folding chairs that had been lined up in the room.

To Riley's relief, the elderly preacher finished his remarks pretty quickly. Even so, she found herself puzzling over some of things he had said—about how Rhea was free from the evils of this world, and how everyone who loved her could take comfort in the knowledge that she was now living in eternal happiness.

The truth was, Riley had never had any idea whether Rhea was religious or not.

Would Rhea be happy to hear the preacher saying such things?

Riley had no idea.

Again, she was tugged by a sad realization that she simply hadn't gotten to know Rhea nearly as well as she should have.

Friends and relatives were now taking turns stepping to the front of the room and sharing memories of Rhea. Most were happy memories of school and play and picnics and family vacations and the like. Some of the funnier stories stirred the group to wistful laughter.

Even so, muffled weeping broke out now and then. Nobody could quite forget their grief, nor the horrible evil that had befallen their community, even if nobody would talk about it.

This morning before leaving, Riley had worried about what to wear for the occasion. Would everybody be wearing black? The closest she could get to that was a solid navy-blue dress, which she'd hoped would be solemn enough.

But as things turned out, Riley was dressed more formally than most of the people here. Generally they were casually, comfortably dressed, as if this were an everyday gathering—as if Rhea herself might walk in at any moment.

Riley guessed that the earlier small service and burial that Kyra had mentioned must have been decidedly more somber. This group seemed touchingly determined to convince themselves of that old proverb …

"Life goes on."

If only that were true, Riley sadly thought.

Still, the presence of such mutually caring people deeply affected her. She found herself thinking about how few people she felt so deeply connected to.

Was there anybody like that in her life at all? If so, it would almost have to be college friends like Trudy and Heather and Gina and …

Rhea.

She shuddered as the name passed through her mind.

It was terrifying to think of how fragile her human connections were.

And there were so few of them.

She thought about her older sister, Wendy, who had run away from home as a teenager. That had been years ago, and Riley had seldom seen her since then. They hadn't talked for a long time and Riley didn't even know where Wendy might live anymore.

Then there were Uncle Deke and Aunt Ruth. She'd lived with them in the little town of Larned during much of her childhood and all of her adolescence. She owed them what little stability she'd had in her young life. She felt bad that she'd given them so much trouble during her teen years. They'd deserved better from her.

She wondered—would she ever be able to make it up to them?

She wasn't sure how. When Uncle Deke had retired, he and Aunt Ruth had moved to Florida, and Riley didn't have much contact with them anymore.

And then there was Riley's father.

As troubled as their relationship had always been, she couldn't convince herself that she hated him. And she suspected that, in his own cold, ruthless way, he still cared deeply for her.

And right now she keenly realized …

Nobody is promised a tomorrow.

Her father wouldn't live forever. Whenever he died, how would Riley feel about all the things they had left unsettled and unsaid?

Was it possible that they could somehow make peace with one another?

Riley found herself thinking …

Maybe it's time to try.

But how could she even start?

As these questions flowed through her mind, Riley noticed that only one person here appeared as uncomfortably out of place as she herself felt, and that was Kyra. For one thing, Kyra looked markedly more sophisticated than anyone else, wearing a sleek rose-colored dress and comfortable but classy flats accompanied by large, elegant earrings and stylishly crimped hair.

Kyra kept glancing at Riley, as if for emotional support.

Riley remembered what Kyra had said over the phone about her family and friends here in Herborn …

"I don't even feel like I know them anymore, and they sure don't know me."

Riley knew that Kyra had become an airline attendant not long after graduating from Lanton. Whenever Kyra came to visit Rhea on campus and spent time with Riley and Trudy, she would regale them all with stories about her travels to all parts of the world.

It had always sounded to Riley like an exciting life. Now Riley realized that Kyra's life had made her feel like a stranger in this small town, where everyone knew everyone else and few people traveled very far away or for very long.

Riley noticed that Rhea's immediate family—her father and mother and brothers and sisters, including Kyra—didn't take the opportunity to tell their own stories. Riley wasn't surprised. Their grief was surely too fresh and deep to share their own joyous memories of happier times with Rhea. But at least Rhea's father and mother seemed pleased to hear what the others said.

When the stories came to an end, everybody got up and started to mingle, herding in the general direction of a table that had been spread with potluck dishes that the guests had prepared.

Riley wished she could shrivel up and disappear.

This was the moment she had been most dreading—having to

introduce herself to people she didn't know and find comforting things to say to them.

But she quickly felt someone's hand on her shoulder.

She turned and saw Kyra, who whispered to her …

"Let's get out of here. Please."

Startled, Riley followed Kyra through the house and out the front door to her car, which was parked at the fringes of the mass of vehicles cramped around the house. They both got into Kyra's car, and then she maneuvered away from the other vehicles and drove away.

Riley almost asked …

"Where are we going?"

But she saw that tears were pouring down Kyra's face.

"Oh, God," Kyra gasped. "I couldn't breathe back there. It was too much for me. Thanks for … thanks for coming. I really needed you here, Riley."

Riley was deeply touched.

She said, "I'm glad I came."

And for the first time, she really did feel glad she'd come. It occurred to her that she was sorry Trudy hadn't.

She hoped Trudy had done as she'd promised and emailed that she wouldn't be there. So far Kyra hadn't mentioned anything about Trudy. Riley figured it was best not to say anything about her unless Kyra did.

Soon Kyra drove into the grounds of the town's small cemetery and along a winding road until she finally parked her car.

When Riley and Kyra got out of the car and started to walk among the gravestones, Riley noticed for the first time what a lovely April day it was. There was a pleasant cool breeze in the air and the trees were green and birds were singing. Spring had definitely arrived.

Soon Riley and Kyra stood in front of a tombstone that looked so new it hardly seemed real. On it was engraved …

Rhea Thorson
beloved daughter and sister

Riley felt a renewed pang of sadness that the word "friend" didn't also appear there. Below those words were the dates of Rhea's shockingly short life.

Riley was startled when Kyra put her hand on her shoulder and squeezed it tightly.

Kyra said, "You have no idea how much Rhea cared about you."

Riley gulped hard. These were words she hadn't expected to hear.

Kyra continued, "She'd tell me about you every time she got a chance. She said you were special and smart and strong, and she thought you were going to do amazing things with your life. She didn't know what those things might be, but she was looking forward to finding out. You were really her best friend, Riley."

Riley was staggered with surprise.

Her best friend?

Riley had had no idea that Rhea had felt that way.

The truth was, Riley herself had never felt as close to Rhea as she did to, say, Trudy.

And she had always thought Rhea had felt closer to both Trudy and Heather than she had to her.

Now Riley felt like maybe she understood why Kyra hadn't seemed very concerned that Trudy hadn't come. Although she had invited both of them, apparently it mattered much, much more that Riley be here.

Kyra added, "She said she could count on you for absolutely anything."

Riley suddenly felt as if she'd been punched in the gut.

Did Rhea really feel that way about me? she wondered.

Riley had never known that.

If she had known, might she have watched over her more carefully that night at the Centaur's Den?

Rhea certainly hadn't been able to count on her then—not when it had mattered most.

Now Riley had to fight back the tears.

She remembered some questions she'd left unasked when Kyra had called to invite her here. Now it was time to ask them.

She said, "Kyra, what have the police been telling you? Surely they've been in touch with you. How close are they to catching the man who …?"

Kyra shook her head and said, "I call them just about every day, and they always say the same thing. The killer was some kind of drifter who came and went. They don't think he's still around. He could be anywhere. Maybe he'd committed similar killings elsewhere, and if so maybe the Feds could help track him down.

But so far it just sounds like the local cops are getting nowhere."

Riley thought back to Dr. Zimmerman's conflicting theory that Rhea had known her attacker, and her own deep hunch that he was still watching girls on campus, waiting to kill again.

Should she talk to Kyra about all that?

Probably not, Riley thought.

Then Kyra said …

"The truth is, I don't get the feeling the police are trying very hard."

Riley remembered feeling the same way when she'd gone to the station and tried to get answers out of Officer Steele.

She wondered—were the police even making any serious effort anymore?

Kyra added, "I keep calling Dean Trusler too, and he's worse than useless—like some kind of automatic condolence-vending machine, saying over and over again how sorry he is for our family's loss, and how the case is out of his hands, but he's sure the police will solve it."

Riley had no idea what to say. She and Kyra stood looking down silently at the gravestone for a few long moments.

Then Riley became aware that Kyra was gazing at her. Riley returned her gaze.

Kyra said, "Riley …"

Kyra didn't finish her thought, but Riley sensed what she wanted to say …

"Riley, please do something. Please make things right."

Riley felt a knot of emotion in her throat. She knew she couldn't say no to Kyra's unspoken question.

So she nodded slowly.

Kyra smiled, seeming relieved.

Then she said, "Come on, we'd better get you to the station in time to catch your bus."

As they walked away from the headstone, Riley kept thinking about what Kyra had just said about Rhea …

"She said she could count on you for absolutely anything."

It now seemed almost like a voice for the grave, begging Riley herself for justice.

How can I possibly bring anybody any justice? she wondered.

CHAPTER SIXTEEN

During her classes the next day, Riley found it hard to concentrate. She kept remembering the imploring look she'd gotten from Kyra yesterday—the look that had seemed to say …

"Please do something."

What could she possibly do?

But if the police weren't doing anything, was it ultimately going to be up to Riley to find Rhea's killer?

The idea was too staggering to even consider.

And yet Riley couldn't help thinking about it.

All day long she carried Dr. Zimmerman's book around, thumbing through it whenever she had a chance. She wasn't sure how many times she'd read *Dark Minds* by now. She'd already filled most of a spiral notebook with notes and words jotted down from it.

But she did know that she really ought to have returned it to Professor Hayman by now, and that was something she could take care of this very afternoon.

After her last class, Riley found Professor Hayman's office in the Psychology building, but she was disappointed to find that he'd already left for the day.

As she turned to leave, she heard a voice from nearby.

"Can I help you?"

She turned and saw Dr. Zimmerman himself standing just outside the main office of the Psychology Department. The older professor looked his usual warm, pleasant, rumpled self.

She felt a flush of shyness as she realized she was holding Zimmerman's own book in her hands.

She stammered, "Uh … Professor Hayman lent me your book, and I dropped by to give it back but …"

Dr. Zimmerman winked and said, "Pretty dry reading, I guess. I'm not surprised you didn't get through it."

Riley shook her head emphatically.

"Oh, no, Dr. Zimmerman. It's fascinating. I read it through and through, cover to cover."

Dr. Zimmerman's smile widened with what looked like

surprise.

"Well, I'm flattered. It's not every day that a student reads a book of mine without being forced to! Perhaps you'd like to come in and talk about it?"

You bet I would, Riley thought. She followed him past the department receptionist into his office, a fairly large and comfortable space cluttered with books and papers.

The professor sat down in a chair behind his desk, and nodded to her to take one of the smaller chairs nearby.

Riley sat down and placed the book on the desk in front of her, wondering what she could possibly say to the author of such a fascinating work. But in a matter of seconds she was asking him all kinds of questions about the criminals he'd written about, especially the psychological forces that drove them to kill—sometimes again and again and again. Riley was fascinated by his insights and answers.

It was obvious that Zimmerman was pleased with her curiosity, and probably also with the evidence that she had actually read the book. He soon began talking about cases that he hadn't written about—so-called "cold cases," ones that had never been solved.

These included the 1987 murder and "sexual mutilation" of Peggy Hettrick in Colorado. Recently, over a decade later, a man had been arrested for the murder, and it seemed likely that he would soon be convicted. But Dr. Zimmerman told Riley that he doubted the police had the right man even now.

He also told her about the sexual assault and murder in 1990 of Susan Poupart, a young Native American mother of two whose body was found six months after her disappearance. Two male suspects in her murder had never been convicted.

When Dr. Zimmerman mentioned that Poupart had disappeared after leaving a party, Riley couldn't help but shiver. It reminded her too much of Rhea's murder after leaving the Centaur's Den that awful night.

Dr. Zimmerman seemed to notice her reaction.

He said in a concerned voice, "I'm getting the distinct feeling that your interest in these crimes isn't strictly academic."

Riley silently nodded.

Dr. Zimmerman said, "I remember now—you were close friends with Rhea Thorson, weren't you?"

Riley nodded again.

Dr. Zimmerman fell silent, apparently waiting for Riley to

speak.

She hesitated, then said, "Dr. Zimmerman, do you think that what happened to Rhea …?"

She couldn't bring herself to finish the question.

Dr. Zimmerman said, "You're worried that her killer will never be found—that her murder will turn out to be a cold case, like the others we've been discussing."

Riley nodded.

Dr. Zimmerman's expression showed a trace of worry.

"I'm not sure what to tell you," he said. "The cases we just talked about involved an element of sexual assault. Rhea's murder didn't. It's also typical of cold cases that the victim's body isn't found right away. That wasn't the case with Rhea either."

Shuddering, Riley said, "I was the second person to see her body."

"I'm very sorry," Dr. Zimmerman said.

A silence fell between them.

Finally, Dr. Zimmerman spoke slowly and cautiously.

"Ms. Sweeney, could we keep the conversation we're having private and confidential?"

Riley felt a strange tingle.

What is he about to tell me? she wondered.

"Of course," she said.

Zimmerman sat staring out the window for a moment.

Then he said, "I know what I said in Professor Hayman's class that day—that Rhea surely knew her killer, and he'd soon be apprehended. But now … I'm starting to have my doubts. If I'd been right, I don't see how the killer could still be at large, even after this relatively short period of time. And of course the police …"

His voice faded, but Riley knew what he was about to say.

She spoke up. "The police think it was some drifter—a total stranger. They think he's committed similar murders in other places."

Zimmerman gave her a curious look.

"You've talked to the police?" he asked. "That's interesting."

He shrugged slightly and added, "Well, even if the police were right and I was wrong, some sort of progress ought to have been made by now. That hasn't happened."

Riley struggled with herself for a moment.

Should she tell Zimmerman about her own thoughts and

hunches?

Would he listen to her, or would he just think she was crazy?

Finally she said, "Dr. Zimmerman, I think Rhea knew the killer—not really well, but well enough not to have been frightened of him. I think he's still here in Lanton. And I really, really think he's going to kill again."

Dr. Zimmerman leaned toward her with an expression of keen attention.

"Indeed?" he said. "What makes you think these things?"

Riley gulped hard. Then she slowly and carefully related her two experiences of slipping into the killer's mind—when she'd retraced Rhea's route across the campus that night, and when she'd stood in Rhea's room imagining how he'd felt looking down at his victim's bleeding body.

His eyes widened with interest as he listened.

When she finished, she said, "I'm afraid maybe you think I've lost my mind."

Dr. Zimmerman shook his head slowly.

"Not at all," he said. "Those sound like very powerful experiences. And … I hesitate to say this … but they might be very insightful. I remember you from my Social Psychology class— you've got a very good logical mind. Now I suspect that you've got exceptional intuition as well."

Riley felt a flood of relief to be able to finally talk to someone about all this—someone who really seemed to understand.

She said, "Dr. Zimmerman, I'm feeling really scared—of myself, I mean. You talked about the importance of empathy in Dr. Hayman's class that day. What does it say about me that I can empathize with a killer?"

"It might mean that you have a unique talent," Dr. Zimmerman said. "It might not be a talent you'd choose to have, but it might prove to be very valuable. Really good criminal profilers are sometimes prone to the same kinds of perceptions you've just described. Have you ever thought about pursuing a career in law enforcement?"

Riley couldn't help but wince as she remembered what Ryan had said to her …

"You should be a cop."

She hadn't liked the idea then, and she wasn't sure how she felt about it now.

"No," Riley said.

Zimmerman said, "Well, maybe you should. As far as empathy is concerned—there are many kinds of empathy, and not all of them are pretty. In my opinion, it's something of a myth that all sadistic killers lack empathy. You have to be keenly *aware* of someone else's suffering if you're going to enjoy it. Contrary to conventional wisdom, I think that many killers are fully aware of their victims' humanity. That's what makes them truly ..." He seemed to search for the right word, then he simply said, "evil."

Riley suppressed a shudder at his words.

Then he added, "As I said before, I hope we can keep this conversation confidential. You see, I now pretty much agree with you that the killer is most likely still among us and intends to kill again. But so far our notion is only a hunch, and we've got no evidence or reasoning to support it. We mustn't cause a panic by spreading our suspicions around."

"But what can we do?" Riley said.

"Let's just keep in touch about all this," Zimmerman said. "If you come to any new insights, please tell me, and I'll do the same with you. I'm in regular contact with the police. I can convey any thoughts and ideas we might come up with to them."

As he got up from his chair, Riley was nagged by a new and much less serious worry.

She remembered how touchy-feely Dr. Zimmerman could be in the class she'd taken from him, and how he'd told all the students in Professor Hayman's class to hug Riley and Trudy.

"You're not going to hug me, are you?" Riley said.

He smiled at her mischievously.

"Don't worry," he said. "I only make students hug other students."

Then he added with a chuckle, "I'm a bit sadistic myself that way."

Riley laughed as well. She found herself liking Dr. Zimmerman more and more every moment.

He held out his hand and said, "Leave the book with me. I'll make sure Professor Hayman gets it back."

Riley handed him the book and left his office.

As she headed away, she found herself confused by her feelings.

She remembered Kyra telling her something about Rhea ...

"... she thought you were going to do amazing things with your life."

Solving murders would certainly be amazing, but the idea troubled her. It didn't sound like a very desirable life.

Even so, maybe she could help solve at least *one* murder—the murder of her friend Rhea.

Riley was really glad that she'd had a chance to talk with Dr. Zimmerman.

She felt relieved to have such a valuable ally.

CHAPTER SEVENTEEN

Trudy was feeling fairly proud of herself as she walked from the library back to the dorm. It was about nine o'clock at night, just six weeks after the horrible night that had turned her final semester of college into a time of fear and dread. For many long days, she'd found it impossible to make a trip like this alone. Even now, although other students were out and about, she still found it frightening to be outside after dark.

Weeks had gone by since her counselor first suggested she do this kind of thing in order to conquer her fears. Since then she'd forced herself to make this nighttime walk many times, and she'd still felt terrified every time. She'd been wondering if her fear would ever go away.

Then she realized that tonight seemed different. At the moment, she didn't feel frightened.

Have I done it at last? she wondered.

She smiled and waved cheerfully to other students who were also walking along the lighted campus paths. A few of them gave her odd looks, but she didn't care.

I'm back, she thought. *I'm my old self again.*

But as she walked along she passed fewer and fewer students, until at last she noticed that there weren't any other people in sight. She knew they hadn't magically disappeared. It was just that, at the moment, there didn't happen to be any other people nearby.

Perfectly natural, Trudy reassured herself.

Then something really weird began to happen.

Suddenly she couldn't walk. She stood frozen, unable to move.

What's happening to me? she wondered.

Worse, she felt her muscles weakening, and her legs started to wobble.

She worried that she might collapse in a heap right here on the pavement.

It reminded her of one of those nightmares when danger was approaching but she couldn't move or scream and …

That's it! she thought. *I'm dreaming! All I've got to do is wake up and …*

But she didn't wake up.

This wasn't a dream.

And here she stood all alone and trembling, like some kind of little animal surrendering to larger beast of prey.

Fear really kicked in as she realized how vulnerable she was.

If the killer was really somewhere in the surrounding darkness, was she just going to stand here and let him kill her?

I can't just stay here. I can't fall down.

Trudy concentrated fiercely, focusing on her left foot. Finally she managed to take one step. Then she forced her right foot to move. She took another step, then another, then another …

And then she was running.

She ran the rest of the way to the dorm, headed straight to her room, and shut the door behind her.

Gasping for breath, she collapsed on the bed.

What happened? she wondered. *What just happened to me?*

Then she remembered something Professor Hayman had talked about in Psych class earlier that semester. He'd been interested in the ways that humans respond when horrible things happened—not to themselves but to other people. He'd discussed the ways that severe anxiety could be converted into physical symptoms such as memory loss, abnormal movements, seizures, or …

Weakness or paralysis, she remembered.

Professor Hayman had called it "conversion disorder."

No doubt about it—she had just suffered an episode of conversion disorder.

She hadn't conquered her fears at all. Her fears had simply taken a new and even more debilitating shape.

Trudy was nearly overcome with a terrible feeling of hopelessness and futility, which soon gave way to a rising sense of shame. None of her other friends seemed to be so deeply traumatized. Yes, they still admitted to spells of fear and grief. Even so, they were managing somehow to deal with it.

For most people on campus, life seemed to be going on much as it always had—for everybody, it seemed, except Trudy.

She pulled her knees up under her chin and started to sob uncontrollably. She asked herself aloud in a choking voice …

"How am I ever going to get over this?"

But it seemed like a stupid question, because the answer was obvious.

She had to get away from Lanton University.

This whole place would always be unbearably haunted as far as Trudy was concerned.

She figured Rhea's roommate, Heather, had had the right idea. Heather had dropped out of school altogether to take a whole year off before enrolling in another college.

Trudy wondered—why hadn't she done the same?

Why hadn't she accepted the simple fact that she'd *never* conquer her fears—not as long as she tried to stay here?

One reason was her parents, she realized. They'd been sympathetic when she phoned them, but she knew they'd be furious if she didn't graduate on schedule.

But she didn't want to stay at college any longer either. She had never been much of a student—not like Riley—and her grades had plummeted since Rhea's murder. She knew she didn't have the grades to transfer into a good school, so it would mean at least another summer here and maybe another semester.

Trudy was sure she couldn't take that.

Her sobbing ebbed as she reminded herself ...

Only one more month.

That was how long was left of the last semester of her senior year.

And then finals, and then graduation.

Now she was starting to feel a wave of renewed determination. She really had to graduate, no matter what.

She reached for one of her textbooks.

She had to study.

*

Riley looked at her watch. She'd spent several hours studying in the common room, but when she saw what time it was she decided ...

It's party time.

According to what her friends had been telling her, things ought to be heating up at the Centaur's Den right about now. She needed to get moving.

Not that Riley was in a party mood. She hadn't felt like partying for many weeks now. Still, she felt the need to respect that little white lie that everyone around her kept telling themselves and seemed to believe ...

Life goes on.

She closed her book and headed down the hallway to her dorm room. As she passed the closed door of the still-empty room, she remembered Dr. Zimmerman's words when they'd discussed Rhea's murder.

"If you come to any new insights, please tell me, and I'll do the same with you."

Riley had tried many times to get back into the killer's psyche, but it hadn't worked for her again. Although she still felt sure that she'd had a glimpse into his mind, she wasn't able to repeat it at will.

She'd fallen into the habit of stopping by Dr. Zimmerman's office every now and then to check in with him. They continued to discuss the homicidal mind, and Riley had read the additional books and papers he'd recommended on the subject. But neither she nor the professor had any new ideas to share.

She'd felt discouraged about that. She felt a continuous ache inside—the desire to bring Rhea's killer to justice.

But after all …

I'm not a cop.

And contrary to Dr. Zimmerman's suggestion, Riley felt more and more sure that she was never going to be.

When she walked into her dorm room, Riley saw that Trudy was curled up on her bed poring over a textbook. Trudy had told her earlier where she planned to go after dinner.

"How was the library?" Riley asked.

"OK," Trudy replied without looking up at Riley.

Riley could tell by her dull tone of voice …

It wasn't OK.

But then, Trudy's little nightly excursions outside the dorm were never OK these days.

Not for the first time, Riley felt a trace of impatience.

"Trudy, I'm going out for a while," she said.

"OK. Have a good time."

"You should come too."

Trudy let out a long, weary sigh.

"Oh, Riley, we've talked about this …"

Riley put her hands on her hips. She decided …

I'm not going to put up with this anymore.

"We're done talking," Riley said. "You're coming with me."

Trudy turned a page of her book, trying to pretend that Riley wasn't there.

Riley said, "This isn't good for you, Trudy. You're getting to be downright agoraphobic."

"Yeah," Trudy said without looking up from her book. "With a good bit of conversion disorder tossed in for good measure."

Conversion disorder? Riley thought.

She remembered Professor Hayman talking about it in class, but she couldn't remember exactly what it was.

Instead of asking her roommate anything more, Riley said, "There's a party at the Centaur's Den tonight."

"When isn't there?" Trudy said.

"Yeah, but this one's kind of special," Riley said.

Trudy just stared at her book until Riley added, "Bricks and Crystal is playing tonight." Riley knew that Bricks and Crystal was one of Trudy's favorite local bands.

Trudy looked up at her.

"Bricks and Crystal?" Trudy said. "I thought they'd broken up."

"Not yet, apparently. Tonight they say they're doing something different—some kind of special 'Grunge-Is-Dead' performance. Because grunge really *is* dead, you know. Anyway, nobody knows what to expect them to do. It could get really intense and angsty and weird and hilarious."

Riley could see a flash of interest in Trudy's eyes. Riley couldn't help but smile a little.

The party animal is still in there somewhere, she thought.

Riley sat down on the bed beside Trudy and patted her hand.

She said, "And of course, there *will* be guys. And excessive and gratuitous drinkage."

Trudy finally gave a slight smile.

"Come on, let's go," Riley said.

Trudy's smiled faded a little.

She said, "Promise you'll stay close by. Don't let me out of your sight. And whatever you do, don't leave without me."

"I promise," Riley said. "But we're going right now."

Trudy hesitated, then she smiled again. She shut her book and got up.

"I have to comb my hair," she said.

Riley waited patiently while Trudy got ready. She was feeling pretty pleased with herself when they stepped outside into the night air.

It was a pleasant walk, but when they had almost reached their destination Riley was struck with an all too-familiar feeling—that sense of being watched.

CHAPTER EIGHTEEN

Riley tried to shake off that unsettling feeling as she and Trudy made their way across the campus. But her sense of being watched wouldn't go away. The killer felt like an invisible but palpable presence. Riley hoped this outing didn't turn out to be a bad idea. After all, she and Dr. Zimmerman agreed that the killer was still around somewhere.

But now she found herself thinking …

It's been six weeks now.

Maybe he's through killing after all.

It seemed only logical. Would a killer who was going to strike again really wait this long? She made a mental note to herself to talk about this possibility with Dr. Zimmerman the next time she saw him.

But even if it was true that there weren't going to be any more murders, Riley was far from satisfied.

The monster who had killed Rhea simply had to be caught and brought to justice.

Who was going to make that happen? As far as she knew, the police weren't even working on the case.

Was catching the killer somehow going to be up to Riley? Was she the only one who'd gotten even a hint of his thinking?

The idea was too overwhelming to even think about.

She murmured aloud to that unseen presence …

"I'm watching you too."

She heard Trudy say, "Huh?"

For a moment, Riley had forgotten that her roommate was walking right beside her.

When she glanced to that side, she realized Trudy had a renewed spring in her step.

"Nothing," Riley said. "Just talking to myself."

Trudy giggled and that made Riley laugh too.

"You know," Trudy said, "you've been pretty tightly wound yourself lately. Maybe you need some kind of an unhinged, riotous blowout even more than I do."

Riley laughed again. It felt good to laugh at herself, at

107

anything.

"Maybe I do," she said.

Trudy grew more animated and cheerful as they made their way across campus, wisecracking and singing and bouncing along. Riley was relieved that her roommate was at least trying to get into the party spirit.

As they neared the front entrance to the Centaur's Den, Riley felt stress kick back in. The last time she'd been here was the Monday after Rhea's murder—the night when she'd talked with the distraught Rory Burdon about his guilt over not walking Rhea home.

Strange, she thought.

It seemed that she'd been avoiding this place without actually thinking about it.

Was she really ready to go back in there?

Beside her, Trudy had frozen in her tracks and was staring at the door.

No surprise that this is tough for her, Riley thought. She was sure that Trudy hadn't been back here at all since the murder.

But now was no time to turn back.

Riley grabbed Trudy by the hand and said, "Come on, what are we waiting for?"

She opened the door and pulled Trudy inside.

The smell of cigarette smoke hit Riley full in the face along with a blast of music. Bricks and Crystal was playing Nirvana's "Smells Like Teen Spirit," and a small mob of college students writhed on the glittering dance floor.

Riley felt a smile form across her face.

Gone was any hesitation she might have felt about being here. It was good to be back. This made everything feel normal again.

She shouted to Trudy over the music.

"Beer! We've gotta get beer!"

Riley dragged Trudy through the crowd to the bar. As Trudy ordered a pitcher of beer, Riley looked all around for some possible place to sit. They'd obviously arrived a bit late for the festivities, and there wasn't a lot of room. But then Riley noticed that the door that led out back onto the patio was open. It looked like there might still be room out there.

Once the beer was poured and paid for, Riley grabbed the pitcher and Trudy grabbed two glasses. Then Riley escorted her friend out onto the patio.

Riley felt her smile widen. It was much nicer here than it was inside. There was still the smell of cigarette smoke, but it was diluted by the fresh night air. The patio was cheerfully lit with hanging lanterns. The band's music was playing on outdoor speakers—not as loud as it was inside, but still loud enough to enjoy, and people were dancing out here too.

Riley heard a familiar voice call out …

"Hey, Riley! Trudy! Over here!"

Gina and Cassie were waving frantically, and they already had a table.

Riley and Trudy wended their way among the dancers and saw that their friends had even held on to two extra chairs at their table.

"Excellent foresight," Riley said as she and Trudy sat down.

Gina and Cassie were halfway through a pitcher of beer, and judging from Cassie's goofy expression, Riley felt pretty sure it wasn't the first they'd had tonight.

Gina said, "It's great to see you here!"

"It's been a while," Cassie added.

"Yeah, I guess it has," Riley said.

She realized that Gina and Cassie hadn't been avoiding the Centaur's Den all this time. She found herself thinking that maybe there was some truth to that dopey old saying after all …

Life goes on.

Maybe it was time to get back into the swing of things.

The band finished playing "Smells Like Teen Spirit" and started into one of its own original songs. Riley had heard them play it before—an anarchic tune with nihilistic lyrics, performed in a semi-humorous, semi-self-satirical style.

Perfect party music, Riley thought.

With a stern look, Cassie planted her empty glass on the table and poured herself another beer.

She said, "Guys, I hate to bring everybody down, but it's time to get serious here. We just can't pretend everything is normal. This is a very solemn night."

Riley was startled.

Maybe her friends weren't in such a party mood after all.

Maybe they, too, were still struggling with fear and grief.

Then Cassie said, "The guys in Bricks and Crystal say they're going to give up playing grunge tonight."

Gina said, "I don't know—maybe they're bluffing."

Cassie shook her head and frowned.

"I don't think so," she said. "Grunge really is dead, you know—or at least it's on its last legs. And the guys are playing even more angsty than usual tonight. I think they really mean it. And you know what that means …"

Cassie suddenly threw back her head and laughed.

"We've got to dance like there's no tomorrow!" she said.

Then Cassie grabbed Trudy by the hand and dragged her onto the dance floor, leaving Riley and Gina alone at the table. In a matter of seconds, Riley saw that Trudy was having a great time flailing away to the music.

That's what we came here for, Riley thought.

Before she could decide whether to join them, Gina asked Riley, "How are you holding up?"

Riley saw real concern in Gina's expression.

"I'm not sure these days," Riley said.

"Me neither," Gina said, pouring herself another beer. "I keep thinking that maybe enough beer and grunge and dancing will make me forget …"

Her voice trailed off.

Riley flashed back to that terrible night when she'd found Rhea's body in the dorm room, then had turned around to see Gina standing just outside the door, her eyes bulging, pale with shock, and trembling all over.

It was hardly any surprise that Gina was still having a rough time.

Riley and Gina sat watching their friends dance for a few moments.

Then Gina said, "I know Cassie looks like she's put it behind her. But she really hasn't. I can tell she hasn't, even if she won't talk about it …"

Gina described how she and Cassie kept going out nights, trying to party their grief and fear away. The truth was, what they'd been doing sounded rather brave to Riley—braver, maybe, than obsessing about murder like she herself had been doing. It seemed too bad that it didn't seem to be making much difference, at least not for Gina.

Gina went on to tell Riley how she kept expecting to see Rhea all the time, and about how her grades were slipping, and she wasn't sure whether it was because of all the forced partying or just poor concentration. Gina said that her campus counselor didn't seem to know either. In fact, she didn't feel like the counselor was doing her much good at all.

Riley was glad to just sit and listen to Gina talk, and it was obvious that Gina felt glad to have someone listen.

Finally Gina smiled sheepishly and said, "Wow, listen to me talk! Like I was the only person on campus who was having a hard time. How about you? Have you been getting any counseling? What are you doing to cope?"

Riley swallowed hard.

As comfortable as she felt sharing this moment with Gina, did she really want to tell her everything that had been going on with her?

How would Gina react if Riley told her how she'd been reading obsessively about homicidal killers, and her weird feelings of connection with Rhea's murderer?

Instead, Riley smiled and said, "Come on, let's dance."

Gina smiled too, and they both got up and headed over to join the mass of gyrating bodies. Riley saw Cassie wandering among the other dancers, dancing so hard that her long hair waved all about.

But where was Trudy?

She hurried over to Cassie and grabbed her by the arm.

"Where's Trudy?" she asked.

Cassie stopped dancing and glanced over toward the table.

"I don't know," Cassie said. "I thought she'd gone back to sit with you guys."

Riley felt a wave of panic rise up inside her.

She remembered what Trudy had said before they'd left their room …

"Promise you'll stay close by. Don't let me out of your sight."

Riley shuddered.

She'd broken her promise.

And now Trudy was gone.

CHAPTER NINETEEN

Riley struggled to fight down her rising panic.

She could see no sign of Trudy among the people dancing on the patio.

She wouldn't go anywhere else without telling me. Riley thought. *She'd never leave without me,*

But where was she?

As Riley stood there surveying the crowd, Cassie grabbed Gina by the hand and the two of them rejoined the dancing crowd. They certainly didn't seem to be alarmed by Trudy's absence. Riley tried to tell herself that she shouldn't be alarmed either.

But she knew that her panic wouldn't wane until she'd located her roommate. She had to be sure that Trudy was safe and sound.

Riley pushed her way out among the dancers to check more closely. She felt someone take hold of her hand, but when she whirled around she saw that it was a guy from one of her classes.

"C'mon," he said.

Riley pulled her hand away and said, "Sorry, I'm just looking for …"

He moved off before she could even finish her sentence. As she made her way off the dance floor she saw him dancing in a threesome with Cassie and Gina. It was obvious they were all having a good time. This was exactly the kind of partying she had promised Trudy tonight, so why would Trudy skip out without a word?

Her roommate definitely wasn't among the dancers or at any of the outdoor tables, so Riley made her way inside the club. She found that it was actually a lot more crowded indoors than on the patio. She couldn't see over the heads of people who surrounded her. The music was also a lot louder in here, so nobody heard Riley groan aloud with despair.

If Trudy was here, would Riley be able to find her among this mob?

As she ventured across the glittering dance floor, Riley was buffeted by dancers flailing away to a particularly frantic and angsty song. She didn't see Trudy anywhere, but she couldn't be at all sure she hadn't missed her in this crush.

She made her way toward the bar, where partiers swarmed and pushed their way toward the beleaguered bartender to make their orders. Riley knew it would be impossible to squeeze her way among them.

She tried to reason with herself ...

If Trudy's over there ordering a drink, she'll show up before long.

But Riley couldn't persuade herself to relax and wait until Trudy reappeared.

She headed into the women's restroom, which was crowded with female students waiting to use the occupied stalls.

Fully aware that she was making a spectacle of herself, she yelled, "Trudy! Trudy! Are you in here?"

The other young women looked at Riley as if she'd lost her mind.

Maybe I have lost my mind, she thought.

But Riley wasn't worried about what anybody thought of her at the moment.

She yelled, "Does anybody here know Trudy Lanier? Has anybody seen her? Does anybody know where she is?"

There were a lot of shaking heads and dropped jaws and quite a few no's.

The only other place that Trudy could be was downstairs. Riley hurried in that direction and dashed down the stairs two steps at a time. When she got to the bottom she came to a sudden halt, not sure whether she was relieved or pissed off at what she saw.

Her roommate was perfectly safe, and apparently perfectly happy.

Trudy was sitting in a booth—the same that booth Riley had occupied on the night of Rhea's murder. And sitting across the table from her was Harry Rampling, Lanton University's star quarterback.

Riley's stress flooded out of her body.

As she steadied herself and walked over to the table, she could see that Harry was talking interminably while Trudy just sat there gazing at him with doe-like eyes and her chin cradled in her hands.

Riley had to nudge Trudy in the shoulder to get her attention. Harry stopped talking, and Trudy looked up at her with apparent surprise.

"Hey, Riley," Trudy said. "Where've you been?"

With a slight growl in her voice, Riley said, "I could ask you the same thing."

Trudy shrugged and smiled and said, "I've been right here. Hey, have you met Harry Rampling? Harry, this is my roommate, Riley Sweeney."

Harry looked anything but pleased to see Riley.

"I don't think we've met," he lied.

"Oh, I think maybe we have," Riley said disdainfully.

Trudy was shifting around nervously. Riley was pretty sure she understood her roommate's body language. Trudy was silently trying to tell Riley that she was emphatically *not* invited to sit down with her and her newfound date.

Harry shrugged and started talking again, apparently where he had left off—regaling Trudy with a story of an especially impressive football play. Trudy was obviously falling for him completely.

She's practically drooling, Riley thought with disgust.

Interrupting Harry again, Riley said to Trudy, "I'm thinking maybe it's time we headed back to the dorm."

Trudy gave her look of childish irritation, like a little girl being told it was long past her bedtime.

"Aw, come on, Riley," she said. "The night is young. Don't spoil the party."

Riley remembered how she'd practically had to pry Trudy loose from their room in order to get her here. Now it seemed that it would take a whole lot of effort to get Trudy out of here. Would it even be worth the trouble?

"I'm staying for a while," Trudy said. "You can go on back to the dorm if you like. But stay safe, don't go back alone. I'm sure you can get Cassie or Gina to walk with you."

Then she added with a wink, "I'll be fine. Don't worry about me."

Trudy resumed gazing at Harry, and Harry started talking again.

Riley shook her head and walked back up the stairs.

Well, at least I don't need to worry about Trudy anymore, she thought with a mixture of annoyance and relief.

As much as Riley loathed Harry Rampling, she was sure he wasn't a killer. She was also sure Trudy was safe from any killer as long as she stuck with a big jock like Harry. And it certainly looked like Trudy was going to stick with him.

Maybe even for the night, Riley thought, cringing at the idea.

Riley made her way back upstairs and out to the patio. Cassie was still dancing with cheerful abandon and Gina seemed to have attached herself to the guy who'd been with them. Riley felt slightly abandoned—a childish feeling, she realized. It was really good that all her friends were having such a good time.

She found the table where they'd all been sitting. Through some miracle, no one had cleared away the pitcher and glasses, and no one had taken their place. Riley sat down there alone and poured herself a glass of beer.

She took a long sip, then closed her eyes and breathed in the semi-fresh outdoor air, feeling a lot better herself.

She just sat there for a while, tapping her foot to the tongue-in-cheek torment of the song Bricks and Crystal was playing.

Her eyes were still closed when she heard a familiar male voice beside her table.

"Um, hello. My name is Ryan Paige. Who might you be?"

Riley's eyes snapped open. He was standing there, holding an almost-empty glass of beer and looking rather shy and tentative.

She grinned broadly.

"I think we've met," she said.

Ryan shrugged and said, "Yeah, but I happened to see you sitting alone here, and I thought maybe we could start from scratch. I'm afraid I didn't handle things all that well the last time we met."

Riley said, "Oh, I don't know why you'd think that."

Of course, she *did* know exactly why he thought that. Ryan had freaked out a little over her ability to "read" him. But Riley couldn't entirely blame him. Maybe she shouldn't have pried so much.

Maybe starting from scratch isn't such a bad idea, she thought.

She said, "Anyway, my name is Riley Sweeney—in case you'd forgotten."

He grinned impishly and said, "Glad to make your re-acquaintance, Riley Sweeney."

"Why don't you sit down?" Riley said.

"I'd like that," Ryan said.

He sat down at the table across from her and refilled his beer from the pitcher.

Just then, the song came to an end, and they heard Bricks and Crystal's lead singer yelling over the outdoor speaker …

"OK, gang. The rumors are true. Bricks and Crystal is over. Through. Defunct."

The crowd was booing now—but not at all seriously. Everybody knew what Riley knew, that the guys were just pulling some kind of stunt.

The singer yelled over the booing, "Grunge is dead—and we just did the songs that killed it!"

There was more booing. Ryan laughed, and so did Riley.

The lead singer went on yelling …

"No, no, don't beg and plead and grovel. Please, you're only embarrassing yourselves. You can't stop us. We're making a few changes—including our name. We're no longer Bricks and Crystal …"

The guitarist blasted out an ominous power chord as the singer shouted, "Now our name is Hog Wild, the bomb-throwing anarchists of country and western!"

The band immediately launched into Johnny Cash's "Ring of Fire"—sounding for all the world as grungy and angsty as they ever had, and not the least bit country. The crowd went wild with shouting and applause, and some of the dancers on the patio started crashing into each other mosh-style.

Riley and Ryan were both laughing hard now.

Ryan said to her, "The more things change …"

Riley finished his thought …

"… the more things stay the same!"

Riley clicked her glass against Ryan's in a toast and added, "Grunge is dead!"

"Long live grunge!" Ryan said.

Their laughter died down and Riley and Ryan just sat there enjoying the song for a few moments.

Then Ryan said, "You may have noticed that I've made a few changes myself. Care to comment?"

Riley shook her head with a grin.

"Oh, no," she said. "Let's not start down that road again."

"Come on, I can take it this time. Really."

Feeling more than a little apprehensive, Riley looked him over.

"Hmm," she said. "No vest anymore, no expensive shirt, and your hair isn't quite so flawlessly coiffed. Instead, jeans and an ordinary cotton shirt, a more casual look—but still well dressed, not at all scruffy."

And handsome too, she thought to herself.

Ryan nodded and said, "What does that tell you about me?"

The changes were telling Riley quite a lot, but she didn't want to say so.

"Why don't you tell me?" she said.

Ryan took a long, slow breath.

He said, "I've given a lot of thought to some of the things you said last time. Especially—how did you put it?—how I figure that the best way to *become* successful is to *act* successful."

Riley said, "I didn't mean that in a bad way. It's actually kind of a good thing."

Ryan tilted his head modestly.

He said, "Yeah, but I didn't realize I was being so obvious about it. I figured it was time to be less … well, transparent, I guess."

Then he laughed and added, "Like maybe I could be a bit more of a man of mystery."

Riley laughed too and said, "Well, you certainly keep me guessing."

Then, with an expression of mock worry, she added, "I hope you didn't sell that nice car of yours."

Ryan laughed some more and said, "Oh, no. I'm still a Ford Mustang kind of guy."

Riley had to admit to herself, Ryan was really pushing all of her buttons—and in a really nice way. It was truly flattering to know that he was making personal changes on her account.

Riley realized that she was smiling with delight.

Nothing mysterious about me at the moment, she thought, too amused by herself to feel embarrassed.

Ryan's smile faded.

He asked, "How have you been doing?"

Riley sensed real concern behind those words. Of course he was asking how she'd been holding up since Rhea's death.

She didn't answer right away.

She was really feeling comfortable with this guy at long last— more than comfortable, really. It was almost as though they'd known each other for a long time.

She felt as though she could talk to him about just about anything.

Did that include her obsession about Rhea's killer and her recent studies about the homicidal mind?

Maybe, she thought.

On the other hand, that kind of talk might scare him off all over again, and she really didn't want to do that.

Before she could make up her mind, the band started playing another song—the old Patsy Cline love ballad, "Crazy." Riley felt herself melt a little, surprised at how soft and mellow and sensitive the normally abrasive band suddenly sounded—no longer like "bomb-throwing anarchists" at all.

With some grumbling, most of the patio dancers started to head back to their tables. They didn't seem to know what to do with themselves now.

But Riley knew what *she* wanted to do.

As if reading her thoughts, Ryan asked, "May I have this dance?"

Riley smiled and nodded. Ryan got up and took her hand and led her out into the dance area, which was no longer the least bit crowded. Ryan put his arm around her waist and pulled her close.

Before she knew it, they were swaying together in perfect harmony with the music.

Riley felt so warm all over, she thought she might dissolve into thin air.

Her body seemed to fit together seamlessly with Ryan's, as if they were both becoming part of the song.

Riley wanted more of this—a whole lot more.

Her whole body felt like one big warm smile as she thought …

I don't guess I'll be going back to the dorm tonight.

CHAPTER TWENTY

The smells of sizzling bacon and fresh coffee woke Riley up the next morning.

She opened her eyes and looked around.

She wasn't in her dorm room. She was lying in bed in Ryan's apartment.

She smiled as she remembered how she'd gotten here ...

It all started with the dancing.

... and then things had continued effortlessly from there.

She heard Ryan's voice say, "I think you told me you're not vegan. I hope I heard right."

Riley turned over in the bed and saw Ryan standing over a stove. His apartment was actually one big room, with appropriate furnishings in designated areas.

"You heard right," Riley said.

Riley then noticed that Ryan had laid out a bathrobe on the pillow next to her—his bathrobe, of course, and too large for her, but she knew that it would be all the more comfortable because of that.

How considerate, she thought.

In fact, his considerateness had been one of last night's major revelations. Memories came flowing back to Riley ... their naked bodies together, making love slowly and languorously. Ryan had been both amorous and thoughtful, focusing on her pleasure as well as his own.

It had certainly been different from her earlier sexual experiences. But then, most of those had been perfunctory acts of teenaged rebellion, and this kind of pleasure had hardly been the point. She remembered what she used to say to anyone who criticized her reckless behavior ...

"It's just sex."

She smiled now as she thought ...

I had no idea what I was missing.

Ryan was whistling as he broke eggs into a frying pan. Riley recognized the tune—it was "Crazy," the song they had started dancing to last night at the Centaur's Den. Ryan whistled with style and grace, and Riley enjoyed hearing the tune again.

She looked around at the apartment, remembering that she hadn't paid much attention to her surroundings when they'd gotten here. She and Ryan had pretty much become tangled up together as soon as they'd walked through the door, promptly dispensing with their clothes and tumbling weightlessly into bed.

The place now looked pleasant in the sunlight that poured in through the large windows of the old building. Riley was sure that Ryan had bought most of furnishings at thrift stores, but also that he had put a lot of time and good judgment into their selection.

The result was an agreeably bohemian look—which seemed all the more charming because Ryan didn't strike Riley as a bohemian sort of guy at all. He'd surely arrived at the style out of budgetary necessity, which rather impressed her.

Except for their clothes, which were scattered on the floor around the bed, the place was also neat and tidy. Ryan was definitely not a slob—considerably more fastidious, actually, than Riley herself.

Unless …

Well, it could be that Ryan had straightened everything up in hopes of bringing Riley home that night.

Or maybe some other woman, she thought.

If so, Riley didn't much mind. She didn't feel the least bit possessive of him—or at least she didn't *think* she did.

I guess we both got lucky.

Ryan was setting the table now, so Riley pulled on the bathrobe, got out of bed, and sat down to breakfast. In addition to fried eggs, bacon, toast, and coffee, there was also a box of fresh donuts. Since Ryan was wearing jeans and a T-shirt, she realized that he must have slipped out quietly for the donuts, and that she had slept right through this brief absence.

As Riley took a sip of coffee, she remembered what Trudy said to her before they'd gone out …

"Whatever you do, don't leave without me."

Riley felt a tingle of alarm.

She'd made a promise to Trudy, and she hadn't kept it.

But she reminded herself of how things had developed. The fearful Trudy had evaporated when she'd gotten to the Centaur's Den. The party animal Trudy had come back with a vengeance, and she'd wound up sitting in a booth fairly slobbering over the campus quarterback. The last thing Trudy had wanted was for Riley to walk her home.

Trudy had even said so ...

"I'll be fine. Don't worry about me."

Still, might Trudy be worried about Riley by now?

Riley certainly hadn't gone to find her roommate again to notify her that she might stay out for the whole night.

She asked Ryan, "I'm sorry, but ... I've got to make a phone call. Is it OK for me to use your phone?"

"Go right ahead," Ryan said, pointing to the phone that was mounted on a nearby wall.

Riley went to it and dialed their dorm room number. She soon heard Trudy's voice on the outgoing message. When she heard the beep she said, "Hey, Trudy, if you're there, pick up."

No one answered. Riley glanced at the clock and saw that it was still pretty early. It was also Saturday, and Trudy might well be fast asleep.

Or ...

Riley smiled as she remembered Trudy's doe-like eyes as she'd sat staring at Harry Rampling.

Maybe she got lucky too, she thought.

As much as Riley disliked the campus super jock, she knew that most other girls didn't share her personal distaste for him. To a lot of them, he was a hero. How could she blame Trudy for being like those other college girls?

She said into the phone, "Well, in case you didn't notice, I didn't make it back to the room last night. And, uh, I'm fine."

She almost added, *"I guess we'll need to compare notes."*

But she reminded herself that Ryan was right there within earshot, and it might be kind of a tacky thing for him to hear her say.

So she simply said, "I'll see you soon. Bye."

She hung up the phone and headed back over to the table. She gave Ryan a quick kiss on the forehead and sat down again to eat.

Ryan sat looking at her for a moment.

Then, a bit timidly, he said, "You were fantastic last night."

Riley smiled back at him, again remembering their lovemaking. Surely it went without saying that she felt the same way, but ...

Say it, Riley, she thought.

After all, he might feel insecure.

"You were fantastic too," she said. "I really mean that."

She took a bite of food and added, "And breakfast ... wow, this is great."

The two of them didn't talk as they devoured the food. But Riley felt that the silence was OK, not the least bit awkward. It was only natural that they'd both be a little shy after last night. The shyness would surely pass.

She was right about that. Before long, conversation started to flow easily between them. Ryan opened up about his working-class background and his hard work and ambitions, and Riley found herself admiring him more and more.

Riley told him the bare bones of her own life story, skipping most of the unpleasant parts. She mentioned that her mother had died when she was little, but not that her mother had been murdered right in front of her. Riley appreciated that he didn't press her for details. He seemed to be aware that it was a painful topic for her.

She surprised herself by opening up to him about her rebellious teenage years. Soon both of them were laughing at her stories of those wild times. It hadn't occurred to Riley that those stories were really quite funny, but they were—at least in hindsight, now that that turbulent part of her life was over.

It felt good to be able to laugh about all that at long last.

One topic that neither of them broached was Rhea's death, and Riley was relieved about that. Everything else was so lovely that morning, she figured it would be a shame to spoil it by talking about how obsessed she'd been about the crime and the monster who had committed it.

Riley soon sensed that she and Ryan weren't going to spend the whole day together. That was fine with her. It would have felt forced somehow, and she was just as glad for them to go their separate ways. She got dressed, and Ryan drove her back to the dorm. When he stopped the car, they looked at each other for a moment, and Riley found herself wondering …

Are we going to make plans for a "next time"?

She sensed that Ryan was wondering the same thing.

But she didn't want to push the issue, and she could tell that he didn't either.

Neither one of us wants to seem clingy, she thought.

And that seemed to her like a good thing. It boded well for whatever times they might share together later on.

She leaned over to Ryan and gave him a lingering kiss, then got out of the car and went into the dorm. As she walked down the hall toward her room, she again wondered about Trudy …

Did she come home last night?

If so, Trudy was going to want to hear all about Riley's night.

And Riley suddenly felt oddly shy about the possibility of having to tell Trudy any details. What she and Ryan had shared together had seemed so effortless, warm, and pleasant ...

Why spoil the memory by talking about it? she thought.

Riley pulled out her room key as she neared her door, but then she noticed ...

The door was already open just a crack. Trudy must be home after all.

Riley hesitated there in the hallway. Her heart was pounding, and she found it hard to breathe.

She wondered where her feeling of alarm could be coming from.

This makes no sense, she told herself.

Still, Riley stood frozen for another long moment.

"Trudy?" she called through the door.

No answer came.

Riley pushed the door open.

When she saw the blood on the floor, her whole world seemed to disappear.

CHAPTER TWENTY ONE

Riley sat very still. She was staring at an open doorway, watching uniformed people coming and going, crowding in and out with ghostly efficiency.

They must be making a lot of noise, she thought.

But she couldn't hear it. Her brain must have been shutting out the noise.

Like so much else, she thought vaguely.

With a lot of effort, she realized that she was sitting on the edge of her own bed in her dorm room. Those people she could see were rushing in and out of her room.

She didn't dare move her head or her eyes for fear of what else she'd see.

She felt as if her body were uninhabited—as if she herself wasn't in it.

Where am I? she wondered.

If not here in her body, in her room, then where?

It was the weirdest feeling Riley could remember ever having.

Or was it?

She thought she'd felt just this way at one other time in her life, a long, long time ago.

But she couldn't remember when that was. The truth was, she was having trouble remembering anything at all.

She kept reminding herself of her own name …

Riley. My name is Riley.

The numbness that gripped her whole body began to ebb a little, and she felt a terrible pain in her chest and head.

I'm not breathing, she realized.

Then she felt her lips silently shape the word …

"Good."

She didn't want to breathe.

Someone else wasn't breathing anymore, and Riley had failed to make that person start breathing again, so she thought she shouldn't be breathing either.

She had no business breathing. In fact, she wanted to stop everything else as well—especially time.

She wanted to freeze time, make everything stop moving, and then maybe she could find some way to turn time backward to …

When?

Before *it* had happened—whatever *it* was.

But the precious numbness that shielded her from reality was fading rapidly, and her chest hurt more and more, and her lungs were burning.

Finally her body betrayed her and she gasped for air.

She felt overcome with horror and guilt.

I failed, she thought. *I breathed.*

But she couldn't stop the gasping and panting now, and she felt her *self* sliding unwillingly back into her body.

She heard somebody say, "Where are you wounded?"

Who said that? she wondered.

Then she realized—someone was prodding her body in different places.

It was a white-uniformed man crouching beside her.

"Where are you wounded?" he repeated.

Wounded? she thought.

She wasn't wounded—or at least she didn't think she was.

She clenched her fists as she tried to understand, quickly noticing how sticky her hands felt. She lifted up her hands and looked at them.

They were covered with blood.

But how?

Why?

Now she could hear all the noise in the room. There must be lots of people packed in there with her.

She started to turn her head to look around, but the man who had been prodding her grabbed her chin to stop her and said sharply but sympathetically, "No. You don't want to do that."

Then the man held her eyelids open and shined a light into her pupils.

"Can you tell me your name?" he said.

It now seemed like a lucky thing that she'd already gone to the trouble of remembering.

"Riley Sweeney," she said.

Then the man asked other questions—about what day it was, what town they were in, who was the President of the United States …

It took some effort, but Riley managed to answer all the

questions.

Then the man rose to his feet and called out to the others present, "I don't think this one is injured. She's in a bad state of shock, though."

Riley was horrified to feel a spasm of laughter trying to make its way up through her windpipe.

Why?

Was anything funny about what was happening right now?

No, but she felt some kind of grotesque irony in the words that the man had just said …

"I don't think this one is injured."

She managed to push the laughter back down into her abdomen. As confused as she was, she knew she mustn't laugh.

She looked at her hands again and wondered …

If I'm not injured, where did this blood come from?

Then memories started flooding back.

She remembered someone screaming—very loudly, for a long time.

It was me, she thought. *I screamed.*

The whole dorm must have heard her screaming.

Still screaming, she had crouched down by the bleeding body on the floor.

Whose body? she wondered. *Mommy's body?*

Horror came crashing down on her like a tsunami.

It had been Trudy's body.

She'd found Trudy's body.

And Trudy hadn't been bleeding from her chest like Mommy had, but out of a huge wound in her throat.

Riley's screaming had waned and she'd tried to decide what to do.

Try to stop the bleeding?

No, even though blood had been everywhere, it hadn't looked like Trudy was bleeding anymore.

Which had meant Trudy must be dead.

But Riley hadn't been able to make herself believe that.

She'd yelled at Trudy and shaken her. She'd tried to perform CPR, pressing down on Trudy's chest, but she'd had to stop when blood started to bubble from the wound again. Could she have done anything else?

There must have been something, she thought. *I failed.*

But all these people hadn't been able to bring Trudy back

either.

And how had they all gotten here?

Had she called 911?

No, she was sure she hadn't. Somebody else had done that—somebody who had heard her screaming.

Once again, she almost turned her head to see Trudy's body. But she managed to stop herself. The memory of what she had seen was already more horror than she could handle.

Now she noticed that lights were flashing in the room. She didn't know what they might be.

She heard someone say to her, "Stand up, please."

She numbly obeyed, and a male cop with a camera moved around her snapping pictures. The flash from the camera hurt her eyes.

But why was the cop taking pictures of *her*?

She looked down at her clothes, which were drenched with blood.

"This is wrong," she whispered aloud. "I shouldn't be breathing."

A terrible sob burst out of her throat, and then another, and then another on top of that, until she was sobbing uncontrollably.

She felt a comforting hand on her shoulder. A woman was looking at her sympathetically. Riley recognized her right away. It was Officer Frisbie, the cop she had spoken with on the night of Rhea's murder.

"Come on," Frisbie said, taking Riley by the hand. "Let's get you out of here."

CHAPTER TWENTY TWO

As Officer Frisbie helped Riley up from the bed, Riley heard her call out something to one of the cops in the hall. It was a simple order of some sort, but at the moment it sounded like gibberish to Riley.

Riley did make out a woman's sharp reply. "Do you think that's a good idea? I mean, isn't she—?"

"Don't argue with me," Frisbie snapped back. "Make it fast."

Officer Frisbie took Riley gently by the arm and led her out of her room. The hallway seemed painfully bright, and Riley had to squint. She couldn't actually feel her legs, but she knew they must be down there, obediently carrying her along. Still, she didn't think she could rely on them, and she was glad that someone was supporting her.

Officer Frisbie led Riley into the bathroom and said, "Get out of those clothes, honey, and give them to me. We're going to get you cleaned up."

Obeying mechanically, Riley removed her clothes. She handed each piece to Officer Frisbie as she took it off.

Frisbie folded the garments carefully and put all of them into a large plastic bag.

Once she was naked, Riley felt strangely unsure of what to do next. Officer Frisbie gently tugged Riley over to a shower stall, turned on the water, and felt it until it seemed like a good temperature, then helped Riley step inside. Frisbie shut the frosted glass door behind her.

As the water sprayed over her Riley realized that she was sobbing—that she'd been sobbing since before she'd left her room, but hadn't been aware of it. The comforting deluge settled her down and the sobs finally stopped.

It felt good to have pellets of hot water pounding her body.

But that also made her feel guilty again. What business did she have feeling good in any way? She shouldn't even be breathing.

The shower stall was supplied with a bar of soap and a bottle of shampoo, so Riley began to scrub herself all over. The blood seemed to dissolve from her hands before reappearing on the tiled floor and vanishing down the drain.

Riley's mind started to clear.

I really lost it for a while, she realized.

She wondered—why was that?

Several weeks ago, when she'd been the second person to see Rhea's body, she'd managed to keep herself under control. She'd even had the presence of mind to keep other students from going into the room and messing up the crime scene.

This time, she'd completely fallen apart.

Of course she had … she had been closer to Trudy.

But why did she feel so guilty this time?

Then she remembered again what Trudy had said to her before they'd gone to the Centaur's Den …

"Whatever you do, don't leave without me."

… to which Riley had replied …

"I promise."

Riley shivered, despite the heat of the water.

Now she understood the difference—she hadn't *promised* Rhea anything. But she'd broken her promise to Trudy. She should have kept that promise, no matter what, no matter how much Trudy protested, even if she'd had to drag Trudy away from that quarterback.

Instead …

A truly sickening realization began to come over her.

Possibly—just possibly—at the very moment when Trudy had been killed …

I was having sex with Ryan.

The thought made her shudder all over.

But this horror ran far too deep for tears. She knew she was going to be carrying this terrible guilt around for a long, long time. Maybe for the rest of her life.

When Riley finally turned off the water and stepped out of the shower stall, Officer Frisbie wasn't there anymore.

Instead, she saw a smaller female cop, a young woman with a pinched and unsympathetic face. She was wearing a nameplate that said B. Danforth, and she was holding a towel and a small pile of clothes.

The woman handed Riley the towel and said in a disagreeably sharp voice, "Dry yourself and get dressed. I got these for you from your room."

Riley remembered that back in her room, Officer Frisbie had

called out some kind of an order to somebody who'd replied …

"Do you think that's a good idea?"

Now Riley understood.

Officer Frisbie had ordered this woman—Officer Danforth—to get a towel and clothes from Riley's closet. Danforth apparently hadn't much liked that idea, and judging from her expression, she still didn't like it.

Riley dried off her body, then towel-dried her hair. She didn't want to ask for Danforth to fetch a hairdryer from her room. Then she put on the clothes Danforth had brought—fresh underwear, jeans, a shirt, and sneakers.

Danforth led Riley back into the hall. Riley saw that cops were still clustered around her dorm room door, including Officer Frisbie. Another was Officer Steele, the overweight, unfriendly cop who had cut off her questions at the police station.

But Riley didn't see any students anywhere.

Where was everybody?

Then she remembered that students had been ordered to stay in their rooms the night of Rhea's murder. They must all be cowering in their rooms right now, wondering what was going on just outside. Riley almost envied them their temporary seclusion.

She herself had no chance to hide away as Danforth led her toward the cops.

As they approached, Officer Steele eyed Riley suspiciously. Frisbie looked up from the notes she'd been jotting down.

Danforth said to Frisbie, "What do you want me to do with her now?"

"Take her to the common room," she said. "Try to help her get comfortable."

Comfortable? Riley thought.

There wasn't much chance of that.

Danforth escorted Riley to the common room, which was as devoid of student life as the hallways were. Riley sat down on a couch, and Danforth sat in a chair across from her.

The cop said nothing. She just sat there staring grimly and silently at Riley.

What's going on? Riley wondered.

Did Danforth suspect her of Trudy's murder? Did all the cops suspect her—except maybe Officer Frisbie?

If so, why?

Then Riley remembered …

I was covered with blood.

They had to pull me away from Trudy's body.

Why wouldn't they suspect me?

Riley wondered—was she going to be arrested?

She felt herself wilt under Danforth's accusing gaze. Should she try to explain to her what had happened?

If I'm under arrest, maybe I should keep quiet, she thought.

Then she heard a pair of quarreling voices outside the common room—the voices of Officers Frisbie and Steele.

She heard Frisbie say, "We should get her to a hospital."

She heard Steele reply, "Why? She's not injured."

"She's still in shock," Frisbie said.

"I just want to ask her some questions," Steele said.

Riley heard Frisbie let out a growl of disapproval and walk away.

Steele strode into the common room. He gave Officer Danforth a nod, which she seemed to take as a silent order to leave. Danforth got up and left the room, and the overweight, red-faced man sat down in her place.

He stared at Riley for a moment.

Then he said, "You're an awfully curious young woman, aren't you?"

Riley didn't know what to say—or even what he meant.

Did he mean "curious" as in wanting to know something, or as in being an unusual person?

Maybe both, she thought.

Steele said, "I remember finding you standing in the first victim's doorway when we showed up that night. Then a couple of days later you came into the station asking questions. 'How is the investigation going?' you wanted to know. And now we've got a second victim—and she just happens to be your roommate."

He fell silent, leaving Riley to wonder ...

Is he asking a question?

If he was, she sure didn't have any idea what to say to him.

Finally Steele added, "Maybe you've got something you'd like to tell me."

Riley was truly baffled now. Then she heard a deeper male voice from the common room door.

"Oh, for God's sake, Steele. What do you think you're doing?"

Riley's head jerked around to see who had spoken. She was relieved to see that Dr. Zimmerman had just walked in the door, accompanied by Officer Frisbie.

Zimmerman crossed his arms and glared at Steele, who looked anything but pleased to see him.

Steele growled, "This is police business, Zimmerman—not yours."

Clearly, the two men knew each other, and they definitely didn't like each other.

"Are you going to arrest this student?" Zimmerman asked. "If so, you'd better read her her rights."

Steele scowled silently.

Zimmerman spoke in a firm voice. "Leave this girl alone. She's not a suspect."

"How do you know?" Steele said.

"Because I happen to know a few things about killers," Zimmerman replied. "And I know this girl. She's sensitive and smart, and she didn't kill anybody, and she doesn't deserve to be bullied."

Officer Frisbie tilted her head at Steele and pointed toward the hallway.

"Come on, Nat," she said. "Leave this poor kid alone. We've got real work to do."

For a moment, Officer Steele looked like he might argue. But then he reluctantly got up and followed Frisbie out of the room.

Dr. Zimmerman sat down on the couch next to Riley and held both of her hands.

"Oh, my dear, I know this is awful for you," he said. "I came as soon as I'd heard about what happened. Is it true? Was it really your roommate this time?"

Riley nodded.

"I'm so terribly sorry," Dr. Zimmerman said.

After the grim coldness of Officers Danforth and Steele, Riley found the professor's kindly presence to be a startling change— even a shock to her system.

How should she deal with it?

How could she help but let her emotional guard down?

As if in reply to her unspoken question, Dr. Zimmerman said, "You can talk to me. It's all right."

Tears trickled down Riley's cheeks.

She said, "I didn't do this, Dr. Zimmerman. I didn't kill Trudy."

"I know you didn't," Dr. Zimmerman said.

"But …"

She couldn't say the rest of what she meant.

Dr. Zimmerman spoke her thought for her.

"You think it was your fault. You think you're responsible."

Riley nodded again and choked down a sob.

Dr. Zimmerman squeezed her hands.

"Tell me the truth," he said. "Was there any part of you that *wanted* this to happen? Did you feel even the slightest trace of such a wish, even for a fleeting moment?"

"No," Riley said.

"Of course you didn't," Dr. Zimmerman said. "Someone else did this, not you. You're not responsible. It wasn't your fault."

Dr. Zimmerman lifted her chin and looked into her eyes.

"It wasn't your fault," he said again. "I'm liable to keep saying that like a broken record. You might even get sick of hearing me say it. But it's true, and you've got to believe it. It's not your fault."

Riley wanted to believe him. But she found herself remembering their conversation in his office a few weeks ago, when he'd said …

"We mustn't cause a panic by spreading our suspicions around."

She said, "Were we wrong, Dr. Zimmerman? Should we have let everybody know what we were thinking? About the killer, I mean. That he was likely to kill again."

She noticed a flash of uncertainty in Dr. Zimmerman's eyes.

He took a long breath and said, "We were just two people with a hunch. We mustn't second-guess ourselves. We have to deal with the here and now."

Riley paused for a moment, then said, "Do they suspect me? The cops, I mean?"

Zimmerman thought for a moment, then said, "Did you see a knife in the room? Did the killer leave the murder weapon?"

Riley tried to think—*had* she seen a murder weapon?

Would she have even noticed if it had been there?

"I don't think so," she said. "I'm not sure."

Zimmerman scratched his chin and said, "We'll have to see. But if it's at all possible, I want to get you away from here. You're still in shock. Would you like me to take you to the hospital?"

Riley shuddered as she imagined spending the night in such a cold and impersonal environment.

"No," she said.

Zimmerman thought again, then said, "I could put you up at my place, just for the night. I've got a guest room."

Riley had trouble deciding for a few seconds.

Then she said, "I guess that would be all right."

Zimmerman helped her up from the couch.

"Come on," he said. "Let's go talk to them, see if it's all right for you to leave."

As Dr. Zimmerman took her arm and escorted her out of the common room, Riley felt markedly stronger than when she'd come in. Zimmerman's presence had been more than helpful. In fact, she wondered how she could have coped if he hadn't shown up.

Once they were out in the hallway, Riley could see that some new people had arrived.

One of them was striding toward her and Dr. Zimmerman—a short, vigorous, barrel-chested man who appeared to be in his mid-fifties.

As the man approached, he called out to her, "Is your name Riley Sweeney?"

Riley nodded.

The man pulled out a badge with identification.

He said, "I'm Special Agent Jake Crivaro, FBI."

Riley stopped in her tracks with a renewed flash of alarm.

I really am going to be arrested, she thought.

CHAPTER TWENTY THREE

Riley more than half expected the FBI agent to pull out a pair of handcuffs and arrest her right there. Then Dr. Zimmerman spoke up.

"Agent Crivaro, I'm personally concerned about this young woman. She's experienced a terrible trauma. She's been through more than enough today, and she'll be better able to answer questions tomorrow. I'd really like to get her away from here."

Crivaro frowned at Dr. Zimmerman.

"You would, huh?" he asked. "And who might you be?"

"Dr. Dexter Zimmermann."

Crivaro's eyes widened.

"Holy shit," he said. "*The* Dexter Zimmerman, the criminal pathologist? Yeah, now I remember—you teach here at Lanton."

Zimmerman nodded and said, "I'm head of the Psychology Department."

Crivaro shook his hand vigorously.

"Man oh man!" Crivaro said. "I must have read everything you've ever written, Dr. Zimmerman. I'm a great admirer of yours. But then, who in the Bureau isn't?"

Zimmerman said, "I wish we could have met under better circumstances. I take it this is now an FBI case. How did you get here so quickly?"

"My team and I flew in from Quantico by helicopter," Crivaro said. "We landed in the college football field."

Crivaro looked at Riley again, then back at Zimmerman.

He said to Zimmerman, "Listen, do you mind sticking with me for a little while? I might be able to use some help."

"I'd be glad to," Zimmerman said.

"Where can the three of us go to talk?" Crivaro asked.

"The common area," Zimmerman said. "Come with me."

Riley walked between the two men back to the common room, still uncertain as to exactly what was happening. Was her arrest just being delayed?

She felt deeply relieved that Dr. Zimmerman wasn't going away, at least for a while.

Soon the three of them were sitting around the table in the kitchen that adjoined the common room. Crivaro took out a pencil and notepad and got ready to take notes.

He said, "Ms. Sweeney, I understand you were the victim's roommate."

Riley felt a jolt at hearing the word "victim."

"Yes," she managed to say. "Trudy ... *was* ... my best friend."

"And you discovered the body, am I correct?"

Riley felt jolted again by the word "body."

In fact, she cringed a little.

Why can't he just call her Trudy? she thought.

"That's right," she said in a whisper.

Crivaro looked up from his notebook. His expression softened, and so did his voice.

"I know this is hard, Ms. Sweeney, but I need some answers. When and how did you find Trudy after she'd been murdered?"

Riley was startled by the subtle shift in his tone.

More than that ...

He called her Trudy.

Had Crivaro picked up on her discomfort at the words "victim" and "body" and was now trying to exercise a bit more tact?

Riley suddenly sensed that this seemingly gruff man might be a lot more sensitive than he normally let people see—and probably a lot more complicated.

In answer to his question, she said, "I found her when I got back to the room this morning."

"At what time?"

Riley told him the time, as best she could remember.

Crivaro squinted at her and said, "So you were out all night?"

Riley winced and nodded.

Crivaro said, "Where and with whom?"

Riley gulped hard. Was she going to get Ryan in trouble again?

She also felt oddly embarrassed at what Crivaro might think of her for spending a night in a guy's apartment.

It seemed like a weirdly inappropriate thing to worry about.

Why should I care what he thinks?

Who is he, my father?

She said, "I went home last night with Ryan Paige—a law student."

Crivaro thumbed through his notebook.

"Ryan Paige," he said. "Yeah, I see that his name has come up before—with regard to Rhea Thorson's death. When did you last see Trudy Lanier alive?"

Riley took a long, slow breath and explained how she'd coaxed Trudy into coming to the Centaur's Den, and how she'd last seen Trudy sitting in a booth with Harry Rampling. At the mention of Harry's name, Crivaro thumbed through his notes again.

Has Harry's name come up already? she wondered.

It certainly made sense. Riley was surely not the only person to have noticed that Trudy and Harry had been together.

Did that mean Harry was now a suspect?

Riley reminded herself …

I still don't even know whether I'm *a suspect.*

When Riley finished talking, Crivaro paused and sat staring at her, tapping his pencil eraser against the tabletop.

What's he thinking? she wondered.

Then Dr. Zimmerman leaned toward Riley. He spoke slowly and carefully.

"Riley, I think you should tell Agent Crivaro about your experiences."

"Experiences?" Riley asked.

"You know. Those … *moments* you told me about when you …"

He left the sentence unfinished, but Riley knew what he meant.

He was talking about those two experiences she'd had of slipping into the killer's mind.

Riley was shocked by his suggestion. Dr. Zimmerman was the only person in the world she'd told about those moments. Did he really think she should confide them to a total stranger?

She looked at Dr. Zimmerman and silently mouthed …

"Are you sure?"

Dr. Zimmerman nodded with a warm and sympathetic smile, then said to Crivaro, "I think you'll want to hear what she has to say."

Agent Crivaro was now staring at her with keen curiosity.

Haltingly and cautiously, Riley began to tell him everything—first how she'd sensed the killer's thoughts as she'd retraced the route he had taken while following Rhea, then how she'd done the same thing in Rhea's room, imagining how he felt looking down on her dead body.

By the time she was finished, Crivaro was squinting at her with intense interest, and his mouth was hanging slightly open.

Then he and Dr. Zimmerman exchanged a meaningful look.

Obviously they were thinking the same thing.

But what are *they thinking?* Riley wondered.

She remembered something Dr. Zimmerman had said to her the first time they'd talked. He'd said that she might have a "unique talent," and ...

"It might not be a talent you'd choose to have, but it might prove to be very valuable."

Was Agent Crivaro thinking along the same lines—that Riley might have the makings of a good criminal profiler?

The idea scared Riley almost as much as the thought of getting arrested.

Finally Agent Crivaro said, "Ms. Sweeney, I don't want to push you ..."

He paused, and Riley felt cold chills all over.

Then Crivaro added, "But I'd like you to try to get into this state of mind again."

"Oh, no," Riley said, her voice trembling.

She couldn't imagine making such an attempt—not while she was so emotionally devastated by Trudy's death.

But Crivaro's expression was urgent. Riley sensed that he wasn't likely to take no for an answer.

Finally Crivaro said, "I think you really should. Two young women have been murdered—and one of them was your best friend. I'm not sure but ... I really think you might be able to help bring their killer to justice."

Riley felt a knot of panic form in her throat. How could she possibly say no?

She nodded slightly.

"I can talk you through it," Crivaro said. "Come with me."

Without another word, the two men got up from the table. Riley stood uncertainly, then followed Dr. Zimmerman and Agent Crivaro out of the common area and into the hallway.

Local cops and FBI agents were coming and going or standing around talking.

Crivaro barked out to all of them, "I want the crime scene cleared of all personnel. Not just the room, the entire hallway. Everybody go outside and let this girl and me work."

The FBI agents immediately started heading out, but the local cops stood gaping at him with surprise. Officer Steele didn't look like he was going to leave.

"Did you hear me?" Crivaro snapped. "Move!"

Startled, Steele and the rest followed the FBI agents out of the building.

Dr. Zimmerman put a hand on Riley's shoulder.

"I'd better go too," he said. "Don't worry, I'll be right outside."

Riley wanted to beg him …

"Please! Don't go away!"

But Dr. Zimmerman headed on out, leaving Riley and Agent Crivaro standing alone in the hallway.

Riley felt chills running over her body.

What was going to happen now?

CHAPTER TWENTY FOUR

For a few moments, Agent Jake Crivaro stood looking at the frightened young woman wondering …

Am I making a big mistake here?

Maybe he was wrong about her. Maybe she didn't have that rare intuition possessed by only a tiny handful of profilers—including himself. But Jake's own gut feelings told him otherwise. Her descriptions of her experiences had sounded extraordinarily real.

Besides, Dexter Zimmerman obviously sensed the same talent in her, and he was a certified genius when it came to this sort of thing. He had written about this ability of certain individuals to get inside the mind of a criminal.

Most important, her insights just might be a shortcut to nailing the killer. Jake knew that the local cops already had a guy in custody, and maybe the girl could help him figure out whether they had the right man.

But Jake also had more in mind than just this one case.

He really had to find out whether her ability was real—and if so, what she could do with it.

He looked around, wondering where to start the exercise.

Near the dorm entrance, he thought.

After all, the killer must have come in from there—whether in the victim's company or not, Jake didn't yet know.

"Come with me," he said to Riley.

They walked down the hall to just inside the dorm's front door. Through its window Jake could see the local cops and FBI agents milling around outside with nothing to do at the moment.

They'll find themselves back to work soon enough, he thought.

As he and Riley Sweeney stood in the entryway, Jake said, "I want you to close your eyes."

The girl obeyed.

Jake said in a low, steady, calming voice, "Now just breathe for a few moments, nice and slow. Pay close attention to your physical sensations—how the air feels around you, the floor under your feet, the smell of this place—things that you might not normally notice."

Riley Sweeney nodded and breathed. Jake could see that she was readily slipping into the state of mind he was hoping for.

He said, "Now—I want you to think back to that experience you had when you walked across the campus that night, imagining how the killer felt following Rhea Thorson. Try to remember—how did it feel to be inside his mind, if only for a moment? What kind of thoughts did you share? Try to *be* him again."

The girl took a long breath, then shuddered slightly.

It's working, he thought.

He said, "Now go back to last night. You just came inside. How did you get through the door?"

Riley said nothing for a long moment. She seemed to be struggling with the question. Then her face tightened.

"Trudy … let him … let *me* in," she said.

Jake was startled to hear her switch to first person.

He hadn't expected that. Was this exercise about to go too far?

After all, she was just a college kid, not a seasoned profiler.

Just let her follow her gut, he told himself. He'd stop her if the exercise got out of control.

"Why did he let you in?" Jake asked.

Riley shrugged a little.

"Because I asked her to," she said.

After another hesitation, she added, "She knew who I was."

So the victim did know her killer, Jake thought. But he cautioned himself that in a setting like that, that was pretty likely. Was this girl just guessing or was she actually sensing something about the killer?

"How well did she know you?" he asked.

Riley's brow wrinkled as if she were making a mental effort.

"I'm not sure," she said. "I think … no, I'm just not sure."

"Breathe deeply," Jake said. "Just say whatever comes to your mind."

The girl continued, "Not close friends, I don't think. Well enough not to be afraid."

"And how does that make you feel?" Jake asked.

A sinister smile formed on the girl's face.

Jake was startled. He'd never seen a novice get this deeply into the exercise so quickly.

Then he cautioned himself again. *Either that or she already knows more about this killer than she should.*

"It makes me feel good," Riley said. "Everything's going just the way I want it to."

Jake put his hand on her arm.

"Just keep your eyes closed," he said. "I'll help you find your way. Just go where your instincts take you."

Jake kept his hand on Riley Sweeney's arm as she walked through the hallway with her eyes still closed. When they were just outside the girl's room, he tugged her to a halt, uncertain what to try next.

The door was wide open, and Jake didn't want her to open her eyes and see how the room looked right now. The body had been taken away, but blood was still everywhere, and a chalk outline showed the position of the corpse on the floor.

But Riley was speaking again, and she seemed to be immersed even more deeply in the state of mind.

"She unlocks the door to the room and invites me inside. I'm really delighted. I don't even have to ask. She goes on in and I follow her ..."

Jake and the girl stepped inside the room. But now, she seemed a little bit uncertain.

Riley said, "I think ..."

She hesitated. Jake wondered if maybe she was going to slip out of her experience.

Then she said, "The phone rings."

Riley was becoming agitated, her hands shaking. Jake was about to break off the exercise when she blurted out, "That was his moment."

Jake noted the transition back to third person. He realized that whatever this girl was experiencing, it was getting to be too much for her.

It's time to stop now, he thought.

Still holding her by the arm, Jake said gently, "Keep your eyes closed. Come with me."

But before he could lead her safely out of the room, the phone actually *did* ring.

The girl's eyes snapped open. Her head darted around as she took in the grisly scene, and she let out a horrified gasp.

Too late, Jake realized.

He rapidly pushed her out of the room and into the hallway. The girl leaned against a wall and started to sob.

Jake put his arm around her comfortingly.

"It's OK," he said. "It's OK."

From the open door to the room, he heard an outgoing message—her roommate's voice, not hers. After the beep he heard a male voice.

"Hey, Riley—are you there? This is Ryan. Jesus, I just heard what happened. I can't believe it. Are you there? Are you all right? Are you safe?"

Stunned and confused and still sobbing, the girl nodded her head as if to tell the boy yes.

After a pause, the voice continued.

"Listen. Call me when you can. If there's anything I can do … anything …"

The voice faded away, and the caller hung up.

Riley was still breathing hard, but the sobs were coming to a stop.

Jake patted her on the shoulder.

"You did good," he said. "You did real good."

He realized that he meant it. He no longer thought she might be faking, simply reporting something she already knew.

Then Jake heard the front door to the dorm clatter open and the sound of approaching footsteps. He turned to see a member of his own team approaching.

Jake snapped at him, "Walton, what did I tell you?"

Special Agent Tyler Walton said, "I'm sorry, sir, but I thought I'd better come tell you. We got a call from the station. It sounds like the suspect they're holding is ready to talk."

"Has he lawyered up?" Jake asked.

"Not yet," Walton said. "He's pretty cocksure of himself, and he doesn't seem to care about getting a lawyer."

Jake looked into Riley Sweeney's eyes and said, "Listen. I think you could be of help to us there, too. Will you come with us down to the station?"

Riley nodded and followed him down the hallway.

As they headed out of the building, Jake remembered how deeply the girl seemed to have slipped into the killer's mind.

She's good at this, he thought.

But had he done her any favors, bringing this ability out in her?

Jake shuddered as his mind was flooded with horrors he'd seen during his career—internally as well as physically.

He had no idea what kind of future Riley Sweeney might have in mind for herself, but he was pretty sure of one thing …

A normal life isn't in the cards for her.

CHAPTER TWENTY FIVE

Riley's head was reeling as Agent Crivaro led her outside among the cops and agents. The experience she'd just had was much, much more intense than her earlier moments of connection with the killer—and much more terrifying.

Some of it was hard to remember. She knew there had been a feeling of satisfaction that belonged to someone else, not to her. She knew she'd spoken words that weren't hers.

"It makes me feel good," she'd said, although it wasn't herself she was talking about. "Everything's going just the way I want it to," she'd added. Or somebody had added.

As she walked along with Crivaro, Riley saw Dr. Zimmerman standing some distance away among the cops watching her.

She wished he'd come over and talk to her, help her understand what had just happened.

But he kept his distance, as if he didn't want to interfere with

…

What? Riley wondered.

What's going on? What am I doing here?

Crivaro led her toward the nearest street. Police vehicles with flashing lights were parked there.

Riley asked, "What just happened?"

Crivaro hesitated for a moment.

Then he said, "I guess you've talked about this kind of thing with Dr. Zimmerman. What did he tell you?"

Riley thought back again to that conversation in Zimmerman's office.

She said, "He told me I had exceptional intuition for … this sort of thing."

"I'd say he was right," Crivaro said.

Crivaro helped her into the back seat of a waiting police car and sat beside her.

Another agent, Walton, had followed them from the dorm. He got into the passenger seat up front and the local cop drove them away.

Riley still wanted an explanation from Crivaro.

"It was so vivid," she said. "How did I know that stuff?"

"Well, strictly speaking, you didn't know *any* of it. It's not like being a psychic or anything paranormal. You were following your hunches and intuition, and they're just a lot more powerful and vivid for you than they are for most people—and maybe more accurate as well. Actually, what you're doing most of all is using your imagination, exercising a rare kind of creativity."

He paused for a moment, then said, "For example, you imagined the phone ringing when Trudy and the killer went into the room. I doubt that that really happened—I didn't see any messages on your answering machine. Still, *something* made Trudy turn away from the killer. The killer took advantage of that moment and pulled his knife and grabbed her from behind and ..."

Riley was glad he didn't finish the sentence. She'd imagined that moment much too vividly just a few minutes ago. She leaned back against the headrest, wondering what was going to happen next.

Walton had said a suspect was in custody and ready to talk.

Crivaro had said ...

"I think you could be of help to us there, too."

What did he expect from her now?

When the car pulled up to the police station they all got out and headed inside. The first person they ran into was Chief Hintz, the tall, lean, vigorous-looking older man who had interviewed her and four other girls—including Trudy herself—after Rhea's death. He hadn't been very sympathetic, which had made an already awful night even worse.

Hintz nodded toward Agents Crivaro and Walton.

"You must be a couple of the FBI guys," he said.

As they introduced themselves, Riley could see that Chief Hintz seemed to be badly shaken.

The chief confirmed her impression, saying, "I can't believe it. I just can't get it through my head."

Can't believe what? Riley wondered. *Another murder or something more?*

Chief Hintz led them through the station to the interview room. They all stood outside looking through the two-way mirror.

Riley immediately recognized the young man who was sitting handcuffed at the table inside.

It was Harry Rampling.

Now she began to understand why Chief Hintz seemed so

troubled. She remembered Hintz's look of disapproval when she'd mentioned brushing off Harry on the night of Rhea's death.

Gazing sadly through the window at the young jock, Hintz said, "I always thought the best of that kid. I took him to be a real hero. I didn't think he had a bad bone in his body. Well, you never can tell, I suppose …"

Hintz's voice trailed off.

Then he looked at Crivaro and Walton and said, "I guess you guys had better take it from here. Me and my guys are really out of our depth."

Hintz turned and walked away.

Crivaro said to his colleague, "Walton, I want you to go in there and question the suspect."

The younger agent looked surprised.

"Are you sure I'm ready for that?" he asked.

Crivaro said, "You learn as you go in this line of work. Go ahead, get started."

As Walton walked through the door into the interview room, Crivaro said to Riley, "I want you to listen carefully to whatever gets said in there."

"Listen?" Riley asked. "Listen for what?"

"You'll know when you hear it—or *if* you hear it."

Riley could hear sounds over a speaker as Walton scooted a chair and sat down at the table.

Walton said to Harry, "Tell me your name, please."

Harry seemed to be bored and amused at the same time.

"Again?" he said. "I feel like I've already said it a hundred times."

"Yeah, again."

"Harry Rampling. Actually, my full name is Henry Wallace Rampling III. You know, you guys are making a big mistake treating me like this. My dad's the mayor of Baxter."

Walton smirked slightly.

"Baxter?" he said. "Where's that? A big town, is it?"

Riley couldn't help feeling momentary amusement at Harry's deflated expression. She knew perfectly well that Baxter was about a hundred miles away from Lanton—and considerably smaller. Walton seemed appropriately unimpressed, and Harry was visibly stung by that.

Walton said to Harry, "I take it you've been told your rights."

"Yeah," Harry said, rolling his eyes.

146

"Do you want a lawyer?"

"This is so stupid."

"Should I take that as a no?" Walton asked.

"Sure. Fine. Whatever."

Walton began to question Harry about what he'd been doing at specific hours last night.

Harry stretched his legs under the table.

"I was in my room asleep," he said.

Walton looked at some notes and said, "Your room in Gettier Hall? Upstairs from where the murder happened?"

"That's right."

"Can your roommate confirm that?"

Harry yawned—trying a little too hard to look bored, Riley thought.

"Naw, Larry was out all night. He told me he wouldn't be coming in. He had a date with a hot chick with her own place. Which suited me fine."

"Why was that?" Walton asked.

Harry shrugged as if the answer ought to be obvious.

"Larry and I try to coordinate our activities. He told me his plans so I'd know I'd have the room all to myself—and for any company I might want to *entertain*, if you know what I mean."

"Company?" Walton said. "You mean like Trudy Lanier?"

Harry winced at the mention of Trudy's name.

He said, "Terrible what happened to her. Nice chick."

"So you knew her really well?" Walton asked.

"No, but we'd spent some time together earlier that night. But I guess you already know that. I mean, that's why I'm here, right?"

Walton held Harry's gaze for a moment.

During the silence, Riley remembered Trudy sitting in that booth across the table from Harry, practically swooning over his every word and gesture.

Did Harry really kill her? she wondered.

Right now it seemed like a distinct possibility.

She wished more than ever she'd simply dragged Trudy out of that booth and walked her home.

Finally Walton said to Harry, "Tell me about the whole thing with Trudy. I mean, what happened between the two of you last night."

Riley's curiosity quickened.

Harry said, "I'd just arrived at the Centaur's Den and wandered out onto the patio to see what was going on out there when this girl dances right up to me—"

"Trudy Lanier?" Walton asked.

"Yeah, her. And she doesn't say a word, but she makes it real clear that she's not going to leave me alone. So …"

He shrugged again.

"She wouldn't go away and I didn't really feel like dancing, so I said let's go get a couple of drinks."

Riley felt a knot of anger in her chest.

He makes it sound like she was being a pest, she thought.

Then she remembered again Trudy's expression as she sat gazing at him.

Maybe Trudy *had* approached him, and not the other way around.

Not that Harry hadn't been on the make. She'd seen him move in on way too many girls—including herself—to believe otherwise.

Harry said, "I hadn't gotten myself a drink yet, so I told her maybe we could head on over to the bar and I'd buy drinks for both of us. That sounded good to her, she said. So I bought a vodka Collins for her and a double bourbon for me."

Harry paused, then said, "Well, I wasn't sure where things were going just yet…"

Riley bristled. It was the first thing Harry had said so far that she was sure wasn't true. When it came to girls, Harry *always* knew where things were going—or at least where he wanted them to go.

Harry continued, "Then she kind of dragged me downstairs, and we found a booth and sat down and talked for a real long time, and I kept going to the bar to get us drinks now and then."

Riley wondered …

How much did Trudy drink? How clearly was she thinking?

Harry said, "After a while, she said maybe it was about time to leave, and I asked her if she wanted me to walk her back to the dorm."

Walton said, "With perfectly innocent intentions, I suppose."

Harry smirked and said, "Well, I'm not sure I'd put it that way. Let's just say I was keeping my possibilities open."

Walton tapped his pencil against the table and said, "Did she talk to anyone else while the two of you were at the Centaur's Den?"

Harry paused and thought for a moment.

"Now that you mention it—she *did* talk to somebody. Her

roommate came up to the table—Riley Somebody. Yeah, Riley Sweeney."

Riley glanced at Agent Crivaro, who glanced back at her.

Harry continued, "Riley was being really annoying, wanted Trudy to go home with her. Trudy told her to get lost."

Riley stifled a gasp as she remembered what Trudy had actually said …

"The night is young. Don't spoil the party."

She was sure Trudy had never told her to get lost.

Then Harry perked up. He said, "Hey, maybe that's important. That Riley Sweeney was around, I mean. You know, she was around after that other girl got killed. I saw her myself, standing right in the doorway to the girl's room. I thought at the time, 'What the hell is she doing there?' She's a weird girl. You should haul her in here and talk to her instead of wasting time here with me."

Walton just said, "Continue."

Harry thought for a moment and said, "We left the bar and started walking back to the dorm. By the time we got on campus, she was leaning into me, and I could tell she was really interested."

Riley wondered whether that was true. It didn't seem unlikely. But had Trudy started to feel uncomfortable along the way? Had she maybe tried to get away from Harry Rampling?

Harry hesitated.

Walton prompted him, "And then?"

Harry said, "Then I saw two of my pals farther on down the path—Eddie and Monty. They were watching us and they got really rude about seeing me with a good-looking chick. You know, whistling and gestures and stuff. They were as drunk as all get out, and it really pissed me off."

"So what did you do?" Walton asked.

"I told Trudy to stay put while I had a word with them. I went over and told them to knock it off. Then they started asking me all sorts of questions, like how I was getting along with her so far, and what did I think was going to happen."

Harry hunched forward, looking at his handcuffed hands.

He continued, "So I guess I must have talked to them for a couple of minutes, and then they started snickering again like a couple of idiots. I asked them what the hell they thought was so funny, and one of them—Eddie, I think—said, 'Looks like you've been dumped, dude.'"

Harry let out a grunt of annoyance and said, "So I turned

around, and sure enough, Trudy was gone."

"Where did she go?" Walton asked.

"Beats me," Harry said. "Maybe you should ask Eddie and Monty. They watched her go away without telling me. Just trying to make me look like an idiot, if you know what I mean."

Is he telling the truth? Riley wondered.

So far, she couldn't be sure either way.

"And then what happened?" Walton asked.

"Eddie and Monty wandered off again, and I was … well, I was kind of pissed off at everybody. I just wandered around campus for a while until I calmed down. Then I went back to my room and went to sleep."

Walton was staring at Harry with intense interest.

"And so you didn't see Trudy again?" he asked.

"No—the poor kid. I should have gone looking for her, made sure she was safe."

"Why didn't you?" Walton asked.

Harry shrugged and said, "Just because I was mad at her, I guess. Anyway, now you know the whole story—or *my* story, anyway. Can I go now?"

"I don't think so," Walton said, scribbling down notes.

Harry impatiently rapped the tabletop with his knuckles.

"When, then?" he said. "Because this is a real waste of time—both for you and for me. I mean, *please* tell me I get out of here sometime today. I've got a lot of studying to do. My grades aren't so hot, and if I start flunking they'll kick me off the football team."

Riley suddenly felt a powerful tingling all over.

She was sure of something, although she didn't yet know why.

She turned to Agent Crivaro and said …

"He's telling the truth. He didn't kill Trudy."

CHAPTER TWENTY SIX

Riley locked eyes with Agent Crivaro's for a long moment. She let the words she had just spoken sink in …

"He's telling the truth. He didn't kill Trudy."

It now seemed blazingly clear to her, and she felt so certain.

Crivaro didn't look at all surprised by what she'd just said.

"Why do you think that?" he asked.

Riley squinted with thought.

Why do *I think that?* she wondered.

It was just a gut feeling, of course. But where had it come from?

She turned to look again into the interview room, where Agent Walton was still questioning Harry Rampling. She stopped paying attention to what they were saying. That didn't interest her now.

Instead, she thought back to when she had found Trudy and Harry together in the booth at the Centaur's Den last night.

Harry had been regaling her with a story of his athletic prowess.

Trudy had been hanging raptly on his every word …

… or had she?

She really didn't care what he was saying, Riley realized.

Instead, Trudy had been ogling Harry's handsome face and his muscular physique—and she'd been fantasizing like crazy and wondering how the night was going to end. Trudy had been looking for something that might get her mind off her fears.

But what did that tell Riley?

She thought back to her experience back in the dorm, when Agent Crivaro had helped her get into the killer's mind. She remembered that moment when she'd imagined Trudy opening their dorm room door to let the killer inside.

But why had Trudy done that?

Riley had felt that Trudy and her killer weren't close friends.

But there had to be some reason.

Riley brought the imagined scene back as vividly as she could.

She closed her eyes and tried to push it a little farther.

The man had been talking to Trudy …

Now Riley realized that Trudy had been truly interested in what he was saying—so interested that she wanted him to come inside so they could sit down and talk.

So she'd opened the door and invited him in.

Riley felt her brain clicking away in strange new ways, and she remembered something that Harry had said just now …

"My grades aren't so hot, and if I start flunking they'll kick me off the football team."

Riley felt her pulse quicken as her gut feeling suddenly made complete sense.

She said to Agent Crivaro, "The man who killed Trudy was interesting, intelligent. She enjoyed listening to him talk, was fascinated by what he had to say."

"And?" Crivaro said.

Riley pointed to the young man in the interview room.

"Harry is *not* very intelligent, and he's anything but fascinating. In fact, he's kind of dumb, and he only talks about himself. I knew Trudy—and *if* Harry walked her all the way to the dorm, she'd most likely have gotten bored with him before they got there. He's not the one she let into her room."

Riley looked steadily at Jake, who kept staring into the interview room.

Does he believe me? she wondered.

She felt like she had to persuade him.

She said, "Agent Crivaro, I'm *sure* about this. I can't stand Harry Rampling. He's an egocentric asshole. But being an asshole doesn't make him a killer."

Crivaro turned to look at her with a chuckle.

He said, "Kid, you've got no idea how true that is."

"So you believe me?" Riley said.

Crivaro fell silent for a moment.

Then he said, "My own instincts are pretty damn good, if I do say so myself. And I don't think this obnoxious prick has the makings of a murderer."

Riley was feeling quite agitated now.

She said, "We've got to tell Chief Hintz that they've got the wrong guy."

Crivaro rubbed his chin and said, "Oh, I'll talk to him about it. But …"

"But what?" asked Riley.

Crivaro shook his head.

"Hintz isn't going to want to take my word for it—much less yours. And the truth is, there's no good reason why he should. Hunches and intuitions aren't evidence. You and I don't have a single shred of evidence to back ourselves up. Right now, there's a lot of evidence pointing to the guy in there. Sure, it's just circumstantial evidence, but it's pretty persuasive."

Riley could hardly believe her ears.

"But they can't just keep Harry here!" she objected. "He didn't do anything wrong!"

Crivaro patted Riley on the shoulder.

"Kid, there's something you should know," he said. "This talent you and I have both got—this ability to get into a killer's mind—it's not an exact science. I'm right most of the time, but I've also been wrong once in a long while. And at best, what we get is incomplete. If you keep on doing this kind of work, you'll be wrong sooner or later as well."

Riley just stared at him. She didn't know what to say.

Crivaro was now looking at her with deep concern.

"You look awfully tired, kid," he said. "You've been through a lot, and I'm afraid I've only made things worse for you. You've done more than enough for now, and there's no point in your hanging around. You really need to get out of here, try to get some rest. But where are you going to go?"

Riley realized it was a good question.

Her dorm room wasn't available—not that she'd want to go back there if it was. She wondered if she'd ever be able to go back inside the building, much less the room that she'd once shared with Trudy.

She remembered something Dr. Zimmerman had said to her a little while ago …

"I could put you up at my place, just for the night. I've got a guest room."

She wondered—should she take him up on that offer?

She didn't even know how to contact him right now. And even if she did, she somehow felt uncomfortable about imposing on him.

She said to Agent Crivaro, "Don't worry about me. I'll think of something."

She hesitated for a moment, then added, "Just … find whoever did this, OK?"

Crivaro nodded, then handed her a business card.

"This has got my pager number," he said. "Get in touch with

me if ... well, for any reason at all."

Riley thanked Agent Crivaro and walked away down the hall.

Just then she remembered the alarmed message Ryan had left on the answering machine ...

"Are you there? Are you all right? Are you safe?"

It was wrong to let him keep worrying.

I've got to call him, she thought.

She found the nearest payphone and punched in Ryan's number.

When Ryan answered, his voice was shaking.

"Riley? Oh my God! I'm so glad you called. I've been worried sick. How are you? Are you all right?"

Riley wondered how she could possibly answer that question.

Am I all right?

Hardly. She felt as though she'd never be all right again.

Even so ...

"I'm safe," she said.

"*Where* are you?"

"At the police station."

Ryan sounded confused as well as alarmed.

"The police station? Why?"

Riley hesitated. What could she tell him about what had been happening and what she had been doing? She barely understood any of it herself.

Then Ryan said, "Riley, please tell me they don't ..."

He didn't finish his thought, but Riley knew what he wanted to ask.

Do they suspect me?

"No, I'm not a suspect," she said.

Ryan asked, "Have they got anybody else in custody?"

"Yeah," Riley said.

What else was there to say about it? How could she begin to explain her own doubts about Harry Rampling, and Agent Crivaro's doubts as well?

Ryan asked, "Are they holding you for any reason? Because I know quite a bit about the law, you know. You've got your rights, no matter what."

"No, they're not holding me," Riley said. "I'm free to go. But ..."

Her voice trailed off as she thought ...

But I don't know where to go.

A short silence followed.

Then Ryan said, "I'm coming to pick you up. Wait for me outside the police station."

"Ryan, you don't have to—"

Ryan interrupted, "No arguments. I'll be there in a few minutes."

Ryan hung up. Riley stood there holding the phone, suddenly feeling alone, tired, scared, and sad. Then she hung up and walked the rest of the way to the front entrance and went outside.

The bright daylight came as a shock to her.

For some reason, she felt like it ought to be night outside—a deep, dark, starless night.

But today was a bright, cheerful spring day, with a gentle, fresh breeze and chirping birds.

Again she thought of that old cliché …

Life goes on.

Maybe it was true after all.

But right now, Riley couldn't help feel that it shouldn't be true.

Everything should just stop living, she thought. *At least for a little while.*

But that wasn't going to happen—and thousands of unaware and unwary people were going to enjoy this perfectly lovely day without sensing the evil that lurked behind it.

Riley sat down on the steps of the police station and waited.

Her thoughts were strangely suspended now. She wasn't thinking about anything at all. There didn't seem to be any point in it. Thinking wasn't going to change things. Thinking wasn't going to bring Trudy back to life.

But the absence of thought made the moments pass slowly.

It seemed like forever before Ryan pulled up to the curb in his Mustang. For some reason, Riley couldn't seem to get to her feet and simply walk toward the car. Instead, Ryan left the engine running and got out and walked over to her. He gently took her by the arm and helped her to her feet, then led her to the car and helped her into the car.

An uncomfortable silence fell as Ryan drove toward his apartment.

Finally Ryan said, "Riley, please talk to me. Just tell me …"

His voice trailed off and Riley wondered …

Tell him what?

Where could she even begin?

She opened her mouth to speak, but the only words that came out were, "Ryan … I can't tell you … everything … I just can't …"

"It's OK," Ryan said.

Soon they pulled up to the apartment building, and Ryan helped her up the stairs to his apartment. Ryan opened the door and led her inside. As soon as she saw the cozy, pleasant interior something seemed to break inside of her.

The anguish she'd been holding back for hours now erupted through her body.

Sobbing, Riley Sweeney collapsed into Ryan Paige's welcoming arms.

CHAPTER TWENTY SEVEN

Riley was sitting up in bed clutching a glass of bourbon in both hands when Ryan came into the apartment. For a moment she felt confused. Why was he back so soon?

Then she realized that it was later than she had thought. Ryan's morning class was long over.

She couldn't think of anything to say as he shut the door and stood looking at her.

Riley knew she looked terrible. She wasn't even dressed yet. She was wearing the pajamas that her RA had brought over from her dorm room along with a few essential supplies, clothes, and study materials.

She'd been staying in Ryan's apartment for four days and nights now, and she knew she hadn't been a joy to be around. She hadn't wanted to talk much about anything. She and Ryan had had sex a couple of times, and Ryan had been as sensitive and attentive as he'd been the first time, but Riley hadn't enjoyed it much.

She felt too numb to enjoy anything.

It certainly wasn't fair to Ryan. She liked him more and more every day but she was finding it hard to express any feelings at all.

Ryan looked especially concerned about the glass in her hand. She took another swallow of bourbon anyway.

"It's not even lunchtime," Ryan said.

Riley looked over at the wall clock.

"It's all right—it's one o'clock," she said.

"But have you eaten anything for lunch? You barely touched your breakfast this morning. You shouldn't be drinking, Riley."

Riley sighed. He was right, of course, and she had no right to argue. She set the glass down on the side table.

Ryan sat down next to her on the bed.

He asked, "How long has it been since you've been out of the apartment?"

"I don't know," she said.

The truth was, she was pretty sure she hadn't stepped out of the apartment since she'd gotten here on Friday. She knew for sure that she hadn't been out of the building.

Ryan said, "You didn't go to classes yesterday. Aren't you going to any today?"

"I don't know," Riley said. "No. I don't think so."

A silence fell between them.

Then Riley reached out and took hold of Ryan's hand. She added, "That's not a problem. Please don't worry. My grades are good. Missing a few classes isn't going to hurt."

Ryan squeezed her hand and said, "Yeah, Riley, but when …?"

He didn't finish his question.

Riley felt a small flash of resentment.

She said, "When am I going to snap out of it, you mean?"

"I wasn't going to ask you that," Ryan said.

"Well, why not?" Riley said. "It's a good question, isn't it? And I don't know the answer. How long is it supposed to take to get over finding my best friend's corpse in my dorm room?"

Right away, Riley could hardly believe what she'd just said.

"I'm sorry, Ryan. I shouldn't have said—"

Ryan interrupted, "It's OK, Riley. It's OK to vent. Actually, I wish you'd vent a whole lot more."

He paused for a moment, then added, "You can vent to me all you like, you know. I'm OK with it, really. I guess …"

He paused for a moment.

"I guess I've already come to care for you."

Riley was startled.

Do we feel the same way about each other? she wondered.

Then Ryan said, "But you've got to realize you can't get through this without professional help of some sort. If not the campus counselors … well, somebody. I just can't cut it."

He paused for a moment. When she said nothing, he added in a slightly bitter tone …

"Even if you wanted to talk to me, which I guess you don't."

Ryan got up off the bed and said, "I'm fixing you something to eat, and I'm not going to take my eyes off of you until you eat it."

He picked up the bourbon and said, "I'm pouring this out."

Riley almost protested, but quickly told herself …

Arguing will make me seem like a full-blown alcoholic.

She certainly hoped that wasn't what she was turning into. But the truth was, she'd gone through most of Ryan's bourbon since she'd gotten here.

Riley watched as he poured the bourbon down the sink. Then he set to work making grilled cheese sandwiches.

Riley didn't move from the bed. She was thinking about what he'd just said …

He thinks I need professional help.

Of course that must have seemed perfectly obvious—at least to him.

She understood why he felt like she was shutting him out. She hadn't told him about a lot of things. She'd told him a little about finding the bodies of both Rhea and Trudy. But nothing about the hours after she'd found Trudy. Nothing about what she'd been doing at the police station.

He knew that her mother had died, but not that she'd been murdered—much less that Riley had watched it happen when she was only a little girl. He certainly didn't know how images of her mother's bleeding body kept merging in her mind with Rhea's body—and now Trudy's.

Sometimes these days, it seemed as though her imagination was drowning in blood.

As for getting professional help, she couldn't begin to imagine confiding in just any old shrink. Maybe she could talk to Dr. Zimmerman about it. Or Agent Crivaro. Or even Professor Hayman, whom Riley admired a lot, and who had inspired her to major in psychology. They'd surely understand. And yet in order to talk to them …

She suppressed a sigh and thought …

I'd have to get out bed. Even out of this apartment.

And right now, that seemed like no easy feat.

She reminded herself that Agent Crivaro was actually just a pager call away. She had reached him that way a couple of times. The first time was to give him Ryan's phone number. The second time was yesterday, just to check in with him.

He'd told her that the local cops were letting Harry Rampling go. The two guys Harry had named for his alibi had given conflicting accounts of his actions that night, but Crivaro figured that was just because they'd been seriously drunk. In any case, the cops didn't have nearly enough evidence to keep Harry in custody.

Still, the local cops were still sure that Harry was the killer, and they were keeping an eye on him. Riley was worried about that. As far as she knew, she and Agent Crivaro were the only people who believed the real killer was still at large. The team from Quantico would have to leave if Chief Hintz decided he didn't need their help anymore.

What would happen if Crivaro and his team went away?

Would more people die?

Ryan came back over to the bed with two grilled cheese sandwiches and two cups of coffee. He sat down beside Riley again. Suddenly, she felt overwhelmed by the kindness and patience he'd been showing toward her.

And what was he getting in return? She was bringing nothing into his life except her own misery.

He deserves better, she thought.

She hesitated for a moment, then said, "Ryan, I need to talk to you about a few things. I mean ... there's some stuff you should know ... about me."

Ryan set his sandwich aside.

"You can tell me anything," he said.

Anything? Riley thought. *I guess we'll find out if that's true.*

She began at what seemed to her the beginning—her mother's brutal murder in the candy store all those many years ago. She was surprised at how calmly she was able to talk about the event that most haunted her in life.

Ryan listened with a dazed expression.

"I'm sorry," he said. "I had no idea."

Riley sighed deeply.

"There's more," she said.

She tried to describe that weird night soon after Rhea's murder—the night when she first slipped into the killer's brain and walked in his footsteps, feeling what it was like to stalk his prey across the campus. She told him about standing in Rhea's room later on, imagining how the killer had felt looking down at Rhea's dead and bleeding body.

Ryan said nothing as she explained how Agent Crivaro had guided her through her most alarming experience so far—her terrifyingly vivid peek into the killer's psyche as he charmed Trudy into letting him into her room.

But when she got to being at the police station, listening to the interview, and feeling sure that Harry Rampling wasn't the killer, he broke in.

"Riley, stop. This is crazy. Are you listening to yourself? You've really, really got to talk to somebody about all this."

His voice was shaking with alarm now.

"Are you telling me that FBI guy—Crivaro—played mind games with you? Why? Just for fun?"

Ryan sounded really angry now. Riley wished she could make him understand.

"No," she said. "He wanted my help. He thinks I've got a unique talent. So does Dr. Zimmerman."

"A talent for what?" Ryan said. "For empathizing with cold-blooded killers?"

Riley almost answered …

"Exactly."

… but thought better of it.

Ryan got up from the bed and started to pace.

"Riley, are you blind or something? What Crivaro did to you was wrong. He was exploiting you, preying on your vulnerabilities. I doubt that it was even legal. You've got to file a complaint."

Riley was truly shocked now.

Was I exploited? she wondered. The possibility hadn't occurred to her for a single second.

In fact, she'd do it again in a minute if Agent Crivaro wanted her to.

She felt like she'd do anything to catch the man who had killed Rhea and Trudy.

She was even willing to *become* the killer, at least for a little while.

What does that say about me? she thought.

Finally she asked, "Ryan, what are we doing here?"

She wasn't surprised when he didn't reply. It was a truly enormous question, one that they'd never discussed during the days they'd spent together.

Then she said, "Ryan, I really, really like you."

Ryan put his arm around her and held her close.

"I really, really like you too," he said.

Riley gently pulled herself out of his embrace.

"I don't know why you like me," she said. "I'm not at my best. Actually, I'm pretty much a basket case. And you're being so nice to me …"

Her words trailed off.

"What are you trying to say?" Ryan asked.

Riley wasn't sure. But she knew it was something important. And it needed to be said. She struggled to find the right words.

"You're a smart guy, Ryan, and you're really going to go

places in life. But tell me the truth. Right now you're worried, aren't you? You're wondering how you can keep up your grades with me around distracting you, with having to take care of me and all. You feel like you're stuck with me. You could … *I* could … ruin everything—your whole future."

Ryan shook his head.

"Riley, that's not—"

Riley interrupted, "It *is* true, and we both know it."

They were both silent for a moment. Riley could see by his expression that she'd touched on the truth.

Finally Ryan said haltingly, "Maybe … it would be best … if we kept this … kind of temporary."

Riley couldn't help feeling stung.

What did I expect him to say? she wondered.

Trying to keep bitterness out of her voice, Riley said, "I'm thinking … maybe I should get out of here now."

Another silence fell between them.

He doesn't disagree, Riley realized.

In fact, she could sense that he was deliberately detaching himself from her now.

It was an emotional ability she'd never noticed in him before. Oddly, she couldn't help admiring him for it. She figured it would help make him a really good lawyer someday.

Finally Ryan said, "Look, maybe we can try again someday later on, when you've got all this stuff straightened out …"

As Ryan's voice faded, Riley found herself remembering again what her father had told her over the phone …

"You're just not cut out for a normal life. It's not in your nature."

Now those words hit her like a thunderbolt.

He's so right.

Daddy's so right.

She said to Ryan, "Yeah, maybe someday later on."

Then she got up from the bed.

She said, "I've got to get dressed. I've got to go now."

Ryan's mouth dropped open.

"Where are you going to go?" he asked.

Riley didn't answer his question. The truth was, she was still struggling with that very question.

Instead, she said, "First I've got to use your phone."

She picked up the phone and called a cab company and ordered

162

a cab to come to Ryan's address in ten minutes.

When she hung up, Ryan was pacing.

"Riley, you don't need to catch a cab. I can drive you anywhere you want to go."

Riley ignored him and picked up some clothes and headed toward the bathroom. She was dressed and ready in just a few minutes. She gathered up her toiletries, then came out and picked up the rest of her things.

Ryan seemed to be really upset now.

"Riley, talk to me please. What the hell is this all about? Where are you going?"

Riley walked over to him and gave him a truly affectionate, caring kiss.

"Don't worry about me," she said. "Let's stay in touch."

Without another word, she walked out of the apartment and left the building. The cab was already waiting for her.

When she got in, the driver asked, "Where to?"

Riley hesitated for a moment. She felt strangely dizzy and frightened, as if she were about to step off a cliff.

She said, "I need to go to the nearest car rental place."

"Got it," the driver said.

He started the meter and began to drive.

Riley wondered whether she'd lost her mind.

Maybe I have, she thought.

Or maybe it's something a whole lot worse than that.

The truth was, she really didn't know, and she felt like she didn't understand anything at all—least of all herself.

And as much as the thought horrified her, she could think of just one person in the world she actually wanted to see.

She had to go visit her father—right now.

CHAPTER TWENTY EIGHT

After the cab dropped her off, Riley quickly settled on one of the cheapest cars in rental lot. It was a beat-up little hatchback, a no-fringe vehicle even its better days, and those days were in the past. But at least Riley could afford the one-day rent on this one.

After just a few minutes on the road, the engine grumbled a little. It seemed almost as if the car was reluctant and apprehensive—just like Riley herself felt.

Riley's visits to her father's cabin had seldom ended well. Her father was anything but a kindly, nurturing presence in her life—or in anyone else's life, for that matter.

So why am I going up there to see him? she asked herself. Then she laughed lightly, realizing that she asked herself that every time she drove up this mountain.

Maybe because he was the only living relative she had nearby. She didn't even know where her older sister was at this point, and there was no one else.

She wasn't yet sure that was reason enough. But she felt strongly that this visit was important.

At least it wasn't a long drive. After a short while going westward, Riley left the main highway and followed country roads where the Appalachian Mountains sloped closely all around her. The day was pleasant and warm, so she rolled down the window and breathed in the clean, refreshing spring air. She always enjoyed the sights of family farms, rocky passes, and flowing streams.

She passed through just a tiny town called Milladore before her final steep ascent toward her father's cabin.

Then the car coughed a few times. Riley patted the dashboard and said aloud, "Hang on, little buddy. We can both get through this. The hard part is getting there. It'll be downhill all the way back. That will be easy."

Or will it? she wondered. *For the car, maybe.*

But maybe not for her. She hoped she wouldn't leave the cabin feeling bitter, angry, and lost, as she often had in the past.

The final turn was onto a winding dirt road that ended at her father's property. His small cabin came into view, standing in a small clearing that had been cut out of the dense surrounding forest.

Riley had no idea how long the cabin had been there. Her father had bought it when he retired from the Marines. He'd made repairs on it himself. He had cleaned up the old spring and repaired its covering. There was no electricity up here, but she knew that he liked it that way. He could have arranged for electrical and telephone lines to brought near enough for him to connect to, but hadn't bothered.

As she approached, she saw her father standing beside a large tree stump. He had a pile of short logs that he was splitting into smaller pieces on the stump. He barely paused from his work while Riley parked the car—barely even looked in her direction.

You'd think I came here every day, Riley thought.

He didn't stop his work as she got out of the car and walked toward him.

He was powerfully built man in his late fifties who had kept both his military haircut and his military bearing. Riley always sensed a lot of anger and fierce independence in his physical deportment.

"Hi, Daddy," she said.

He glanced at her, nodded, and split another log.

Riley stifled a sigh. It was a familiar task, trying to draw her father out, to get his attention, even to get him to acknowledge her presence.

Riley noticed that a new utility vehicle was parked to one side of the cabin.

"I see you got some new wheels," she said.

"Yeah, hated to spend the money," he said, finally stopping for a moment and wiping his brow. "But the other one gave out on me."

Then he let out a tough, raspy laugh.

"Don't know why," he said. "I never drove it anywhere except to church."

Riley was surprised to feel herself smile at the joke. Daddy was anything but a churchgoing man. But he needed a tough vehicle to navigate these mountains, especially in difficult weather.

He went back to his work. Riley crossed her arms and watched him for a moment.

She said, "Do you really need to cut firewood this time of year?"

"Yeah, if I want to survive the winter. I need a lot of wood for that. Can't get started chopping too soon. And the wood needs time

165

to season."

Riley walked toward him and held out her hand.

"Why don't you let me give you a break for a minute?" she suggested.

Daddy willingly handed her the axe. Riley set a log upright on the stump, raised the axe high, and split the wood cleanly. She was startled at how good the burst of exertion felt. Her father had taught her to split logs from the time she was big enough to wield an axe. Now she realized that she'd missed this kind of mindless physical effort.

Daddy put his hands on his hips and watched her work. He actually smiled a little.

He said, "Isn't this a school day? Or did you drop out of school?"

"Nah, I'm still at that damn college, getting that useless degree you don't think I should get. I just felt some kind of urge to come up here and see you."

"That's downright kind of you," he said.

Riley was startled by a hint of softness in his voice.

He sounds almost like he means it, she thought.

Riley split a couple more logs, and then her father said, "I hear there's been another murder."

Riley planted the axe in the stump and turned toward him.

"How did you find out?" she said. "I thought you stayed off the grid."

He shrugged as if trying to look unconcerned.

"I do pretty much. But I go down to Milladore now and again, pick up a newspaper, catch a little TV news at the VFW bar. Just happened to catch word of it."

Those words really caught Riley's attention ...

"Just happened to catch word of it."

She sensed that he hadn't "just happened" to do anything.

Since she'd last talked to him and told him about Rhea's murder, he must have been spending more time in Milladore keeping track of the news from Lanton.

He's been worried about me, she realized.

They stood looking at each other for a moment.

He asked, "Another friend of yours?"

Riley nodded, determined not to show any emotion.

"My roommate, Trudy."

"Damn," her father said.

"I found her body. And I was the second person to find the other girl's body. Both of their throats were slashed."

"Damn," he repeated.

Then Daddy turned his head toward the woods and said nothing.

Well, I guess that's all we're going to say about it, she thought with a flash of disappointment.

She felt like she ought to know better than to expect Daddy to express concern about her safety for more than a minute or two.

She reached for the axe to start chopping again. Suddenly, she felt her father's arm snap tightly around her throat. Before she knew it, she lay flat on her back on the ground. Her father planted his knee on her chest and held a hunting knife to her throat. The tip of the blade felt sharp against her skin.

Riley gasped with horror.

She wondered …

Has he lost his mind?

Is he going to kill me?

CHAPTER TWENTY NINE

Pinned down by her father, Riley felt like a small trapped animal staring into the eyes of its overpowering prey. For a moment neither of them moved. He held the knifepoint perfectly steady against her throat.

Riley's thoughts raced.

Where had the knife come from?

Then she remembered—her father always carried a hunting knife strapped to his ankle. He'd grabbed it so quickly she hadn't even noticed.

But why did he attack?

She had no idea. But if he intended to kill her, she had no way to stop him now.

Their gazes stayed locked. She saw no bloodlust in his eyes. His expression was grim, but hardly murderous—canny, not crazed.

As suddenly as he had struck her down, he pulled the knife away, took his knee off his chest, and rose to his feet.

He said, "You're dead, girl. Or at least you should be. I'd say you deserve to be."

Shakily, Riley got up off the ground.

"What the hell was that all about?" she demanded.

"You tell me," her father said. "First a good friend of yours got killed. Then it was your roommate. What's the matter with you? Hasn't it occurred to you that you're as likely as anybody to be next?"

Riley squinted with surprise.

No, it really hadn't occurred to me, she realized.

She'd been so devastated by both deaths—especially Trudy's—and so obsessed with what she could learn about the killer's mind that she hadn't even thought about her own safety.

Her father shook his head with a growl of disapproval.

"If that's the best you can do, you're a goner for sure," he said.

Now he stood facing her arm with his legs slightly apart. He tossed the knife to her. Riley was a little surprised—and relieved—that she caught it neatly by the handle. Then her father waved his arms.

"Come on," he said. "Attack me."

Fueled by the recent adrenaline rush and by rising anger, Riley raised the knife and charged toward him. She didn't care if she did wound him.

In a flash, she was buffeted by a blinding tangle of blows, and she found herself on the ground again.

"What the hell kind of fighting is that?" she asked, gasping as he helped her back to her feet.

"It's called Krav Maga," her father said. "It's an Israeli fighting system."

He cut the air with wild and aggressive movements as he explained, "It originated in the years just before World War Two. Jews in Eastern Europe used it to defend themselves against fascist attackers. It combines elements of several disciplines, including Aikido, judo, and karate. But mostly, it's just plain down-and-dirty street fighting. Anything goes—anything that works. That's why I like it."

Riley stood watching his gestures with her mouth hanging open.

It dawned on her that she'd had good reason to make this visit after all.

She remembered again what her father had said to her over the phone ...

"You're just not cut out for a normal life. It's not in your nature."

Despite her earlier doubts about even coming up here, this trip was beginning to make sense. There were things her father could teach her—and maybe not just about fighting.

Maybe he could help her understand herself.

Right now, he was obviously waiting to see how she would respond.

Riley said, "Show me what I should have done when you attacked me."

Her father guided her through a series of violent motions—all carried out slowly and carefully so as not to cause injury. Bit by bit, she started to get the hang of certain maneuvers.

Following his instructions, she went into slow-motion action as he locked one arm around her neck and wielded the knife with the other. She brought one arm down as if to strike his groin, and almost simultaneously grabbed him by the hair with her other hand and yanked him back, then finally switched hands again to smash him in the face, breaking his grip and forcing him backward as the knife flew from his hand.

"Not bad," he snapped. "Now speed it up."

They carried out the same sequence several times, each time a little faster than before. Riley was almost alarmed at how quickly it began to seem natural to her.

Then her father showed her how to deal with a series of possible attacks—pushing, lunging, and grabbing from behind and in front. As they worked through each situation, he explained the core ideas of Krav Maga.

"Sheer aggression is the key thing," he said. "In most kinds of fighting, you defend and attack separately. With Krav Maga, you do both simultaneously, and you move fast. You don't give your opponent time to breathe. And you don't stop until he's debilitated—or dead. If someone really wants to kill you, you'd better kill him first and get it done with. It's not a game."

Riley was both fascinated and frightened by the fierceness of Krav Maga. It was based on street fighting, after all. She learned that the idea was to attack the most sensitive parts of an opponent's body—eyes, throat, groin, solar plexus, and so forth, causing a lot of physical harm as quickly as possible. One also grabbed whatever objects one could use in combat—rocks, bottles, sticks, or anything else that happened to be within reach.

After teaching Riley one especially ruthless maneuver, her father suddenly turned and walked away.

"I guess it's time for you to get back to school," he said. "And it's time for me to get back to work."

He turned away and walked back to the stump where he'd been splitting logs.

Riley felt baffled.

"That's it?" she said. "That's all you're going to teach me?"

Daddy picked up his axe, glanced back at her, and shrugged.

"What do you think I'm here for?" he said.

That's a good question, Riley thought.

As Daddy set up a log to split, he said, "If you want to learn how to fight, take some lessons. You can't get it all in one afternoon."

As he swung the axe, he added, "As you can see, I'm busy getting ready to survive the winter."

Riley was about to protest, but quickly realized it was pointless.

Her father was chopping wood with a relentless rhythm.

It's like I'm not even here anymore, she thought.

She said, "Well, goodbye, Daddy."

Then she added with some bitter sarcasm, "It's been great seeing you."

He didn't reply, just kept splitting logs.

As Riley got back into her car and drove away, she felt her eyes stinging a little.

Don't cry, damn it, she told herself.

After all, what did she expect to have happen? Did she think a little hand-to-hand combat training was going to magically change their relationship for the better?

At least the car seemed to be doing better as she drove it along the winding road down the mountain. As she took in the beautiful scenery again, she asked herself …

Was it worth it?

Should I have bothered coming here at all?

As she thought it over, she began to realize that the answer was yes.

She'd learned some useful self-defense tactics, but she'd learned something else as well—something that was harder for her to put her finger on.

Then she remembered something her father had said a little while ago …

"If someone really wants to kill you, you'd better kill him first and get it done with."

The sheer aggressiveness of Krav Maga had already worked its way into her system.

"It's not a game."

And understanding that grim fact made her feel somehow closer than ever to the killer himself.

*

Riley's spirits began to sink during the short drive home.

Now she had real, mundane, everyday problems to deal with.

She'd been in a hurry to leave Ryan's apartment, to get out before things got any worse between them. Then she'd been focused on going to see her dad and on everything that had happened there. During all that, she hadn't given any serious thought to where she was going to live now.

She only knew one thing for certain. She'd never be able to

sleep in the dorm room she'd shared with Trudy again. Perhaps, if she called her floor's RA, she could get assigned another room with another roommate. But the idea of even setting foot inside the dorm building made her stomach feel queasy.

Sooner or later, of course, she'd have no choice. Most of her clothes and belongings were still in that room, and she'd have to get them somehow. Meanwhile, the few necessities she'd had brought over to Ryan's apartment—toiletries, books, and changes of clothes—were right here in the car with her.

I'm like some kind of nomad, she thought as she drove into Lanton.

But where was she going to stay next? She couldn't even sleep in the car, which she'd rented just for today.

When she pulled into the rental car lot, she remembered something. A couple of days ago she'd called Gina from Ryan's house. Gina had said that she and her roommate, Cassie, couldn't deal with the dorm anymore either, and they'd found somewhere else to stay. She'd given Riley their new phone number.

Wherever they were living right now, could they make room for Riley?

She turned in the car keys at the rental office and got her deposit back. Then she lugged her bags of belongs outside the building, where she'd seen a payphone. She dialed the number Gina had given her.

An unfamiliar female voice answered the phone.

"Hello?"

Riley stammered awkwardly, "Um—could I speak to Gina Formaro?"

"May I ask who's calling?"

The voice sounded none too friendly.

"Riley Sweeney," she said.

"I'll go check."

Riley heard the rattle of the receiver being set down. Then she heard voices and knocking. Finally came the welcome sound of Gina's voice.

"Hey, Riley! What's up? How are things going with that guy of yours?"

Riley gulped a little.

"Um, things didn't work out so good with Ryan, and I ..."

She hesitated, feeling more embarrassed by the moment.

Then she said, "Gina, I can't go back to the dorm."

Gina let out a sympathetic-sounding sigh.

"I hear you," she said. "Cassie and I feel the same way."

Riley said, "I was wondering … what are *your* living arrangements these days?"

Gina said, "Remember Stephanie White and Aurora Young? They lived on our floor in the dorm until last year."

Riley remembered Stephanie and Aurora. They'd hated dorm life and had decided to find a cheap place off campus.

Gina continued, "Well, Cassie and I moved in with them. It gets a little crowded and nerves get frayed once in a while. Still, it looks like maybe it's going to work out OK, with four of us to pay the rent and all."

Riley stifled a discouraged sigh.

Four girls are living there already, she thought.

There didn't seem to be any point in even asking if she could join them.

But then Gina said, "Hang on just a minute, I'll go talk to Steph. She's kind of the mother hen around here." She added in a whisper, "She's kind of a tyrant, if you want to know the truth."

Again Riley heard the phone receiver rattling, then Gina talking with someone who sounded like the girl who had answered the phone in the first place.

Finally Gina got back on the phone.

"Steph says you can move in. We've got a little room in the attic that nobody's using. We can work out your share of the rent when you get here."

Riley suddenly breathed more easily.

"Oh, thank you," she said. "That would be great."

"Where are you? I'll come and pick you up."

Riley had almost forgotten that Gina had a car. Maybe her luck was starting to take a turn for the better. She told Gina that she was at the rental car place, and they ended the call.

Flanked by her bags of belongings, Riley slouched against the wall of the car rental building. She was suddenly seized by a wave of helplessness and futility as she thought …

I must look like some kind of bag lady.

And in a way, she couldn't help thinking that that was pretty much what she was …

Just some homeless bum hoping people will be kind to me.

She choked down a sob and blinked back her tears.

It wouldn't be good to be crying when Gina pulled up.

It just seemed hard to remember how she'd felt a little while ago, sparring so aggressively with her father, feeling truly powerful.

She certainly didn't feel powerful now. She felt like a breath of wind would carry her away like a speck of dust.

She reminded herself …

He's still out there.

And she felt in her gut that she was somehow fated to confront him someday.

And whenever that day came …

I've got to be strong, she thought.

CHAPTER THIRTY

Although Riley knew that the physical attack was coming, she felt eerily calm.

Even her breathing was perfectly under control.

As her larger assailant lunged and grabbed her by the left wrist, Riley's own movements became eerily dancelike. Time seemed to slow down.

Is this really fighting? she thought.

It seemed more like dreaming.

She turned her own left hand in a small, graceful semicircle, twisting his hand loose from her wrist. Then she took hold of his hand with her right hand and subtly moved her hips, hands, and feet simultaneously. She raised her right hand up to his elbow and lifted it up over his head.

His whole body turned forward as if he were hinged at the waist. He fell to his knees and she held his arm up behind his now helpless body.

Both Riley and her attacker froze in that position for a moment.

Then she let him go, and he stood up and smiled at her—a bit flirtatiously, she thought.

Not that she minded.

She found him charming, good-looking, and likeable.

This was Riley's first time attending the Aikido class in the campus gymnasium. When she'd gotten here, she'd been surprised to find out that the certified instructor was her psychology professor, Brant Hayman.

Professor Hayman called out to the class, "All right, everybody—switch *ukes* and *toris.*"

Riley had learned enough Aikido terminology to know that he was telling all the partners in the room to switch roles. The *uke* was the designated attacker, and the *tori* was the designated defender.

Now it was Riley's turn to be the *uke.*

She and her partner had spent just as much time learning to attack and fall as they had learning the defensive maneuver.

At Professor Hayman's command, she reached out and grabbed her partner's wrist, and he turned his own hand exactly as she had a moment before. She felt her grip loosen, and then felt his right hand come up to her elbow. Her whole body cooperated with his as he lifted her elbow over her head and she slipped down to her knees.

They froze again. This time her partner was holding her arm up behind her.

"Very good," Professor Hayman called out to the class. "Now let's do some more breathing."

Riley and her partner and the other ten people in the class moved into rows. Professor Hayman began to lead them in an exercise of gentle arm movements accompanied by deep breathing. Hayman had explained earlier that this exercise was all about increasing one's *ch'i*—an Asian concept having to do with energy and flow.

As Riley breathed and moved, she found herself wondering ...

Do I really believe all this stuff?

All during the class, Hayman had been using words that seemed to her to have nothing to do with fighting—harmony, creativity, spirit, and even peace.

She found it all strange and unfamiliar.

The brief Krav Maga lesson her father had given her several days ago had been all about sheer aggression—attacking fast and brutally. There was nothing brutal about what she was doing now.

Still, she had to admit, everything she was doing felt very good. It made her feel both relaxed and energized.

As the class continued, Professor Hayman led them through several more maneuvers interspersed with breathing exercises. Finally the class ended just as it had begun—with formal group bows.

As the other students left the gym, Riley walked over to talk with Professor Hayman.

He smiled and said, "Hello, Riley. What do you think of Aikido?"

"I'm not sure," she admitted.

Hayman's brow knitted inquisitively.

"What's troubling you about it?" he asked.

Riley thought for a moment, then said, "Well, not to sound uncouth about it, but ... will this stuff actually do me any good if I'm physically attacked?"

Hayman smiled again.

"That's a good question," he said.

"Well?"

Hayman looked away rather dreamily.

"Tell me, Riley," he said. "*If* you were attacked—in a dark alley, say—wouldn't it be good to be able to turn your attacker's own aggression against him? To end the confrontation without having to fight at all?"

Riley couldn't help but smirk a little.

She said, "I think I'd just as soon beat him to a bloody pulp."

She was relieved when Hayman let out a hearty laugh.

"Well, that would work too, I guess," he said.

His laughter died down and he added, "What path you choose to take is up to you. The thing is, Aikido is as much a *philosophy* as a self-defense system. You could even call it a way of life—a life in which violence and aggression evaporate in your very hands, with your every breath."

Riley didn't know how to reply to that.

Finally Professor Hayman added, "Give it a try for a couple of lessons. See if it grows on you. Whether it does or not, I'm pleased to have you in my class. You're always a pleasure to teach, Riley."

Riley felt herself blush a little. She remembered something Trudy had once said about her …

"Riley likes to impress Professor Hayman. She's got a thing for him."

As she stood looking at her handsome teacher, Riley wondered …

Do I have a "thing" for him?

If so, she figured she'd better keep it to herself. Professor Hayman didn't seem like the kind of professor who'd get romantically involved with a female student. And if he *were* that kind of professor, Riley knew she ought to steer clear of him.

She said goodbye and headed out of the gym.

She found someone waiting for her in the hallway—the guy who had been her sparring partner during the class.

He grinned at her shyly and said, "I don't think we've really been introduced. I'm Leon Heffernan."

"I'm Riley Sweeney," she said, offering him her hand to shake. "Are you a student here at Lanton?"

"Yeah, I'm a philosophy major. And you?"

"Psychology."

Leon shuffled his feet nervously, then said, "Listen, I hope you don't mind my asking … but would you like to go somewhere for coffee or something?"

Riley realized she would very much like to do that, but unfortunately, Gina had agreed to pick her up in her car right now. They had errands to run for their housemates.

"Sorry, I'm afraid I can't," she said.

But then something occurred to her.

She said, "My housemates and I are planning a big party for tonight. Pretty much anybody and everybody is invited. Would you like to come? If you're not too busy, I mean?"

Leon's eyes twinkled.

"Thanks, that sounds great," he said.

Riley wrote down the address on a slip of paper and handed it to him. Then she heard a car horn honk outside the building.

"That's my ride, so I've got to go," she said. "I'll see you tonight."

She hurried out the door and got into Gina's car.

Gina grumbled, "I thought you weren't ever coming out."

"Sorry, I got kind of detained," Riley said.

She added to herself …

By two handsome men, one of whom I have a date with.

It was almost enough to make her forget how badly things had ended with Ryan.

"We'd better get a move on," Gina said. "We've got a lot of stuff to buy for the party, and not a lot of time."

As Gina started driving, Riley suddenly felt a weird chill.

It was a palpable feeling of the killer's presence, as if he were watching her right now.

She was startled. She hadn't felt anything like this lately. She'd been doing whatever she could to put the murders out of her mind. She hadn't even talked to Agent Crivaro for the last couple of days. The last time they'd spoken, he'd assured her that he and his team were staying in Lanton for a while longer.

Riley was glad of that.

She was also glad she was learning something about self-defense.

Deep down in her gut, she felt sure she was going to need it—perhaps sometime very soon.

CHAPTER THIRTY ONE

Riley felt trapped and isolated.

The house that she shared with four other girls always felt pretty crowded ...

But not like tonight, Riley thought.

She looked around at the partiers jam-packed into the downstairs living-dining area and wondered ...

Am I having fun yet?

She really didn't think so.

A big blowout before finals week had certainly seemed like a good idea when she and her housemates planned it. Riley herself was plenty ready for exams. Last-minute studying was never her style. And a party should be a good way for Lanton students to let off some of the anxiety still hanging over the campus after two murders.

It seemed to be working for just about everybody except Riley.

The music was deafening.

Beer was flowing freely from the two kegs she and Gina had brought home with the other party supplies, and there was a strong scent of pot in the air. A lot of dancing and chattering and making out was going on, and Riley's four housemates were mingling among the guests.

By contrast, Riley stood alone in a corner drinking beer from a plastic cup. She wasn't feeling any kind of a buzz in spite of consuming quite a lot of beer. Pot normally wasn't her thing, but she thought maybe she'd give it a try soon if she didn't feel herself loosening up a little.

Meanwhile, she really wasn't crazy about this party—and after several days in this house, she wasn't all that happy about her new living arrangement.

She and Gina and Cassie got along just fine, just like they had back at the dorm. But as far as Riley was concerned, Aurora was a shallow twit who talked endlessly about things that bored her to death, and Stephanie certainly lived up to what Gina had said about her over the phone ...

"She's kind of a tyrant, if you want to know the truth."

Stephanie was a stickler for rules and organization, and she'd posted lists of chores and obligations all over the place. And right now, she was even going around telling guests what to do ...

Like she's directing a movie or something.

Riley reminded herself that this was temporary. Exams began next week and graduation would come soon after that.

At the moment, she couldn't help wondering—would everything seem better if Ryan Paige walked through the door? She hadn't been in touch with him since she left his apartment, and she felt the loss more than she'd expected.

She knew that law school graduation was earlier than it was for undergraduates. So maybe he wasn't even in school anymore. Maybe he'd already finished up and left.

Would she ever see him again?

The idea really saddened her.

Then all of a sudden, a familiar song blared over the stereo.

It was "Whiskey in the Jar" by Metallica—the same song she'd heard at the Centaur's Den the night of Rhea's murder.

Riley shuddered deep inside, trying to fight down a flood of horrifying memories.

Should she go over to the stereo and change songs?

No, everyone else seemed to be enjoying the music, so it would be a rude thing to do.

Maybe I should just get out of here, Riley thought with a sigh.

She was trying to decide where else she might go when the front door opened and someone she recognized came in.

She smiled. It was Leon Heffernan, the guy who had been her sparring partner in the Aikido class.

Riley had almost forgotten that she'd invited him, but here he was—and at the moment, he was looking as out of place as Riley felt.

Riley pushed her way among the partiers toward him.

When she got within earshot, she spoke loudly over the music, "Hey, Leon! Glad you could make it!"

He smiled, looking relieved to see a familiar face.

"I'm glad too," he said loudly back.

"Come on, let's get you some beer," Riley said.

She tugged him by the hand toward the kegs, where he poured himself a plastic cup of beer and Riley refilled her own. Then they retreated to the corner where Riley had been standing before.

Riley held up her cup and said, "Here's to finals."

He tapped his cup against hers and said, "Yeah, to finals."

They both sipped their beers.

Then Leon looked around and said, "Some party, huh?"

Riley smiled at the clumsy remark.

"You could say that," she replied unenthusiastically.

Then they were both silent for a few moments. The awkwardness between them didn't surprise Riley—she and Leon barely knew each other, after all. Still, one of them needed to say something instead of just standing there.

What did he say his major was?

Then she remembered.

She said, "So. Philosophy."

Leon nodded and said, "Yeah."

"Sounds like pretty deep stuff," Riley said.

Leon's eyes seemed to light up a little.

"Not so deep," he said. "And actually, there's a lot of overlap between philosophy and your major—psychology, right?"

"Right."

Leon said, "I mean, think about colors. What are they, really?"

Riley felt an odd flash of *déjà vu.*

Have I had this conversation before? she wondered.

"I give up," she said. "What *are* colors?"

Leon shrugged and said, "Well, scientifically, there's no such thing as color. There are only varying wavelengths of light. And yet … we *experience* color all the time. Red, green, blue—all the colors of the rainbow seem plenty real to us. But how do we experience something that doesn't exist in the real world? And what are colors, really?"

Riley throat caught a little as she remembered …

Trudy used to talk about this same topic sometimes when she'd had a few too many drinks. She'd been fascinated by the nature of color and how people experienced it.

Leon took another sip of his beer and added, "So it sure seems to me that whole question of color has to do with both psychology and philosophy."

Riley thought back to how she and her friends used to tease Trudy whenever she started talking like that.

Now she really wished they hadn't.

In fact, it suddenly seemed like a really interesting topic, and she wished Trudy were here to join in the conversation.

The thought of Trudy made her sad.

Leon said loudly, "Don't you think it's kind of hard having a conversation with so much noise?"

Riley nodded in agreement.

Leon added, "Why don't we go somewhere more quiet?"

Riley studied his face for a moment.

Is that a pickup line? she wondered.

If so, was that a good thing or a bad thing?

She looked Leon over and observed again how good-looking he was—tall and muscular with a handsome face. But he didn't seem the least bit vain.

And smart too, she thought.

Maybe what she needed tonight was a little excitement.

She smiled at him and said, "Come on, let's go to my room. It'll be quieter there."

She led Leon by the hand up the stairs to the second floor, then up the narrower flight of stairs into her attic room. She suddenly felt a little embarrassed by how modest her room was. The ceiling was slanted on either side, so there wasn't much space for a tall guy like Leon to even walk around. Even with the window open, it was also stuffy.

There was also hardly any furniture—just a couple of chairs and a table and a fold-out futon.

At least the noise from downstairs was more muffled here.

Riley said, "I'm sorry this place is so …"

Before she could get out an apology, Leon grabbed her and pulled her against him and kissed her.

Riley was startled—but not displeased.

She felt a raw heat rising up inside her—feelings that she'd been repressing lately out of anxiety and fear.

She reminded herself …

You don't really know him.

But somehow, she couldn't make herself care. It was almost like being a reckless teenager again.

And she liked that feeling.

As the kiss continued, Leon started to maneuver Riley over to the futon.

She started to get uneasy.

Things are moving awfully fast, she thought.

Vague, wordless worries started to crowd into her mind.

Riley struggled to put her thoughts together …

A good-looking guy …

... interesting conversation ...

So good-looking and interesting, in fact, that she'd felt OK inviting him into her room.

Then with a shock she remembered imagining how the killer had made his way into the dorm room with Trudy—all charm and fascinating talk.

It's him! she thought with horror.

She tried to pull herself away from him, but he held her fast.

And he was a lot stronger than she was.

CHAPTER THIRTY TWO

Riley struggled to pull free, but Leon was much bigger and stronger than she was. She could feel buttons tearing loose as he yanked at her blouse. Then he was clawing at her bra.

"Stop it!" she yelled breathlessly. "Stop!"

But instead of stopping, he wrapped Riley in a bear hug that pinned her arms at her sides. The harder she struggled, the tighter he held her. It was almost like one of those Chinese finger traps that tightened the harder one tried to pull one's fingers apart.

He tried to kiss her again, but she twisted her head away.

Gasping for air now, she yelled as loudly as she could …

"Somebody help!"

But the music from the party below vibrated through the whole house. She knew that nobody down there could hear her voice.

Maneuvers she'd learned in the class today flashed through her mind. But they had been dancelike, graceful on the part of the defender and even of the attacker. She hadn't yet learned how those smooth actions could help her now.

There was nothing graceful about what was going on. It was clumsy, ugly, and dangerous.

And it was about to get worse.

She could feel Leon trying to lift her off her feet. If he threw her onto the futon, she would be truly helpless.

A harsh voice seemed to ring in her head …

"Sheer aggression is the key thing."

Her father had told her to fight aggression with aggression—with Krav Maga. She had to be more aggressive than her attacker.

Now she clearly remembered what he had taught her about fighting off a hold from the front.

First, make myself heavier …

She let herself go limp at the knees, using her weight to pull both of them downward a little. That made a slight separation between their two bodies, but her upper arms were still held tight.

She turned both hands into fists and slammed them together into his groin.

Leon let out a loud gasp of pain.

But Riley knew she wasn't through yet. He was still holding her, still determined to take her down. And she knew that hurting him could make him more dangerous.

She brought her right knee up to his groin twice, producing a sharp groan each time, then slammed the side of her foot into his instep.

This made him stagger and almost fall, but not quite.

She heard her dad's voice again …

"It's just plain down-and-dirty street fighting."

Go dirty, she told herself.

She bit violently into the side of her attacker's neck.

Leon let out a yelp of shock and pain and backed away from her.

He touched his neck and realized she'd drawn blood.

"You fucking bit me, bitch!" he growled.

As he reared up to lunge at her again, Riley was feeling around for the nearest physical object—a lamp on the top of a dresser. As Leon charged, she swung the lamp in his face. The cheap plastic shade crumpled and fell off, and the light bulb shattered against his face.

He was gripping his bleeding face now, staggering.

With a yell of rage, Riley rushed at him and kicked his shin as hard as she could. He collapsed to his knees, and she kicked him again in the chest. He fell backward, flat on his back.

Now Riley *literally* could taste Leon's blood on her tongue from when she bit him.

It tasted good.

She remembered something else her father had said …

"If someone really wants to kill you, you'd better kill him first and get it done with.

"It's not a game."

She felt a cruel grin form on her face.

Killing him seemed like a fine idea.

She crouched over him and planted her knee on his chest. Then she raised her fist, planning to use it to crush his windpipe. He would suffocate to death in terrible agony.

But a familiar voice stopped her.

Riley looked up and saw that Gina was standing at the top of the attic stairs, with several partiers crowded behind her.

Riley reluctantly removed her knee from Leon's chest and stood up. He stayed on the ground.

Gina and the others were staring at her, and at her torn blouse.

"He attacked me," she gasped. "Call the police."

Gina headed back down the stairs. Three guys rushed to grab Leon and hold him down on the floor.

Leon looked at the guys as if appealing for sympathy.

"This crazy chick just tried to kill me!" he said.

The guys only laughed.

"I guess you got off lucky," one said.

Leon's bleeding face flashed with anger, and for a moment he looked like he might try to jump up and start the fight again. But then his face softened as he seemed to think better of it. There was no way he could successfully take on all of the three big guys holding him.

Riley stood with her arms crossed, not trying to hide a smile of deep satisfaction.

But then she noticed a glimpse of something shiny poking out of his pants pocket. She stepped toward him and reached for it.

Leon yelled in a shrill voice, "Don't touch me, bitch!"

"Relax," Riley said in a mock-kindly voice. "This won't hurt a bit."

She pulled the shiny thing out of his pocket.

She gasped when she saw what it was.

A large, folded pocketknife.

Her hands started shaking so much that she almost dropped it.

This is it, she thought.

This is the knife he used to kill Rhea and Trudy.

And if I hadn't stopped him …

She put the knife in her own pocket, shuddering at the thought that she'd surely have been his next victim. The guys were still holding Leon on the floor, so she stepped back and sat down on her futon. She could hear the other students muttering to each other, but didn't even try to understand what they were saying.

Riley was grateful when she heard the sound of approaching sirens. Everybody in the room was quiet now, waiting for the police to take over.

Soon there came the loud stomping of feet coming up the stairs and then several cops pushed their way past everybody. Riley wasn't happy to see Officer Steele, who charged into the room and demanded to know what was going on. She was glad to see that he was followed by the woman cop, Officer Frisbie. Then came Officer White and the little room was absolutely jammed with people.

It took Riley a few moments to notice that Agent Crivaro was standing in the doorway. She wanted to explain everything to him, even across the sea of people between them. But no words came.

Riley realized that she was dumbstruck. She simply didn't know what to say. Fortunately, Gina explained that some partiers had heard fighting in the attic. They had come up here to find that Riley had already subdued the man she claimed had attacked him.

Then Steele barked, "I want all you kids out of here."

The students obediently went back downstairs. As Officer White handcuffed Leon, Officer Steele read him his rights. Leon kept protesting that he hadn't done anything wrong, that Riley had attacked him out of the blue.

Even Steele didn't seem to think that likely. He and White led Leon away into custody.

Riley drew a deep sigh of relief. The only people left there with her were Officer Frisbie and Agent Crivaro. Frisbie sat down beside her, taking out a pencil and a notepad. Crivaro sat in a nearby chair.

"Now tell me what happened," Frisbie said to Riley in a gentle voice.

Riley gathered her thoughts and told Frisbie everything, starting with when Leon had arrived at the party and ending when the party guests had poured into the room to find her kneeling on Leon's chest.

As she told her story, she began to worry …

Wasn't this a classic "he said, she said" kind of situation?

Leon was surely telling a different version of the story to the male cops who had arrested him.

Who were they likely to believe—Riley or Leon?

When she finished her account, Riley said to Frisbie …

"You've got to believe me. I'm telling the truth."

Frisbie chuckled as she put her notebook and pencil back in her pocket.

"Oh, I think your story will hold up just fine," she said. "The alternative is to believe that you lured an innocent guy up to your room for the sole purpose of beating the shit out of him. How credible is that?"

Riley laughed a little herself.

"Not very," she agreed.

Then Riley remembered Leon's pocketknife.

She took it out of her pocket and said, "Officer Frisbie, I found this in Leon's pocket."

Frisbie took the knife, opened it, and looked at the blade with keen interest.

Agent Crivaro got up from his chair and said to Officer Frisbie, "I'd like to see that knife."

Officer Frisbie handed it to him, and he stepped away to study it closely.

Riley said to Officer Frisbie, "He's the killer, isn't he? Leon killed Rhea and Trudy."

Frisbie tilted her head and said, "It doesn't seem unlikely."

She patted Riley on the shoulder and said, "You did good, young lady. You did real good. We may have more questions for you later, but don't worry about it."

Then Frisbie got up from the futon and took a camera out of her bag.

She said, "Your blouse is torn, and you're pretty bruised up. I need to get pictures of all that."

Riley stood up and let Officer Frisbie take pictures.

When she finished, Crivaro said, "Officer Frisbie, I'd like to speak to the girl alone, if I may."

Officer Frisbie gave him a questioning look, but then she nodded and left the attic. Crivaro paced back and forth in front of Riley, examining the knife.

His silence worried Riley. She wished he'd say something.

Finally she asked, "It's over, isn't it? We've caught the killer. He'll never kill anyone again."

Crivaro shook his head slowly.

He said, "Riley …"

"What?"

"It wasn't him. That kid never killed anyone in his life."

Riley's mouth dropped opened with disbelief.

"How do you know?" she asked.

Crivaro shrugged a little.

"I've known more than my share of killers. I can tell. For one thing, he obviously tried to *sexually* assault you. There was no sexual component to either of the other murders—none at all. And …"

He fingered the knife blade.

"This knife has never been used as a murder weapon. It's too small and too dull for that kind of thing. The wounds on the victims had to have been made by a much bigger, sharper weapon."

Riley felt a flash of anger.

She said, "Are you trying to tell me it's just a coincidence that the guy who attacked me happened to be carrying a knife?"

"That's exactly what I'm telling you," Crivaro said.

Riley started to shake all over.

"I don't believe in coincidences," she said.

"Well, you better start believing in them," he said, sounding a bit angry himself. "In my line of work, coincidences are a fact of life. So is a little thing called 'confirmation bias.' That's when you interpret everything you see as evidence for what you want to believe."

Riley was really shocked now.

Is he patronizing me? she thought.

"It's him," she said. "Leon's the killer."

Crivaro sighed bitterly.

"You've got a decision to make, Riley. Leon is definitely a sexual predator, and he'll attack more young women if he isn't stopped right now. Are you willing to bring a charge of attempted rape against him? He'll get five years to life. And he'll damn sure deserve it."

"It was attempted murder," Riley said. "I'm sure of it."

Crivaro folded the knife and said, "Yeah, and the local cops are going to think the same thing. They'll charge him with murder, all right. But they'll be wrong. And you'll be wrong too."

Riley felt her face redden with rage. She was too angry to even speak.

Finally Crivaro said, "I'm going down to the station now. Whatever you decide to do, I'm going to put the fear of God into that bastard. You gave Frisbie a good solid report of what he tried to do to you. If nothing else, I'll let him know that this incident will be used against him if he ever tries anything like this again."

He paused for a moment, then said, "Think it over, Riley. Sleep on it."

Then he went downstairs, leaving Riley alone.

Riley could hardly believe what had just happened.

"Sleep on it," he told me.

He's really got some nerve.

She collapsed onto the futon, aching and exhausted, wondering what to do next.

She surely needed to go downstairs and check on things there. The party guests must have dispersed by now, but she needed to

189

find out how her housemates were doing. Then she needed a shower and a good night's sleep.

If that's even possible, she thought.

She didn't feel like anything in her life was any good right now.

There was only one thing that could make things right.

I've got to prove I'm right, she thought.

I've got to prove that Leon's the killer.

CHAPTER THIRTY THREE

Riley recognized the familiar sound of Bricks and Crystal blasting out their grunge rendition of "Ring of Fire."

It was night. The air reeked with odors of beer and cigarette smoke.

It took her a few moments to realize that she was sitting alone at a table on the patio at the Centaur's Den. She was watching a crowd of young people thrashing to the music in the dance area.

But the dancers weren't smiling and happy.

They all looked frightened.

Their movements seemed convulsive and involuntary, as if they didn't want to be dancing.

She wondered what awful inner force was driving them.

Then the belting music began to get under her own skin. She felt the pull of the dancing, a powerful urge to join the others.

Don't, *she told herself.* It's dangerous. Don't go out there.

She breathed slowly, deeply, trying to smooth that terrible urge away ...

Connect with that ch'i energy, *she told herself.*

She knew she might need it soon.

As she watched, she saw something dark spreading on the floor, under the feet of the increasingly desperate dancers.

It was blood!

Pools of blood were spreading and widening on the floor where the people were dancing.

She knew she would have to go out there now. She had to find out where the blood was coming from.

Riley rose shakily to her feet and walked toward the dancers. She felt her own shoes sticking in the blood. She kept breathing slowly, resisting the urge to start dancing.

She was among the dancers now, studying their faces closely.

She realized that she had seen them all here before. She didn't know their names, but their faces were imprinted in her brain.

Then she came across a figure lying on the floor.

It was a girl. Dark, glistening blood was pouring out of a large wound in her throat.

Riley gasped.

Then she saw one of the dancing girls grip her throat as blood spurted out, and she fell writhing to the ground.

The same thing happened to another girl ... then another ... then another ...

While the rest of the dancers kept thrashing to the music, the floor was littered by more girls with their throats cut open, and the blood got deeper.

Someone was murdering them.

Where was he?

How could she stop him?

Her eye darted from one male face to another. If she could just see him, she would know him ...

Riley's eyes snapped open. Daylight was pouring through her attic window.

It was morning, and she'd been asleep in her open futon.

She sat up slowly, startled by the aches and pains she felt. She looked around and saw that the room was a mess. Pieces of the broken lamp were still scattered on the floor.

Memories flooded back of her desperate struggle against her larger male attacker.

She smiled a little as she remembered ...

I beat him. I took him down.

But much of the rest of what had happened last night was foggy and vague.

Her head and stomach hurt—and not just from fighting. She remembered that she'd had more than a few beers last night. She might be just a little bit hungover.

I need to get up, she thought. *I need coffee.*

She pulled on some clothes, straightened herself up a bit in the second-floor bathroom, then continued on to the downstairs kitchen.

There, Gina was busily cooking at the stove.

When Gina saw Riley, she ran over and gave her a big hug. Riley groaned and winced.

"Oh, I'm sorry," Gina said, letting go of Riley. "You must hurt all over. I'm fixing some scrambled eggs. Would you like some?"

"Sure, thanks," Riley said.

Riley made her way around the kitchen, fetching orange juice from the refrigerator and a cup of freshly brewed coffee. Then she sat down at the kitchen table.

"How did you sleep last night?" Gina asked, dishing out scrambled eggs and slices of toast onto a couple of plates.

"Like a log," Riley said.

"I'm so glad," Gina said. "I had a lot of nightmares, myself."

Riley shuddered as she remembered her dream, but she decided not to mention it.

Gina put the plates on the table and sat down with Riley. Riley realized that she hadn't yet seen the other three housemates.

"Where is everybody?" Riley asked, starting to eat.

"You missed them, they left a little while ago to get some breakfast somewhere else. They were pretty shaken up, wanted to get out of the house."

Riley ate in silence for a few moments. She wondered if the others had wanted to avoid seeing her. Maybe they weren't happy that she had invited a killer to their party and had the cops invade their house.

"Are you sure you're OK?" Gina asked. Then she added with a nervous giggle, "I mean, it's OK if you're *not* OK. Perfectly understandable. Maybe I should just keep my mouth shut."

Riley shook her head and said, "I'm still trying to sort it all out—everything that happened last night, I mean."

Gina reached over and touched Riley on the shoulder.

"What happened was—you're some kind of a hero, Riley! You took out that guy all by yourself! It was amazing. How did you do it?"

Riley felt shrugged. Right now it seemed like a good question ...

How did *I do it?*

Gina continued, "Anyway, you did something really, really good. The cops have got that guy now. He'll never kill anybody again."

Riley felt a jolt as she remembered what Agent Crivaro had said ...

"It wasn't him. That kid never killed anyone in his life."

She remembered how angry his words had made her. And now she started feeling angry all over again.

Crivaro just had to be wrong. How could Leon *not* be the killer?

He even had a knife! Riley thought.

The local police had seemed as sure of his guilt as she did. It troubled her a lot that Crivaro didn't think so as well. What if he convinced the local cops that Leon wasn't the killer after all?

What if they just let him go?

Somehow, she felt responsible for keeping that from happening.

Riley kept on eating, not really paying attention to Gina's continuing chatter. When she was finished, she thanked Gina for breakfast and left the house.

But she wondered, where did she want to go, and what did she want to do?

All she knew for sure was that she'd left something unfinished—something she had to take care of.

If Leon was really the killer—and Riley felt sure that he was—it was up to her to prove it once and for all. If she didn't, other people would surely die.

But she had no idea at all how to go about it.

For a while, Riley wandered aimlessly along the tree-lined streets near the campus. Then she was startled to realize that her rambling steps had taken her right past the Centaur's Den. She stopped and looked around, not sure whether she had come here on purpose or by accident.

She was surprised to see the front door wide open. She was sure the Centaur's Den didn't open this early on a Sunday.

But that open door seemed to invite her in.

She shuddered. That was where last night's dream had taken place. Did she really want to go in there today?

Without answering her own question, Riley went to the open door and peeked inside.

A man in coveralls was mopping the floor. She guessed that he'd left the door open just to air the place out while he cleaned.

She felt a strange tingle of curiosity. She stepped inside and called out to the cleaning man …

"Excuse me, sir …"

The man looked up from his mopping.

Riley thought fast, trying to decide what to say.

"Um, I think I lost a piece of jewelry here last night. Could I come in and have a look?"

"What kind of jewelry?" the man asked.

"A pretty earring. My aunt gave it to me. It would be awful if I lost it."

The man shook his head.

He said, "I've been cleaning up here, and I haven't run across anything like that."

Trying to sound more insistent, Riley said, "It's really little, you might have missed it. I might have dropped it out on the patio. It might have fallen into one of the potted plants. Please let me have a look."

The man shrugged.

"Suit yourself, go have a look," he said, resuming his mopping.

Riley thanked him and walked through the bar toward the patio. When she got to the outside dance floor, she stood there wondering ...

What am I trying to do?

What am I looking for?

Then she realized—she needed to re-create what had happened to Trudy on that awful night.

She remembered arriving here with Trudy, then later her alarm at not seeing Trudy among the dancers, followed by her rising panic as she made her way through the bar until she'd finally found her downstairs in the booth with Harry Rampling.

She also remembered what Harry had said about what had happened afterward—how he'd started walking Trudy back to the dorm until he'd been distracted by a couple of buddies, and then Trudy was gone.

He'd been telling the truth, of course. But now Riley found herself wondering ...

Was Leon also here that night?

Had he been watching Trudy, stalking her, waiting for a chance to catch her alone?

The nightmare she'd had this morning began to come back to her. In that dream, she'd been able to clearly visualize the dancers' faces.

Could she do that now?

Standing in the middle of the patio, she closed her eyes and thought back to that terrifying moment when she'd noticed that Trudy was missing. Riley had waded among the dancers looking for her.

She was startled at how vividly the scene came back to her. Just like in her dream, she could see faces clearly—the faces of those who had been on the dance floor that night.

But everything was moving too fast.

She slowed down her impressions, trying to remember, trying to see the individual faces again, one at a time until ...

No, she realized. *He wasn't out here dancing.*

But on the periphery of her mental vision, something at a nearby table caught her attention.

In her mind, she turned to look. There Leon was, sitting with a girl, chatting her up.

Riley eyes snapped open and she saw the table, now empty in the sunlight.

Was that real? she asked herself.

Or did she just imagine that she had seen Leon there?

She closed her eyes again. And there he was, his attention entirely focused on the attractive young woman sitting across the table from him.

Now Riley was sure of it. She really had glimpsed Leon during those panic-filled moments when she'd been looking for Trudy.

But now Riley knew—Leon hadn't been stalking Trudy at all.

He hadn't even been aware of her. His whole attention had been focused on the girl he had been sitting with.

Riley shuddered deeply as she remembered again what Agent Crivaro had said …

"That kid never killed anyone in his life."

And now Riley knew …

Crivaro was right, and I was wrong.

I should have believed him.

Suddenly, her head was spinning and she felt horribly dizzy and nauseous.

Without stopping to think, she dashed to the restroom, went inside, and shut the door behind her.

Then she threw up violently in the toilet.

What's wrong with me? she wondered.

What's happening?

CHAPTER THIRTY FOUR

When the vomiting stopped, Riley leaned gasping over the toilet bowl.

What's wrong with me? she wondered again. She was seldom ill. Why was this happening now?

Of course she'd just had a terrible shock, realizing how wrong she'd been about Leon.

She was hit with a gnawing discouragement that the murders were far from solved, and nearly overwhelmed with horror to realize the killer was still out there.

And, she also reminded herself, there was the fact that she still had a bit of a hangover …

Her thoughts were interrupted by the sound of knocking on the restroom door.

She heard the cleaning man's voice …

"Hey, miss—are you OK in there?"

Riley sighed and coughed.

"I'm fine," she said in a raspy voice.

She went to the sink and rinsed off her face and tried to straighten herself up a little. Then she went out of the restroom, where the cleaning man was still standing with his mouth hanging open.

"Did you find what you were looking for?" the man asked.

"No, but thanks for letting me have a look," Riley said.

Without another word, she hurried past him and headed on outside. As she walked along the street, her stomach settled a little, but her brain was still reeling.

I was wrong, she told herself yet again.

The killer's still free.

And the cops didn't know that. But Agent Crivaro knew, and now she did too. Riley felt desperate to do something to fix her mistake—and to do it right now.

But what could she do? How could she find out anything that the FBI agent didn't already know?

Her mind felt wiped clean of any ideas about the killer. She had to start thinking again, look for fresh insights, start all over.

She walked faster as it dawned on her where she might look for the insights she needed. With a new sense of purpose, she headed to the campus library, which had just opened for the day. Once inside, she went straight to the long table filled with library catalogue computers. As she sat down at one and started to search, she heard a voice whisper from across the table …

"Riley Paige!"

She looked up and saw Professor Hayman, who was peeking at her around his own terminal.

He smiled at her and whispered, "Good to see you studying on this lovely Sunday morning!"

But his cheerful expression shifted to one of concern.

"Riley—are you all right? What happened?"

For a moment, Riley wondered what he could possibly mean.

But then she remembered the bruises still on her face.

Riley smiled weakly at him and said, "I'm fine, Professor Hayman.

Then she lowered her head to focus on her own computer screen.

As much as she liked her psychology professor, she didn't want to talk to him or anybody else right now.

She typed in a search for the book she wanted and was relieved to see that it wasn't checked out.

Then she got up and went upstairs to the shelf location and took down the book— *Dark Minds: The Homicidal Personality Revealed,* by Dr. Dexter Zimmerman. Already thumbing through the pages, she headed for the nearest study table and sat down.

Of course she'd read and reread the book many times before she had returned Professor Hayman's copy. But she'd found it so rich in ideas and insights, she'd seemed to find new revelations in its pages every time she opened it.

And that was what she needed right now …

A fresh revelation about a murderer's mind.

She found herself flipping to the last chapter of the book, where Dr. Zimmerman had summed up his discoveries and provided further thoughts. A particular paragraph quickly caught her eye …

In this book I have explored the homicidal personality in some depth. Alas, there are many aspects of serial murder that remain unresearched, including some that have nothing to do directly with the criminal's mind. What sort of mental trauma does a community experience when it is plagued by serial murders? Does a victimized group, whether large or small, heal from its collective psychic wounds quickly, slowly, or not at all?

Riley almost turned to another page, thinking that this passage had nothing to do with what her current dilemma. But she was seized by an uncanny gut feeling that she'd found what she was looking for.

She kept on reading ...

It is a matter that I would like to study myself. And yet I confess that I don't know at this juncture how to go about it. The ethical problems alone are enough to perplex the academic mind. How does one transform a particular community—a neighborhood, small town, or even a college campus—into a laboratory setting for such a survey? One cannot very well turn a serial killer loose among a group of people just to find out how that group will react. And yet there must be some way to examine this important question ...

Zimmerman then went on to raise other questions that he thought deserved more research. But Riley ignored them and read the same passage several times. A gnawing horror built up inside her as she felt herself on the verge of thinking the unthinkable.

No, she told herself, trying to keep such thoughts out of her mind.

I've got to be wrong.

It's not possible.

But now she found herself remembering how she'd felt about Dr. Zimmerman before she'd gotten to know him—how disagreeably touchy-feely and cuddly she'd found him, so obsessed with hugs and good feelings.

She'd changed her mind after their first conversation—had come to like, respect, and admire him. He even seemed to understand and appreciate her in ways that nobody else except Agent Crivaro did.

Most of all, Riley had come to trust him.

She felt like she could talk to him about anything.

How many other students felt the same way?

How many students—even coeds—might not feel the least bit

alarmed if they happened to encounter this kindly, rumpled, smiling gentleman on the campus paths by night?

If they knew him even just a little, wouldn't they be pleased to strike up an interesting conversation with this very interesting man?

Mightn't they even invite him into their rooms just to keep talking to him?

After all, how could they possibly suspect any danger?

Riley shivered deeply as she reread a sentence ...

How does one transform a particular community—a neighborhood, small town, or even a college campus—into a laboratory setting for such a survey?

Riley shook her head, trying to drive away the idea.

No, she thought. *It's just too crazy.*

Surely *nobody* could be sick enough to kill people for the sake of an academic study, least of all a kindly, sensitive man like Dr. Zimmerman.

And yet ...

Didn't she see it right here in his book, printed in black and white?

Was it possible that he had turned Lanton University into his perfect laboratory?

Riley was shaking all over now. Even the spacious library suddenly seemed cramped and claustrophobic—and at the same time lonely.

I've got to talk to somebody, she thought. *Somebody who can tell me that I'm wrong.*

Because I've got to be wrong.

But who could she possibly talk to about such an insanely twisted idea?

Then it occurred to her—Professor Hayman sometimes kept Sunday office hours. She had his office number written down in her purse. She head straight to the library's payphone and punched in that number.

She was relieved that Professor Hayman answered instead of his outgoing message.

When she told him who it was, he said, "Hey, Riley, I'm surprised to hear from you today. What can I do for you?"

Riley gulped hard.

Could she really talk about this over the phone?

She stammered, "Professor Hayman, if—if you're in your office, could I—?"

Professor Hayman's voice sounded concerned now.

"Come on over to talk? Sure. Where are you right now?"

"The library."

"Come on over then."

As she hung up the phone, Riley realized that she didn't feel the least bit relieved to have someone to talk to about her terrible hunch.

What would Hayman think of her for even imagining such a possibility?

Riley took Dr. Zimmerman's book to the front desk and checked it out. She left the library and headed toward the psychology building. Before she reached her destination, she was surprised to that see Professor Hayman had come out to meet her along the way.

"Riley, you sounded upset," he said as they approached each other. He took a closer look at her and added, "What's the matter? What happened to you? Were you attacked?"

Riley suddenly realized how awful she must look. Aside from her bruises, she was sure that she now was as white as a sheet from shock.

She tried to explain as they walked along together...

"A guy tried to jump me at a party last night. Tried to rape me, actually. Don't worry, I fought him off."

She laughed nervously and added, "Believe me, he looks a lot worse than I do right now. The police came and got him."

Hayman said, "Do the police think ... I mean ..."

Riley understood what he wanted to ask.

She replied carefully, "The police are pretty sure he's the guy who killed those girls."

Hayman breathed an audible sigh of relief.

"Then it's over, thank God. He'll never kill again. And you took him down! Do you realize how amazing that is, Riley? You're a hero!"

Riley felt a stab of emotion at those words ...

"A hero."

That's what Gina had said this morning.

She hadn't been displeased to hear it then.

But now she didn't feel like a hero.

In fact, she felt like she was anything but a hero.

The very word made her feel guilty and wrong.

I've been wrong—so wrong—about everything.

To her own surprise, she felt tears trickling down her cheeks. A sob forced its way out of her throat.

Hayman said, "Riley, you're crying."

Riley nodded and more sobs came.

Hayman took her gently by the arm and said, "Come on, let's sit down and talk."

Riley again wondered …

Can I really talk to him about this?

Then she thought that maybe Professor Hayman could talk sense to her, explain how wrong she was about Dr. Zimmerman. Surely she could be wrong yet again.

That would be wonderful, she thought.

When they arrived at the Psychology building, Professor Hayman unlocked the front door. When they got inside, he locked the door again. He led her to his office and offered her a seat in front of his desk.

Then he walked around the desk and sat in his swivel chair, leaning toward her with a look of empathy and compassion.

He spoke a bit cautiously …

"Riley, you know I'm not a clinical psychologist. I hope it's not a mistake—talking to me, I mean. All I want to do is help. If you like, I could refer you to a professional therapist …"

Riley shook her head, her sobbing starting to wane a little.

"It's OK," she said. "Maybe you can understand. You see …"

Her mind suddenly reeled.

How could she begin to explain what she was thinking?

She began to speak very slowly …

"Professor Hayman … could you tell me …. How do you feel about Dr. Zimmerman?"

Hayman looked surprised by the question.

But then his expression turned to one of almost awed reverence.

"I think the whole world of him," he said. "He's my mentor, my inspiration. I feel like I owe him … well, simply everything. He's been like a father to me."

Riley's spirits sank as she remembered something Hayman had said about Zimmerman in class …

"He's just about the most insightful guy I've ever known in my life."

He really will think I'm crazy, she thought.

But who else did she have to talk to about this?

She opened Dr. Zimmerman's book and found the passage that had disturbed her. With shaking hands, she passed the open book across the table to Professor Hayman.

She said, "Could you please read the third paragraph and ... tell me what you think?"

Hayman slipped on a pair of reading glasses and read silently until he came to a phrase that he spoke aloud ...

"'... a laboratory setting for such a survey.'"

His expression changed as he kept reading. Now he seemed sad and troubled.

Does he understand? Riley wondered.

Hayman slowly closed the book and tilted down his reading glasses and stared into space for a few moments.

Then he looked at Riley and said, "Riley ... do you really think ... ?"

Riley's heart quickened.

He does *understand!* she thought.

She said, "I know it sounds crazy ..."

Professor Hayman slowly shook his head.

"No, I'm afraid it doesn't sound crazy. I've often wondered ... I've often thought .... It has occurred to me ..."

He got up from his chair, raised his glasses back up, and picked up the heavy book and opened it again.

He began pacing a little as he read bits of the text, "'The ethical problems alone ...' 'How does one transform a particular community ...' 'One cannot very well turn a serial killer loose ...'"

Still peering into the book, he began to walk around his desk.

"That's the question, isn't it? Why *can't* one turn a serial killer loose on a college campus—if it's for the good of scientific knowledge? If the insights are of enough value? Not Dr. Zimmerman, of course ... not such a kindly, innocent, scholarly man ..."

As he stepped nearer her, Riley began to feel a strange tingle of discomfort.

Hayman continued, "But someone else, someone fascinated by his ideas, could very well take up his proposal ..."

Without warning, Hayman slammed the book shut and swung it against the side of Riley's head, sending her hurtling off the chair. She banged her head sharply against the hardwood floor.

She was seeing stars now, and her mind was unclear.

She tried to focus on what was happening, but her thoughts were scrambled.

Professor Hayman crouched down beside her and looked her in the eyes with a malevolent expression.

He said, "It would take someone with an exceptionally strong will."

CHAPTER THIRTY FIVE

Riley lay in a dazed heap on the floor, flat on her face and unable to move.

Thoughts and memories swirled through her aching head.

She heard again Trudy saying to Rhea ...

"Riley likes to impress Prof. Hayman. She's got a thing for him."

... and she heard herself protesting sharply that she *didn't* have a thing for him.

And she remembered thinking at the same time ...

He's cute and smart.

Every other girl in the class has a crush on him.

Fragments of the truth were coming together in her mind.

She remembered imagining Trudy's murder from the killer's point of view—how delighted she seemed to be in his company, how eager to continue the conversation they'd been having.

Surely Trudy had thought nothing of being alone with the charming, handsome, and intelligent young professor.

"What coed wouldn't feel that way?" Riley asked herself.

"Surely not Rhea."

And now ...

Not even me, she realized.

Now she heard Professor Hayman speaking, and realized that this time the voice was real, right here in the room. He was standing somewhere above her.

Riley feebly clawed at the floor trying to move. But Hayman planted one foot squarely in the center of her back, pinning her helplessly as he kept speaking calmly ...

"It's been going well—the experiment, I mean. I've been writing it all down, all my observations, the collective trauma of the campus—especially among the close friends of the victims. I've got a whole chapter's worth of material about you alone. It'll be a fine study, a fine book. Dr. Zimmerman will be so proud."

Hayman paused for a moment, then added ...

"I guess you must be wondering—why do I care so much about impressing him? Well, I guess you wouldn't know. You were probably brought up in a nice little nurturing middle-class family. You have no idea what it's like, not having a mother—just a father whose expectations are impossible to fulfill."

Riley was seized by the palpable irony …

Yes, I do know.

I know exactly what it's like.

Then Hayman said, "Of course, Dr. Zimmerman need never know the lengths I went to carry out his study. One day the killings will stop, and no one will know why. No one need ever know the truth—except you, of course."

As Riley listened, she slowly brought her breath under control …

Find that ch'i energy, she kept telling herself.

… until she mustered enough strength to shift her body abruptly, sending Hayman slightly off balance so she could slip out from under his foot. She started to rise to her feet and he grabbed her by the arm. An Aikido move flashed through her mind …

… a turn of the hand in a graceful semicircle …

… but as she tried to execute the move, Hayman's arm remained immobile.

He sneered at her and said, "Don't try that move with me—I taught it to you."

Then she remembered her father's lessons …

… attack the most sensitive parts of the body …

Hayman's throat was exposed and vulnerable.

Riley raised her free hand, formed a fist, and struck out—but the blow was weak. Hayman caught her fist with his own free hand and held it fast.

He snickered now.

"A street fighter, eh? I can do that too."

He released her hands, but before she could make another move, he punched her brutally in the forehead, and the back of her head crashed against the floor again.

The world swirled around her again, and Riley felt too weak to make another attempt to fight back.

She couldn't hold back a groan of despair.

She remembered something her father had said up at the cabin when he'd first taken her by surprise and struck her down …

"You're dead, girl. Or at least you should be. I'd say you deserve to be."

It was no use.

She couldn't save herself.

She couldn't even keep her eyes open.

Stay awake, damn it, she told herself. *Don't give up!*

She forced her eyes open and everything looked blurry for a moment. But as her vision cleared, she saw that Hayman was crouched over her holding a large, gleaming knife near her throat.

He said, "But you do present me with a bit of a problem, don't you, Riley? You got too close to the truth, and that sealed your fate. But I can't very well do to you what I did to the others. The circumstances are different—and totally unplanned. Your body mustn't be found here. And anyway, I don't want my office drenched in your blood. I'd never get things clean. And I'm rather obsessed by tidiness."

He tilted his head in thought.

"Still, I'm sure I can make good use of you. On top of the routine slashings—the two coeds so far, and the others yet to come—how will my experimental community respond to the mysterious *disappearance* of another coed? Especially one who was known to be too curious for her own good—a would-be Nancy Drew, if you will? Would it discourage others from following in her ill-fated footsteps? I'd like to think so."

To Riley's surprise, Hayman raised the knife toward his own throat.

Has he gone crazy? she wondered. *Is he going to kill himself?*

Instead, he slipped the blade under his collar and slashed through his necktie.

The only thing she could think was how sharp that blade must be.

He chuckled grimly and said, "An expensive tie—but any sacrifice for the cause of science."

He held a long piece of the severed tie in his hands.

Now Riley understood.

He wouldn't use the blade on her. He was going to strangle her and dispose of her body where it would never be found.

Before she could summon up strength for a final burst of resistance, he flipped her over on her face again, pulled the tie around her neck, and yanked hard.

Riley couldn't breathe, and she felt as though she were leaving her body.

Her head filled up with what sounded like radio static, and the world rapidly slipped away.

She thought the familiar voice she heard must be another hallucination,

"Let go of her! And get on your feet!"

… then everything went black and she was gone.

*

When Riley's eyes opened again, she seemed to be surrounded by a deep, thick fog.

She heard the weirdly noisy sound of her own breathing.

"She's coming to," a male voice said.

"Take off the oxygen mask," another said.

Riley felt the release of some physical pressure around her mouth and nose.

Her vision became clearer, and she found herself looking up into the faces of three men.

Two were dressed in white uniforms.

The third was Agent Crivaro.

Then she became aware of the sound of a siren and the rumble of a vehicle's engine.

I'm in an ambulance, she realized.

Crivaro smiled and stroked her hair gently and said, "You're going to be OK, Riley. But damn, you had us scared for a little while."

Riley managed to say just one word …

"How?"

Her throat hurt badly uttering the word. In fact, it was painful to breathe.

Crivaro shook his head and said, "No, don't try to talk now. Save your energy."

Riley felt a flash of anger.

To hell with not talking, she thought. *I want some answers!*

She managed to croak out …

"How did you … find me … in time?"

Crivaro said, "I'd been following you all morning."

Riley began, "I didn't …"

"Yeah, I know—you didn't see me. I can be pretty stealthy when I want to be. I had a feeling you were on to something—I didn't know what, but I knew you might get yourself in trouble. Then you followed Hayman into the building, and I got worried, and I called for backup. I broke into the building and heard sounds of struggle. That's how we got to you. And not a second too soon."

Riley could remember none of it.

She asked, "What about Professor Hayman?"

"Don't worry, we've got him in custody. And his office was full of incriminating evidence—piles of notes describing the murders, even the murder weapon. We've got him cold."

Riley's thoughts were still vague and uncertain.

She found herself thinking about all the blunders she'd made—first thinking that the killer was Leon, and then ...

She said to Crivaro, "I thought ... the killer ... was Dr. Zimmerman."

Crivaro chuckled a little.

"We all make mistakes," he said.

Riley tried to shake her head, but found that it was in a brace.

"But Agent Crivaro ... I was *wrong* ... about *everything.*"

Crivaro laughed heartily.

Then he said, "Riley, read my lips ..."

He said slowly and deliberately, "You ... led ... me ... straight ... to ... the ... killer."

He stroked her hair again and added, "Your conclusions weren't perfect, but your *instincts* were right on the money. Do you realize how amazing that is, for someone with no training in law enforcement? Later on you're going to have to tell me exactly how you did it."

Now Riley remembered finding those words in Dr. Zimmerman's book ...

One cannot very well turn a serial killer loose among a group of people just to find out how that group will react.

She'd taken that as a clue ...

... and I was right!

It was like Agent Crivaro had just said—faulty conclusions, but perfect instincts.

Now Crivaro was gazing at her with open admiration.

He said, "You're a diamond in the rough, Riley Sweeney. I've never met anyone like you. You'd make one hell of an FBI agent. Now, I don't know what kind of plans you've got for your career, but ..."

One of the paramedics interrupted and said, "It's really best for her to keep quiet right now."

Crivaro's smile broadened and he said to Riley, "Well, those are the doctor's orders. And he's the one who gives the orders—at least for the time being."

Crivaro fell silent and seemed to be deep in thought.

Riley wished she knew what was on her mind.

She had a feeling whatever he was thinking was going to have a huge effect on her own future.

Then her mind began to wander, and she found herself wondering about something that seemed oddly trivial and irrelevant under the present circumstances …

Why did I get so sick at the Centaur's Den?

CHAPTER THIRTY SIX

Riley sat on her folding chair flanked by other students. They were all wearing their graduation robes. She was also still wearing a neck brace, which made her feel especially stiff and awkward. But she had made it through college, and at this point that seemed fairly miraculous.

Even though she was glad to be here, Riley she couldn't keep her mind on what the guest speaker was saying. He was a prominent and well-respected businessman, and it seemed a shame to miss out on his sage advice.

She caught enough of it to know that he was telling the graduates what a wonderful future awaited them, and how prepared they were go out into the world.

Prepared, ha! Riley thought.

She was anything but prepared for the future.

Her GPA certainly wasn't the problem.

Despite her recent ordeal, she'd done fine on her final exams—at least her academic ones.

Her results on another kind of test had been a different story.

She'd bought the test kit from the drug store, and hadn't believe what it told her.

So she'd taken another test … then another …

The results were the same.

Just as she'd feared when she missed her period, she was pregnant.

She and Ryan hadn't been careful enough during their first night together.

So what was she going to do with her life now?

She hadn't been in touch with Ryan since their bitter parting, so of course he didn't know.

Should she contact him somehow?

Should she tell him?

Again, she remembered something her father had said …

"You're dead, girl. Or at least you should be. I'd say you deserve to be."

Those words now seemed too true for comfort—figuratively

speaking, anyway.

Of course her father hadn't come to the graduation, and Riley was just as happy about that given the circumstances. He hadn't even been in touch since she'd helped catch Brant Hayman, who was due to be tried for murder soon and might well face the death penalty.

Does Daddy even know what happened?

She was sure he did. During her last visit to his cabin, he seemed to be keeping up with the news coming out of Lanton.

She wondered how he felt about what she'd done?

Was he proud of her, maybe relieved that she'd survived, or was he totally unimpressed?

He probably doesn't know himself, Riley thought.

And honestly, she wasn't sure that she cared one way or the other.

And right now, that seemed like a healthy thing.

She remembered what Professor Hayman had said to her …

"You have no idea what it's like, not having a mother—just a father whose expectations are impossible to fulfill."

Of course, she *did* know exactly what that was like.

But it hadn't turned her into a murderer.

She wondered …

What made the difference?

Riley certainly didn't feel like the picture of mental health, but …

Why did Hayman become so horribly twisted?

She stifled a sigh and thought …

Maybe someday I'll understand.

The ceremony passed much too slowly for Riley's taste. When her name was called, she mechanically got to her feet and walked up on the stage to receive her diploma. Then she joined all the other graduates in the orderly procession out of the large hall while the school band played "Pomp and Circumstance."

At the end of the procession, friends and relatives were waiting eagerly for the new graduates, and there were lots of hugs and kisses and congratulations being exchanged. Even though she hadn't expected anyone to be here especially for her, Riley felt a pang of sadness as she wended her way through the crowd.

But then she glimpsed a familiar face beaming at her.

It was Dr. Zimmerman, looking his rumpled and pleasant self.

Riley was thrilled—and relieved.

She'd heard that Dr. Zimmerman had stopped teaching his classes and had even stopped coming to campus after he'd gotten word about what his protégé Brant Hayman had done. Rumor had it that he felt personally responsible for planting such a ghastly idea in Hayman's sick mind.

But here he was—beckoning to Riley as though he was a family member.

Then she saw another familiar face.

Agent Crivaro was standing next to the professor.

Riley was truly surprised now. The last she'd heard, Crivaro and his team had gone back to Quantico because their work here in Lanton was finished. And now here he was, in Dr. Zimmerman's company.

What's up? she wondered.

She walked up to Dr. Zimmerman, who shook her hand warmly.

He said, "Riley, you've made me so proud—so very proud."

Then his expression saddened and he added, "I'm just sorry that …"

His voice faded. Riley gripped his hand with both of hers.

She said, "It wasn't your fault, Dr. Zimmerman. None of it was your fault."

Zimmerman smiled a bittersweet smile.

"So everybody keeps telling me," he said. "Maybe someday I'll believe it."

Then, without warning, he wrapped his arms around Riley in a big hug.

Riley laughed as he held onto her tightly.

"Careful," she said. "My neck's still pretty sore."

Zimmerman released her and said, "Oops. So sorry."

"It's OK," Riley said. "But I thought you didn't hug students."

"You're not a student anymore," Zimmerman said.

Then with a sly grin he added, "Besides, as you know, I *am* a bit of a sadist!"

He and Riley both laughed.

Then with a sideways nod toward Crivaro, Zimmerman said to her, "But I'd better get out of your way. This gentleman needs to talk over a few plans with you."

Plans? Riley wondered.

What had the two men been discussing?

Zimmerman went away and Crivaro walked up to Riley.

He shook her hand and said, "First of all, congratulations. On your graduation, I mean."

Riley thanked him, although she sensed that he had things other than her graduation on his mind.

Then Crivaro handed her a manila envelope.

"This is for you," he said.

"What is it?" Riley said as she took it.

"Papers to apply to FBI Honors Internship Program. It's a great opportunity, Riley, and it's only for very select college students and recent graduates. It'll be ten weeks during this summer. You'll get paid to learn."

Riley was confused. "You want me to apply for this?" she asked. "You think I'd be accepted?"

"I've already put in a strong recommendation for you. You're in."

Riley's mouth dropped open.

I'm in?

She wasn't sure what that even meant.

She began, "But where would it be?"

"There a several locations," Jake replied. "I think the best one for you would be FBI headquarters in Washington, D.C."

She sputtered, "But what if I don't even want—"

Crivaro interrupted, "Think hard about it, Riley. Think really, really hard. And don't expect me to take no for an answer. The FBI needs young people like you—especially women. You'd make a very fine BAU agent."

"BAU?" Riley asked.

She'd couldn't remember ever hearing of that.

"The Behavioral Analysis Unit. It's a part of the FBI that uses behavioral sciences to help with investigations. Your psych degree gives you a great head start. And believe me, you'll be perfect for it."

Riley asked, "Is that what you work for—the BAU?"

"For the time being," Crivaro said. "I'm eligible for retirement, but I might stay on for a while to help someone like you get started. And I'd like to see you get started right away."

Ten weeks during this summer, Riley reminded herself.

She wondered if she should ask …

"What if I'm pregnant?"

But she figured that shouldn't be a problem—not during the early months, anyway.

The real question was …

Is this what I really want?

Crivaro said, "Think about it. And say yes."

Then he added with a chuckle, "Otherwise, I'll have to lean on you. And when I lean, I drill for oil. It won't be pretty, believe me."

Without another word, he turned and walked away.

Riley just stood there for a moment with her mouth hanging open.

What just happened? she wondered.

Did I just get drafted into something called the BAU?

Do I have any choice?

Just then she saw someone else weaving through the crowd toward her. A familiar tall figure. She felt a surge of excitement when she realized who it was.

"Ryan!" she cried, "What are you doing here?"

"I heard what happened," he replied. "At least some of it. I didn't realize you'd been hurt," he added, looking at the brace on her neck.

"I'm fine," she said. "This will come off soon."

Then there was an awkward silence. He shoved his hands in his pockets, and shuffled his feet.

Riley felt an urge to throw her arms around him, but she wasn't sure how he'd react.

Ryan spoke fast, "I just couldn't leave things like … well, like we left them. I can't get you out of my mind, Riley. And listen, I've landed a new job with a really good D.C. law firm. I guess this sounds crazy, but I want you to come with me. I want us to live together. Or maybe even …"

His voice trailed off.

Is he thinking about marriage? Riley wondered.

Her life had suddenly gotten mind-bogglingly complicated. But she realized that she could go into the FBI program and still live with Ryan. Both of them would be in D.C. And she'd be earning money, too. Then maybe they could start a family together—if Ryan wanted that.

The thought of starting a family together reminded her …

Ryan doesn't know yet.

Slowly and carefully, she said, "Ryan, I've got something important to tell you."

WAITING
(The Making of Riley Paige—Book 2)

"A masterpiece of thriller and mystery! The author did a magnificent job developing characters with a psychological side that is so well described that we feel inside their minds, follow their fears and cheer for their success. The plot is very intelligent and will keep you entertained throughout the book. Full of twists, this book will keep you awake until the turn of the last page."
--Books and Movie Reviews, Roberto Mattos (re Once Gone)

WAITING (The Making of Riley Paige—Book Two) is book #2 in a new psychological thriller series by #1 bestselling author Blake Pierce, whose free bestseller Once Gone (Book #1) has received over 1,000 five star reviews.

Brilliant 22 year old FBI intern Riley Paige struggles to decode the riddles of the sadistic serial killer dubbed by media as the "clown killer"—but finds it all becomes too personal when she herself, targeted, is in a battle for her life.

Recent college graduate Riley Paige is accepted into the prestigious FBI summer internship program, and is determined to make a name for herself. Exposed to many departments of the FBI, she thinks it will be a quiet summer—until a serial killer holds Washington by suspense. Dubbed the "clown killer," he dressed and paints his victims as clowns, and mocks the FBI with tantalizing riddles in the media. He leaves everyone to wonder: is he a clown himself?

It seems that only Riley has the mind brilliant enough to decode the answers. And yet the journey into this killer's mind is too dark—and the battle too personal—for Riley to come out unscathed. Can she win this deadly game of cat and mouse?

An action-packed thriller with heart-pounding suspense, WAITING is book #2 in a riveting new series that will leave you turning pages late into the night. It takes readers back 20 plus years—to how Riley's career began—and is the perfect complement to the ONCE

GONE series (A Riley Paige Mystery), which includes 13 books and counting.

Book #3 in THE MAKING OF RILEY PAIGE series will be available soon.

Blake Pierce

Blake Pierce is author of the bestselling RILEY PAGE mystery series, which includes twelve books (and counting). Blake Pierce is also the author of the MACKENZIE WHITE mystery series, comprising eight books; of the AVERY BLACK mystery series, comprising six books; of the KERI LOCKE mystery series, comprising five books; and of the new MAKING OF RILEY PAIGE mystery series, which begins with WATCHING.

An avid reader and lifelong fan of the mystery and thriller genres, Blake loves to hear from you, so please feel free to visit www.blakepierceauthor.com to learn more and stay in touch.

BOOKS BY BLAKE PIERCE

THE MAKING OF RILEY PAIGE SERIES
WATCHING (Book #1)
WAITING (Book #2)

RILEY PAIGE MYSTERY SERIES
ONCE GONE (Book #1)
ONCE TAKEN (Book #2)
ONCE CRAVED (Book #3)
ONCE LURED (Book #4)
ONCE HUNTED (Book #5)
ONCE PINED (Book #6)
ONCE FORSAKEN (Book #7)
ONCE COLD (Book #8)
ONCE STALKED (Book #9)
ONCE LOST (Book #10)
ONCE BURIED (Book #11)
ONCE BOUND (Book #12)
ONCE TRAPPED (Book #13)

MACKENZIE WHITE MYSTERY SERIES
BEFORE HE KILLS (Book #1)
BEFORE HE SEES (Book #2)
BEFORE HE COVETS (Book #3)
BEFORE HE TAKES (Book #4)
BEFORE HE NEEDS (Book #5)
BEFORE HE FEELS (Book #6)
BEFORE HE SINS (Book #7)
BEFORE HE HUNTS (Book #8)
BEFORE HE PREYS (Book #9)

AVERY BLACK MYSTERY SERIES
CAUSE TO KILL (Book #1)
CAUSE TO RUN (Book #2)
CAUSE TO HIDE (Book #3)
CAUSE TO FEAR (Book #4)
CAUSE TO SAVE (Book #5)
CAUSE TO DREAD (Book #6)

KERI LOCKE MYSTERY SERIES

Made in the USA
Monee, IL
11 October 2020